THE DANCER'S PROMISE

THE DANCER'S PROMISE

Olivia Horrox

embla books

First published in Great Britain in 2024 by

 **embla books**

Bonnier Books UK Limited
4th Floor, Victoria House, Bloomsbury Square, London, WC1B 4DA
Owned by Bonnier Books
Sveavägen 56, Stockholm, Sweden

A CIP catalogue record for this book is available from the British Library.

ISBN: 9781471415814

This book is typeset using Atomik ePublisher

Embla Books is an imprint of Bonnier Books UK
www.bonnierbooks.co.uk

For Sophie, I am so lucky to have
a big sister like you

PART ONE

'She'll go and fall in love, and there's an end of peace
and fun, and cosy times together.'

– Louisa May Alcott, *Little Women*

Chapter 1

Autumn 1936

Somebody is finally moving into the old Draper house. I see the removal vans come parading down our leafy residential street as I lean out of my bedroom window. The sight of all those vehicles causes me to lean out, right over the window box, my long hair falling over the last flurry of late summer carnations. The Draper house has sat quiet and empty for as long as I can remember, and I have always wondered what it must look like inside. Is all the old furniture still in there, covered in dust sheets just ready to be unmasked? Or is it an empty shell, stripped bare of any memories of the old Drapers? My sister Grace and I used to make up stories about what happened to the Drapers. Stories from the obscure to the downright grizzly, but it looks like today we might finally get some answers.

I lean out a little further over the window box as the removal men start unloading the vans and carrying in the furniture, all of which looks brand new. They haul in plush velvet armchairs, gilded birdcages, dark mahogany bookcases, and dozens of tropical-looking plants. My curiosity intensifies, and I am hoping to catch a first glimpse of the new owners, but I don't see anybody out of the ordinary on the street below. I spy Mrs Arbuthnot from number twelve quick-walking down the street, her handbag swinging vigorously as she

3

clamours to be the first neighbour to introduce herself. I roll my eyes and rest my chin on my hand, then watch with mild amusement as she looks around a little absently for want of someone to greet, but there is no sign of the newcomers. She keeps trying to stop the removal men and ask them questions, but they just shrug and brush her off. Oh, why does Grace have to be at work today of all days? I can't believe she is missing this momentous occasion, after so many years of the two of us wondering about this mysterious house. This is quite possibly the most interesting thing that has happened on this street since . . . well, probably since our father died and everything that has become of our family since.

'Clementine?' My mother's voice rasps from down the hall and I feel the hairs on the back of my neck stand to attention. She calls my name again and I feel my jaw tighten.

'Coming, Mother!' I call as I tear myself away from the hubbub on the street below and quietly close the sash window.

I take a deep breath, close my eyes and plaster a pleasant smile on my face before making my way to her bedroom. There is a tray outside Mother's door with a rather sad-looking bowl of long-cold porridge and glass of juice, and with a jolt, I remember Grace asking me to make sure I gave Mother her breakfast when I woke up. She must have left it here for me and I completely forgot. I pick up the tray and rush into her bedroom, my eyes adjusting to the gloom. The air in here is stale, and my nose twitches as I disturb the dust with every footstep. I place the tray gently across my mother's lap, and her dark eyes narrow in her pallid face at the sight of me. My mother is in her late forties, but you would find it hard to believe, looking at her now. She is sat up in bed with a shawl wrapped around her shoulders, and she clasps at it with one bony hand. Her long, dark hair, now shot through with silver, is piled in a haphazard bun to the top of her head, but several matted curls have escaped their pins, giving her the look of a slightly deranged Gibson girl. In her heyday, she was a striking beauty, a trait she bequeathed to Grace, but sadly not to me. I look far more like our father, with very serious deep-set eyes and a long (perhaps slightly too long) aquiline nose. I don't mind that Grace inherited the good looks, it makes me quite glad to know that I carry our father's features, almost like keeping a little piece of him alive. To me, that is worth far more than a pretty face.

'Did you call?' I ask sweetly.

'You know very well I did,' she barks, her eyebrows knitting together in disapproval. 'Is that my breakfast? I'm half-starved by now. What have you been doing all morning, selfish girl? And what is happening outside?'

'Someone is moving into the Draper house,' I inform her, and her eyes briefly widen in surprise. Even though Mother hasn't left the house for ten years, she still understands the relevance of this news.

'Who are they?' she asks shrewdly.

'No sign of them yet,' I reply and she nods pensively.

'Let me know when there is, won't you?'

'Of course, Mother.' I respond automatically, bowing my head a little, and a rare smile spreads across her lips.

'There's a good girl,' she says almost fondly, and I hate how much the compliment makes my heart swell. She returns her attention to her breakfast and I linger in the doorway, unsure if I should stay and try to make some more conversation or slink away. I am frozen on the spot with indecision when she looks up at me again with her usual unfeeling glance. 'You can go now.'

I sidle out of the room and close the door softly behind me, stopping for a moment on the landing to catch my breath. My heart is hammering in my chest so quickly that I fear I might take flight, and I clasp the worn edge of the banister for support as I make my way back to my bedroom. I shut the door behind me and return to my perch by the windowsill, but the street below has fallen silent once more, though the vans are still parked outside. I look at the time and my eyes widen with surprise as I realise it is almost midday. I hastily reach under the bed and pull out a small duffel bag, checking over the contents inside: a black tunic, a pair of knitted tights, a handful of scattered hairpins, and most importantly, two pairs of well-worn ballet shoes – my leather ballet slippers for everyday use, and my most prized possession: my satin pointe shoes. All present and correct. I fling the bag over my shoulder and step back out onto the landing, pausing outside Mother's door once more.

'I'm off to ballet now, Mother,' I call through the door, listening intently for a response. 'I'll be back with Grace, in time for supper.'

I hear a muffled murmur of disapproval from the other side, so I fly down the stairs as quickly and quietly as my legs will carry me, ignoring the small ache her displeasure for my dancing brings about in my chest. It was always my father who encouraged me to dance as a little girl. He took both Grace and me to ballet lessons every weekend. Grace could never get on with it, but I fell in love with dancing the very first time I slipped into a pair of ballet slippers. My mother on the other hand quite simply hates the thought of me doing anything that makes me that happy or reminds me of my father. If she had the strength to get out of her bed, I am sure she would put a stop to my lessons in an instant. I already know she is counting down the days until my eighteenth birthday, at which point I will have to get a job and be forced to leave my dancing behind forever. I shake my head roughly, as if I can toss the negative thoughts from my mind. There is no use thinking about it now. A lot could happen between now and my eighteenth birthday, and I will not give up ballet without a fight, for there is no better feeling in the world than the moment when I place my hand on the barre as the piano music starts.

Chapter 2

Madame Lebedev's School of Ballet is located in a small, cobbled street called Montpelier Mews in Fitzrovia, and it is my very own slice of heaven. Each tiny, flat-roofed building is painted a different colour, and they are bedecked with window boxes full of bright, blousy flowers. When you step off the main road onto this secluded little back street, it is quite easy to forget you are in London at all. I round the corner and spy my best friend Rudi leaning against the yellow brick wall, smoking a cigarette with his feet turned out in fifth position. His hooded grey eyes light up as he catches sight of me, and he drops the cigarette, stubbing it out under his black ballet shoe.

'Your mother will kill you if she catches you doing that to your shoes.' I grin as he sweeps me up into his arms and lifts me lightly off my feet. Rudi is my dance partner, so while this sort of interaction may seem odd to the occasional passer-by, to us it is second nature.

'What she doesn't see can't upset her, *solnyshko*,' he says in his beautiful Russian accent, with a wink. Only Rudi calls me *solnyshko*. He once told me it is Russian for 'little sunshine', and that to him, that is what I am. I can't hear it without beaming from ear to ear, and he knows this and occasionally uses it to his advantage. 'I was starting to think you weren't coming,' he continues, 'and I can't bear to be in there alone with all those girls, so I was waiting for you out here . . . You know how they get.'

I *do* know how they get. Almost every girl Rudi meets falls under his spell. Between his athletic physique and full head of bronze curls, he is quite striking. When you add his captivating accent to the mix, they practically fall at his perfectly turned-out feet. My experience of Rudi has been very different. I first met him the day after my father died. I was at school; Mother had insisted upon it.

'You must never show your weakness, girls,' she had said with a stiff upper lip. 'People will use it to exploit you. If you must cry, do it alone in your bedroom.'

Grace nodded stoically, took my hand and walked me to school. She smiled and greeted the neighbours as we passed, she nodded sympathetically at their well wishes, she held it all together, but I felt like I was completely falling apart.

When we reached the school gates, she knelt and retrieved a handkerchief from her satchel to dab my eyes. 'Be strong, little Clem, for Mother.'

She gave me a squeeze and walked me to my classroom. I managed to bottle everything up until lunchtime. I sat in a shady corner of the playground and bawled my eyes out. Grief tore me to shreds like I was nothing more than paper. I cried until my throat was raw with pain and my eyes strained with the effort of producing tears, but I still didn't feel any better. My shoulders were shuddering up and down when a shadow fell over me. I looked up, bleary eyed, and there was Rudi.

He was tall for his age, even then, but he was thin and awkward. His face hadn't grown into his long, sharp nose yet and he was all bones and odd angles. He had the most magnificent head of curls, and they shone like bronze under the dappled autumn light.

'Are you OK?' he asked quietly, then shook his head. 'Obviously you are not OK. I suppose I mean do you want someone to talk to?'

I remembered Mother's warning that people could exploit my weaknesses, but looking at this shy young boy, I couldn't imagine he would. His grey eyes were soft and gentle as he looked down at my huddled form, then he came and sat down beside me. I could smell the soap on his skin, and something else . . . The spicy, smoky scent of cloves.

'Your father died, didn't he?' He cut through the silence. 'That's what everyone is saying. Was it the influenza?'

I nodded, more than a little mortified beneath my grief that everyone was talking about me.

'My father is dead too, but I never knew him, so I guess it's not quite the same,' he said matter-of-factly. 'But I still miss him. Isn't that strange? How can you miss someone you never knew?'

'I don't know. All I know is I miss my father very much,' I croaked. My throat was so sore from crying that it hurt to talk. 'Does it ever stop hurting?' I asked him suddenly and he looked at me in surprise, as if he hadn't expected me to be so forthcoming with my feelings.

'I don't think the pain lessens . . .' he said thoughtfully, 'but you grow stronger and it becomes easier to lug around with you all day.'

'But I'm not strong at all,' I replied dismally.

'You're a ballet dancer, aren't you? You must be stronger than you think!'

'Not anymore. My mother says we cannot afford for me to keep dancing,' I said, the tears welling in my eyes. As if the loss of my father was not enough, knowing I would lose the one thing that would keep him alive in my heart was killing me.

'Well, we may be able to fix that!' he said, brightening. 'My mother is a ballet teacher. Maybe she can teach you and remind you how to be strong.'

'It's kind of you to offer, but it doesn't solve how I would pay for my lessons,' I said at last, my eyes casting down to my lap.

He was silent for a moment, then said, 'Just come along tomorrow after school. Let my ma see what you've got, then we'll see.'

The next day changed my life. I went along to Madame

Lebedev's as Rudi had instructed; I turned up in one of my old leotards that was already getting too small and, sticking firmly to the back of the studio, I followed Madame Lebedev's instructions to the letter. Rudi was there, dancing too, but at the front of the class with a confidence I didn't recognise from the boy I had met at school. He kept looking back and smiling at me encouragingly. For that entire lesson, I was so focused on what I was doing, I didn't think about my father's death for the whole hour. When the class ended, my feet were cramping painfully, but I felt lighter in a way I hadn't been sure I would ever feel again. Even more importantly, I felt connected to my father in a way that didn't cause me pain. That day, I learned something very important – dancing can only ever hurt your feet, never your heart.

Rudi and I have been dancing together ever since that day, and it wasn't long before we started spending all our time at school together. I would often go back to his small apartment above the studio after school, or before class for tea and I soon grew close with Madame Lebedev too. She never asked or pried, but I got the feeling that she knew things weren't great for me at home, so she struck the bargain. She said she saw great potential in me, and that one day she thought I could be a magnificent ballerina if that was what I wished to be. She said that if I was serious about dancing, she would teach me everything I needed to know to get there. She only asked in return that I never forgot to mention where I learned to dance, and that as I grew older, I would help out by cleaning the studios and teaching the younger students. I agreed on the spot. I realised then, even at seven years old, that if Madame Lebedev saw potential in me, that ballet could one day be my ticket to freedom. I knew what I wanted, and I was willing to do whatever it took to get it.

I stop daydreaming about the past and focus my attention back on the present. Rudi's eyes are smouldering as he looks at me curiously. I don't think he even knows he is doing it.

my plimsolls and replacing them with my soft-soled leather ballet shoes.

I overhear a murmur from the group of girls who are stretching over by the barre. 'You know if any of us were late, we'd be getting an extra fifty pliés.'

'Well, it pays to get cosy with Madame's son, doesn't it?' someone says loudly, and I look up to find Alice Blakely staring daggers at me. Her blonde hair is scraped back into a bun and her blue eyes are icy cold. Her gaggle of supportive friends swan around her with their arms crossed, but I just shoot them a placid smile. They can all believe their fantasies about Rudi and me if they please. It makes no difference because when we dance together the magic takes over and I think of little else. Alice is an incredibly talented dancer, her only problem is that she is far more interested in boys than ballet. She often lands a major role in Madam Lebedev's shows, but she never gets to dance with Rudi, which is what she really wants. I am fairly certain that Madame Lebedev (who is very protective of her only son) knows this, and will never allow it to happen.

'Enough chit-chat!' Madame Lebedev calls and steps gracefully into the centre of the room. 'Take your places at the barre and let us begin.'

The music starts, and we all fold in unison into our pliés. I watch our reflections in the floor-length mirrors as we bend and stretch, unfurling our limbs like the petals on a flower.

'Good, now plié, one-two, and straighten, *fondu* . . .' Madame Lebedev calls over the music, and our bodies respond instinctively to her commands. We spend half an hour warming up at the barre, swishing our legs up high, practising our control and studying our balance. Madame Lebedev circles like a vulture, looking for any signs of weakness: a slightly turned in foot, a wobble while elevated, and her biggest pet peeve . . . 'Tuck your pelvis *in*, Alice!' she sighs dramatically, right on cue. 'Where is your head today?'

The class ends all too soon, but when I look at the clock

on the wall, I realise two hours have passed. My body is aching and exhausted, but I have a huge smile on my face as I slip off my ballet shoes and shove my feet back into my plimsolls.

'Remember, everyone, I will be putting up the role sheet for *Giselle* in the coming days. Rehearsals start next week!' Madame Lebedev calls as the rest of the girls begin filtering out, giggling amongst themselves and sharing their weekend plans. Only Alice still lingers around, waiting expectantly near Rudi as he helps his mother tidy up.

'Alice, did you want something?' Madame Lebedev asks brusquely, and Rudi glances over his shoulder as if he has only just noticed she is still there.

Alice turns crimson all the way up to her white-blonde hairline, reminding me of strawberries and cream. 'Oh no, not really,' she mumbles. 'I was wondering if you'd had any thoughts about the casting for *Giselle* yet, Madame, anything you could perhaps let me know now?'

Madame Lebedev gives her a discerning look, then returns to what she was doing. 'What did I just say, Alice?' she snaps. 'You will know when I have made my decision, at the same time as all the other girls.'

Alice nods, but her eyes are fixed firmly on the back of Rudi's head. 'Of course, sorry, Madame, I am so keen to begin rehearsing.' Her sickly sweet voice makes my eyes roll all the way back in my head as I pack my belongings into my bag. 'Oh, um, Rudolf . . . did you have any plans this evening?' she almost squeaks, and I stop lacing my plimsolls in surprise. I almost feel sorry for her when Rudi stops what he is doing and turns around slowly to offer her a gentle smile.

'I'm sorry, I have to help my mother tidy up after class,' he says kindly but firmly, and she nods again before dashing from the room.

Madame Lebedev sighs and straightens her back, giving her son a long, hard look. 'What do you do to these English girls?'

'Not all of them!' he grins mischievously and looks back over his shoulder at me.

'Yes, well, they would probably all find you a lot less attractive if they ever heard you trying to sing, or watched you cry through *Little Women*,' I reply plainly as I pick up a broom and begin sweeping the floor.

'It was a sad movie, Clem! You have no heart,' he scoffs, blushing a little and returning to polishing the mirrors.

'Such a sensible girl, Clementine,' Madame Lebedev purrs. 'You know better than to fall so easily for the charms of men. You will have your work cut out for you when you play Giselle. She was not as smart as you.'

Now it is my turn to blush. It shouldn't come as a surprise that Madame Lebedev has picked me again, but it always does, and I don't really like the pressure of having prior knowledge over the other girls. 'Thank you, Madame Lebedev,' I reply graciously, focusing intently on my sweeping.

'Don't thank me, Clementine, you have always earned your place,' she reminds me. Then with a wink, she adds, 'Just don't forget where you came from when you get whisked off to the Vic-Wells Ballet.' She pats me on the shoulder, an affectionate but affirming gesture, reminding me of our deal. I must make it as a ballerina, and when I do, I will bring her ballet school the prestige she has always dreamed of.

It takes about an hour to sweep and mop the floors, polish the barres and mirrors, and pack everything away. I am practically on my knees by the time I finally stuff the mop and broom back in the cupboard, but it will all have been worth it when I am the prima ballerina at the Vic-Wells Ballet, one of the most prestigious ballet companies in the world. This is one of the reasons why Madame wants me to remember where I came from, why she allows me to have free tutelage. Of course, she has always said she sees great potential in me and she can't bear to watch it go to waste simply because I cannot afford the lessons, but I know I owe her a great debt for her kindness. I want to follow this path for myself, but I would also like more than anything to be able to give that to Madame Lebedev in return for her tireless faith in me. And more than that, I know how proud it would have made my father. Now that I am seventeen, almost eighteen, I know it is time for me to spread my wings and make our dreams reality. Madame says she has a contact, a scout for the Vic-Wells, and she is hoping he will come to our performance of *Giselle*. This performance may well be the one that decides both my fate and Rudi's. Of course she has given us the principal roles.

'Here, I have a treat for you,' Rudi says, handing me a big wedge of cake, and I grab it hungrily. 'It's *sharlotka*, one of my favourites.' He grins through a mouthful.

'Thank you.' I nod appreciatively. 'Did you make it yourself?'

'Ha! Not likely,' he laughs. 'A new bakery has opened around the corner. They make all sorts of foreign delicacies. I've been a few times and the baker's daughter noticed I was Russian, so she asked what my favourite treat from back home was, and she baked it just for me! Can you believe it? Tastes exactly like how my *babushka* used to make it. Ma never did pick up her culinary skills unfortunately, and neither did I . . .' He chews thoughtfully, his eyes closing with a look of delight.

I take a nibble. He is right, the cake is delicious, with an incredibly light and airy crumb, laced with tiny pieces of perfectly sweet apple. I suddenly realise how hungry I am and scoff the lot, letting the crumbs melt on my tongue and licking the grease from my lips.

'Good, huh?' He grins.

'Delicious!' I agree, picking up my dance bag and walking out with him.

'I'll take you with me next time. I think you'll like Anna.'

I glance sideways at him as we walk to the end of the mews. 'On first name terms already, are you?' I tease and he smirks.

'It's nothing, *solnyshko*. You're as bad as my mother.' He wraps one of his strong arms around me and pulls me closer to him as we prepare to go our separate ways, and I breathe in the comforting scent of cloves that clings to his skin. 'The bakery is on Grenville Street. Will you meet me there on Monday before ballet?'

'It must be a little more than nothing if you're willing to introduce me to her,' I remark. 'Just think of all the things I could tell her about the real Rudolf Lebedev.'

'Don't make me change my mind, Clem. As my best friend, it is your duty to lie and tell her what a respectable gentleman I am.' He winks as we pull apart, and I cast him a disparaging look as he lets out a peal of laughter. 'See you tomorrow!' he calls, waving behind him as he struts down the street and I watch him go, the smile melting from my face the moment he looks away. It is sometimes hard to reconcile the Rudi who I have grown up with, my dearest friend, with the Rudi who is anything but a respectable gentleman. I must not think on it now, as there are far more important matters at hand, such as whether or not the new residents of the Draper house have made an appearance yet. And with that in mind, I make my way to the London Library to meet Grace so I can fill her in on everything.

Chapter 3

The London Library is a beautiful, if somewhat inconspicuous building. Tucked away in a corner of St James's Square, you could quite easily walk past it and never realise that behind the great wooden doors is a treasure trove full to bursting with rare books. I think that is what Grace likes about it so much: it is a little secret oasis of calm and knowledge right in the centre of the bustling city. I skip up the stone steps, heave open the door, and steal myself inside before it swings shut again. As the door closes, all the sounds of the outside are vanquished and a heavy silence descends. I spy Grace sitting behind the counter in the middle of the main hall, her large blue eyes are narrowed in concentration, and her bowlike lips are pursed, causing little dimples to form in her cheeks. I make a beeline for her, dashing between tables and chairs, careful not to knock over any piles of books as I fly past, and she finally looks up from what she was reading in startled surprise.

'Grace, the most wonderful, exciting thing happened today!' I exclaim, my voice echoing around the shelves and carrying back to me as I bundle my dance bag onto the counter. Her eyes widen in dismay as I clasp my hand to my mouth and whisper an apology to a couple of disgruntled-looking scholars at a nearby table.

'Clementine Harrington, you are going to get me fired one of these days,' she sighs, tucking a loose tawny curl behind her ear before shelving a pile of returned books onto her trolley. She stops, mid-bend, her interest piqued. 'What happened then?' she asks, turning back with a small smile, her blue eyes twinkling with the intrigue I had originally hoped for.

'Someone is moving into the old Draper house,' I whisper animatedly, leaning as far over the counter as I can.

'You're kidding!' she responds a little too loudly, then blushes as she realises she has broken her own golden rule to never disturb the peace of the library. 'Did you get a good look at them?' she adds more quietly.

'No, not yet . . .' I sigh, then perk up a little as I remember the sight of the rather disgruntled Mrs Arbuthnot traipsing up and down the street, and recount it to Grace. I expect her to find it as funny as I did, but she looks a little unimpressed.

'So, nothing *that* exciting has happened then,' she replies coolly, and I feel a little pang in my chest to have disappointed her.

'Well, I don't know what you were expecting. It is only Hampstead, after all . . .' I reply, slightly stung. I had thought she would be as excited as I was by the revelation. We have dreamt of this moment a thousand times over and it is finally happening.

As if sensing my chagrin, she smiles encouragingly and grabs my hand. 'Who knows, maybe the new owners will have made an appearance by the time we get home.'

I smile back at her, though rather wanly, my initial enthusiasm somewhat doused, just as Grace's colleague Jacob slides round the desk, chewing on a large piece of fruit-studded bread.

'Gracie, I can't find that Proust volume anywhere and someone has called up to request it,' he says. 'Are you sure you put it back in the right place?' Jacob has the warmest, loveliest pair of eyes I have ever seen, and they widen in surprise at the sight of me, like two round conkers. 'Oh, hello, Clem,' he says fondly. 'I didn't hear you arrive. How was ballet?' He tears off a piece of the bread and offers it to me. 'Would you like some challah bread? My mother's secret recipe.'

'I'm surprised you didn't hear her. The rest of the library did,' Grace mutters with a pointed look at me as I take the challah bread from Jacob and pop a piece in my mouth. 'And don't call me Gracie,' she adds with a huff. 'It's not very becoming.'

Jacob and I raise our eyebrows at each other conspiratorially and she folds her arms crossly.

'Oh honestly, when you two get together I always get ganged up on. Jacob, the two gentlemen over at that table were asking about Proust. They probably have what you're looking for. You'll have to prise it off them.'

He nods, his floppy mahogany hair swishing around his face, then sweeps his way over to the table where the two scholars are buried deep in their books. Grace's eyes follow him as he goes, and I watch her observing him with intrigue.

'I don't know why he's friends with you,' I snort, leaning back against the counter. 'You're always so mean to him.'

Her eyes dart back to mine and her cheeks flush a little. 'I am *not*,' she replies indignantly. 'Besides, why don't *you* try working with him all day, then criticise. His head is always off in the clouds . . .' She trails off, her eyes slowly roving back towards where Jacob is still trying to coax the book away from the scholars, then she shakes her head, her petite nose crinkling.

'This bread is delicious,' I say through another mouthful. It is soft and spongy, almost more like a cake than a bread, delicately honey-sweetened and interspersed with the tang of raisins.

Grace turns her attention back to me and tears a piece of the bread off for herself, munching on it thoughtfully. 'Come on, it's time we were getting home. Mother will be wondering where we are.'

I wave goodbye to Jacob, who has finally managed to wrestle the book free, and he waves goodbye enthusiastically at us with a large grin, but Grace doesn't look back as she fiddles with the buttons on her coat.

'Definitely mean,' I murmur under my breath, just loud enough for her to hear, and she rolls her eyes as she loops her arm through mine.

'Forget about the library. Talk me through what has been going on at the Draper house. I want all the details,' she says enthusiastically, and I launch into a blow-by-blow account of everything I saw.

Chapter 4

When Grace and I return home, it is to find that there has been no development in the case of our mysterious new neighbour. The removal vans have all left, and the street is quiet once more, but there is not a single light on in the old Draper house.

'Maybe they sent their belongings ahead of them?' I suggest as we walk past, both our eyes glued to the old three-storey townhouse.

'Maybe the electricity has been cut off . . .' Graces muses. 'Or maybe the Drapers didn't have electricity installed and were still using candles.'

'Well, that doesn't make sense,' I scoff. 'We would still be able to see flickering candlelight if that were the case.'

'Oh, Clem, but what if our new neighbour doesn't have any candles?' she insists, her blue eyes wide and shining. 'Perhaps we should take some round . . .'

'You're beginning to sound like Mrs Arbuthnot,' I warn her, narrowing my eyes, and the two of us burst into fits of giggles as we traipse up the steps to our own front door.

I gaze back across the street at the old Draper house while Grace fiddles with her key in the lock. It really is a very beautiful building. Somehow, despite having been empty for so long, it is dilapidated in a rather romantic way. It is almost as if the old house has been asleep for many years, and is ready to be awoken by its new owner. A wrought-iron fence, bordered with overgrown roses, encircles a chipped and battered mosaic pathway up to the red-brick facade. Each floor boasts a huge bay window, and I imagine how

Thankfully, I have known Rudi for such a long time now, that I consider myself immune to his irresistible charms that have broken the hearts of so many other girls. That is probably why we dance so well together: years of trust, and no awkward attachments to distract us. Of course, half the girls at Madame Lebedev's are convinced we are secretly courting; the other half think we have some sort of complicated romantic past. They assume we get all the principal roles because Rudi is the only boy in our class and Madame Lebedev's son, and that I get to dance with him because I wormed my way into their close family circle. The real truth is that we work the hardest and we want it the most. We have both fantasised of joining the Vic-Wells Ballet from the moment we first danced together and Madame Lebedev said that we were destined for great things. Madame jokes that Rudi was born pointing his feet, but what she really means is that ballet is in his blood. She used to dance in the Bolshoi back in Russia, she even danced for the Tsar on several occasions, but then things in Russia got so treacherous that she and Rudi fled to Europe, before finally settling in London.

Rudi loops his arm in mine and escorts me inside, our footsteps creaking on the worn wooden floorboards as we make our way to the studio. Madame Lebedev is leaning against the piano, speaking in fast fluent Russian with the pianist and pointing animatedly at the sheet music before him. She is an incredibly beautiful woman. Her hair is darker than Rudi's, almost mahogany, but she has the same heavy-lidded grey eyes, like the soft downy feathers of a cygnet. She is tall and willowy, her lithe muscles flexing with every movement beneath her black leotard and long wrap-around skirt. She stops when she sees me and stands up straight.

'Rudi, Clementine, what time do you call this?' she snaps, but her eyes are filled with warmth, and they crinkle at the corners as her lips spread into a reluctant smile. 'Get changed and warmed up.'

'Sorry, Madame, I lost track of time,' I say, kicking off

the daylight must come flooding in each morning, casting splashes of colour from the stained-glass across the floor like scattered boiled sweets. But my favourite part is the gabled attic, right at the very top, where a round window, paned in white, shines like a full moon. It is nothing like our house, which is simply rundown from neglect. Our house was once magnificent too, when Father was still alive. I remember it was always warm, and it felt so full of light. Father was always bringing home interesting new curios too – big brass telescopes, leather-bound books with gold embossed titles, framed collections of iridescent beetles and delicate butterflies. One by one, all of these magnificent memories have been sold off to pay the bills, all to keep this ramshackle ruin of grandeur running. If it weren't for the memories that the house holds, I don't know if I would say it was worth it.

'Clementine?' Grace says, and I spin around in surprise. She has the door open and is already in the hall, pulling off her boots. 'Come in quickly, and shut the door!' she hisses. 'You're letting all the cold in.'

I hurry inside and close the door behind me as quietly as I can, anxious not to disturb Mother.

'Whose turn is it to cook tonight?' Grace asks, shaking off her coat and wandering down the hall towards the kitchen.

'Definitely yours,' I reply firmly, following after her. The kitchen is freezing cold, and I recoil slightly from the drop in temperature, running to the Aga to turn the heat up.

'Fine, but if I cook, *you* have to take it upstairs to Mother,' she reminds me, and I wilt at the prospect. 'And you have to wash the dishes, *and* you have to eat my cooking,' she finishes, listing the consequences like punishments on her fingers.

'In that case, it is definitely my turn to cook.' I grimace, and she squeezes my shoulder affectionately.

'I had better say hello and collect her breakfast tray,' Grace sighs, then glides out of the room.

I rootle through the cupboards in search of inspiration, but they are practically empty. I find a solitary tin of baked beans, half a loaf of rather stale bread and a couple of slightly greying sausages. I give the sausages a sniff and they seem alright, so I chop them into thin slices and pop them in a pan with the last knob of butter. My stomach growls hungrily as I begin slicing up the bread, attempting to make it go round all three of us. I hear Grace's footsteps on the stairs as I empty the beans into a saucepan and pop them on the stove. She sighs as she enters the kitchen and places Mother's tray down by the sink.

'Everything alright?' I ask tentatively, glancing over my shoulder. Her hands are clutching the kitchen counter tightly and her head is hung low, but she whips around to look at me with her classic everything-is-fine smile.

'Yes, of course!' she lies. 'Mother's not hungry, so the good news is there will be more for the two of us.'

'She's cross about breakfast, isn't she?' I cut to the chase, and Grace sighs.

'Is it really so difficult to just check on her when you wake up?' she pleads.

'I didn't do it on purpose!' I snap. Grace always tries to keep the peace, but that so often means bowing to Mother's pressure. 'Is it really so hard for her to get out of bed and collect her own tray?'

'She's not well, Clem.'

'She had energy enough to enquire after the Drapers,' I grumble under my breath.

Grace sighs again and rubs her eyes, then wrinkles her nose. 'Something is burning.'

'Oh, blast!' I cry and turn back to the stove where the beans are boiling furiously in the saucepan.

I scrape as much as I can from the pan onto the toast, avoiding the charred layer of sauce at the bottom, and spoon the sausages on top, then hand a plate to Grace who eyes it suspiciously.

'Bon appetit,' I grin, and her face finally cracks into a genuine smile as we tuck in.

Once Grace and I have cleaned up after dinner, we both drag our tired bodies up the staircase to bed. Grace stops on the landing and gazes wistfully towards the bedroom we once shared. After our father passed away, Mother insisted that Grace move into his bedroom. She swore it was to give us both more space, but we both know Mother would go to any length to keep the two of us apart, terrified that our close bond may lead us to revolt against her. I miss sharing a room with Grace too. We used to have so much fun, lining up our teddy bears and dolls, pretending they were at school. Grace would always teach them English, reading to them from whichever book she currently had her nose in. I would lie on the floor, resting my chin on my hands and join the teddies and dolls in rapt silence as we enjoyed her dramatic reading. Then, afterwards, I would teach them ballet, and Grace would take turns moving their soft limbs into the correct positions. We would swap clothes too, sharing practically everything in our wardrobe, all the lovely dresses that Father bought for us, with satin bows and lace trim, all of which are long gone now.

Grace blinks slowly, then refocuses her gaze on me. I wonder if she is thinking about the same memories as me. 'Night, Clem,' she whispers, then kisses me on the cheek and floats up the second flight of stairs to her bedroom.

I pause where I am for a moment, listening intently for any sound from Mother's bedroom. When I don't hear anything, I creep past her door, careful to avoid the squeaky floorboard in case I wake her, and softly close the door to my bedroom. I look longingly at my bed for a moment, but I can't sleep just yet. I sit on the edge of the bed and pull my ballet shoes from my bag, sliding my feet into the familiar, worn, soft leather slippers. I point and flex my toes a couple of times, then lift myself off the bed and rest one hand on the dresser and begin practising my *tendus*, extending my leg along the floor until only the very tip of my toe remains anchored. I practise my barre exercises diligently every night before I go to sleep and every morning as soon as I wake up. There is something meditative about the process, the control I must exert over my body. I don't think I could sleep if I ever missed a practice, but I wouldn't know as it never happens.

I am halfway through my *fondus* when something outside the window catches my eye and I stop with my leg outstretched in mid-air. There is a warm, flickering light coming from across the street. One of our neighbours must have lit a fire in the grate – nothing out of the ordinary, summer is drawing to an end and the nights are getting cooler, so I don't know why it strikes me as peculiar. I gently bring my foot down to the ground and pad across the floor to the window, and that is when I realise why the light caught my attention. It is coming from the Draper house.

I feel my pulse begin to race and instinctively reach my fingers out as if I could touch the enchanted house from here, but all I feel is the cold glass of my own windowpane. I am rooted to the spot as a million possibilities dance through my mind. Have the new owners moved in? I wonder if anybody saw them arrive. If it had been Mrs Arbuthnot, she would have been sure to inform the whole street. A disturbing thought begins to niggle at the back of my mind: what if an intruder has broken in? I should simply finish my practice, change into my nightgown and go to sleep. I know that is what I *should* do, but my feet make up their mind before my head does, and the next thing I know, I am whisking my way downstairs and out of the front door.

The night air has a bite to it and I wish I had thought to take my coat. My feet, though, aren't bothered by such trivial matters, numb as they are from years of ballet training. The road is bathed in orange light from the tall street lamps, but I keep to the darkness, my leather-soled ballet slippers allowing me to approach the Draper house with the stealth of a cat. I stop at the wrought-iron gate, my fingers on the latch. I look around but the street is deserted, so I push it open and wince as it creaks. I step softly up the mosaic path to the front window where the flickering light is coming from, but the sill is too high and I can't get a good view. I glance around the front garden, then decide to try the back gate. This time, I don't have to worry about making too much noise as the gate is already open and swinging softly on its hinges in the chilling breeze. I slip through and make my way down the side of the house, shrouded in shadow. As I reach the back garden, a fox darts across the lawn and I almost let out a scream, clasping my hand tightly across my mouth just in time as my heart thunders against my ribs. I should turn back, it is a warning, I tell myself, but still I walk on.

The house is built in a similar layout to our own, with the kitchen at the back, leading to the garden. Our own kitchen door is rarely locked, usually because I forget, something which Grace and I quarrel over at least once a week. If there is an intruder, perhaps this is how they got inside. I make a solemn vow under my breath never to leave it unlocked again. I try the door and am unsurprised when it opens with a little shove. I close it quietly behind me, then stop dead in my tracks as it hits me that after years of daydreaming, wondering and speculating, I am *finally* inside the Draper house. I gaze around the kitchen in wonder, running my fingers across the smooth marble countertops. Heat is rolling off the Aga in waves – the new owners are obviously wealthy – and my muscles finally relax as I stop shivering. I pull open a drawer, full of glistening brass cutlery. I reach up on my tiptoes to open a cupboard and find it stuffed to bursting with food. My stomach pangs painfully, hardly satisfied from my meagre supper, as I scan my eyes across tinned peaches, tomatoes, marrowfat peas, baked beans . . . I can almost taste the sugary-sweet sauce and my mouth begins to water. I contemplate taking a tin when I remember that I am here to perhaps *catch* an intruder, not to become one myself. I close the cupboard again firmly and march quickly from the kitchen, leaving the temptation behind.

I fumble around in the darkness of the hallway for a moment, praying that no one is watching me from the shadows. That is when I hear a light groaning sound and stand frozen to the spot. Is it the creaking of the old house or something more sinister? My brain screams at me to turn and flee, I shouldn't be here, but my feet have a mind of their own and they creep along the polished wooden floorboards. Flicking honey-coloured light pours out of a room at the end of the hallway, and I walk 'possessed' towards it. The door is open just enough for me to squeeze inside.

The groaning is louder in here, but I still can't see where it might be coming from. I look around the room, rooted to the spot by the door. A deep velvet sofa sits in the middle of the room, atop a large Persian rug, covered in a bundle of blankets. The walls are hung with the most beautiful botanical illustrations. I quietly cross the parquet floor to look more closely at one of them. It is a fine pen and ink detail of some tropical-looking plant I have never seen before. I reach out and trace my fingers against the fine lines of the stem. A grand fireplace is situated against the wall, and the remains of the fire which caught my attention have burned down to a handful of glowing coals. It is too warm and I begin to feel a little faint as I try to cool my hot cheeks with the back of my hand. The groaning starts again, and I jump in surprise, forgetting why I came here. I spin around, and to my horror, the pile of blankets on the sofa begins to move and unfurl. I am paralysed to the spot as an arm frees itself from the mass of blankets, followed by a bushy head of long dark-blonde hair, and finally a haggard and bearded face. A pair of piercing green eyes lock onto mine and for a moment I am not sure who is more terrified.

The man tries to say something, but whatever it is he wanted to say is drowned out by my scream. My fight or flight response finally kicks in, and I choose flight. I dash from the room as quickly as I can, knocking plants to the floor and tripping over piles of half-unpacked books. I can hear stumbling footsteps growing louder behind me, and I hop down the hallway, trying to remove my ballet slippers so I can throw them at the assailant as he gains on me. The first shoe finds its target, hitting the man square in the face. It is not very heavy, but I think the shock of the action surprises him long enough for me to gain some distance. I race back through the kitchen and turn the door handle, wrenching it open and tearing off into the night. I scarper back down the side of the house to the front garden, leap over the gate, my ballet tunic tearing on the wrought-iron spokes, but I keep going, my heart in my mouth. Thankfully the street is silent at this hour and I rush across the road, up the stone steps to home. I close the front door behind me as quietly as I can and lean against it for a moment, then lock and bolt it fast, my chest heaving up and down as adrenaline courses through me. I look down at my hands and they are shaking as I try to slow my breathing. I turn around and lift my eye to the peephole to see if the man followed me but the street is silent once again.

Chapter 5

The next morning, I lie in bed for a while longer than usual, thinking about the night before and my close encounter with danger. Who was the man in the Draper house? I am not sure what to do about it because I shouldn't have been trespassing in the first place. I feel I should tell Grace; she would know what to do, but I can already picture the disappointed look on her face when she realises I ignored her advice to steer clear of the house. The longer I lie in bed, the more I start to worry. What if that man had been some sort of caretaker? What if he calls the police? I wonder if he realises that I live just across the street.

I roll out of bed and reach underneath it for my dance bag to start my morning stretches. I sift wearily through the contents for my leather ballet slippers, rubbing sleep out of my eyes, but they are not in here. My heart stops, and I cast my eyes around the bedroom. One of them is lying on the floor and I snatch it up to my heart, but where is the other one? I start sifting through drawers and my wardrobe, even stripping the bed sheets back as my panic mounts. Then I remember. I removed my ballet shoe and threw it at the mystery man in the Draper house. It was what gave me the distance to make my escape.

I swallow hard and make my way downstairs to the kitchen, where I can hear an awful clanging and a terrible burnt smell wafting through the hallway. I push open the door and find a harried-looking Grace in an apron, her usually neat hair in tufts and streaked with flour. I let out an involuntary snort and she glares murderously at me.

'Sorry,' I giggle. 'But you do look a state. What on earth are you doing?'

'I'm trying to bake a cake,' she says with exasperation, her cheeks flushed with the effort of beating a rather sloppy-looking batter around the bowl. 'I thought it was supposed to be easy, but this is my third attempt and we're nearly out of eggs.'

I lean over her and glance at the sad excuse for a cake mix. 'You need more flour.'

'How do you know?' she asks sceptically.

'I just do. Here, let me help. I'll sift it in while you keep beating.'

I lift the bag of flour above the bowl and begin shaking it over the bowl while Grace stirs. Once it is all mixed in, we both dip our fingers into the batter and give it a try. 'That's actually not too bad!' she says with pleasant surprise. 'Thanks, Clem, you're a lifesaver.'

'What's it for?' I ask, and her pink cheeks grow even rosier as she opens the oven.

'It's for Jacob's birthday,' she replies hastily, avoiding my gaze. 'He's been going on and on for weeks about how he never gets a birthday cake, and I thought if I made him one he might finally shut up about it.'

'Such a kind sentiment.' I grin, licking the remaining batter off the spoon.

'Did you want something, or did you just come by to offer your criticism?' she replies drily, straightening up again and placing her hands on her hips.

'Ah, well actually, I do need something . . .' I reply sheepishly. 'I think I need a new pair of shoes.'

'Well, why don't you ask Mother? She has your savings book.'

'Not those kind of shoes,' I say quietly, then look over my shoulder to check the coast is clear before whispering, 'ballet shoes. I hate to ask, but you know she won't allow me to spend my savings on anything for ballet.'

'Oh, Clem, I feel like it was only yesterday we bought your last pair. Surely you must have stopped growing by now?'

'I know, I'm sorry!' I groan. 'I haven't outgrown them, I . . . I have worn through them,' I lie, losing the courage to tell her about last night.

She raises her eyebrows. 'What were you *doing* in them?'

'Just dancing,' I reply casually, keeping my eyes fixed on the spoon in my hand as she sighs.

'Well, it will have to wait until this evening. I'll be picking up my pay cheque at the library later on today. Can you make do with your pointe shoes for now? And can you please try and make this pair last a little—!' She stops mid-sentence as I fly at her.

'Thank you, thank you, thank you!' I exclaim with relief. 'You really are the best sister anyone could ever ask for.'

'Well, you did save my bacon with the cake, so we'll call it even,' she says with a smile.

I am finally starting to relax and think I may have got away scot-free with my midnight excursion when there is a sharp rap at the door, and I start in surprise. I leap up to answer it, but Grace is quicker and beats me to the hallway.

'No, Grace, don't!' I cry, but she has the door open before I even make it to the hall. I spy Mrs Arbuthnot at the doorway with a very grave expression on her face; I don't think I have ever been so relieved to see her. Grace is nodding gently while Mrs Arbuthnot lets forth a tirade of information at her before catching my eye.

'Oh good, Clementine, you're here too!' she trills as I step closer. She is holding a pile of pamphlets in her hand and her expression is anxious, but her eyes shine with the kind of excitement she only gets from meddling in other people's business. 'I was just explaining to your sister, there was a break-in on the street last night.'

'Oh,' I say guiltily, dropping my gaze to my feet.

'Oh, indeed!' she replies. 'I've never heard anything like

it in all my years living here. Poor Mr Draper, what must he think of his neighbours . . .'

'Mr Draper?' I ask sharply, my head snapping back up.

'Why, yes. The break-in was at his house. Poor man has only just moved in, and he's been frightfully unwell apparently.'

So that must have been our elusive new neighbour who I threw my ballet slipper at. My stomach churns uncomfortably.

'I didn't realise anybody had moved in yet,' Grace replies. 'Is he related to the original Drapers or is it coincidence?'

'He's their grandson apparently, an American though.' She whispers the word 'American' like it is a slur. 'Oh, you should hear how he says coffee! Most peculiar, but not to be helped . . . He is from New York originally, and he has only been in London for a couple of days. He's recently back from some overseas expedition apparently. He's a botanist, don't you know? An important one,' Mrs Arbuthnot says proudly, in the same way she goes on about her son Archie, rather than a new neighbour who is barely more than a stranger. I must admit, I am impressed with how much information she has managed to garner on him already when most of us have seen hide nor hair of him. 'Anyway, I have taken it upon myself to set up a neighbourhood lookout,' she continues, handing one of the pamphlets to Grace. 'We all must do our bit to keep this street safe. Just think if the perpetrator had broken in here where you three ladies are all alone, or worse, into *my* house! No, it won't do. We must snuff these culprits out at once.'

Grace takes the pamphlet and scans over it. 'Thank you, Mrs Arbuthnot,' she says in her most polite voice. 'We'll be sure to share this with our mother.'

Mrs Arbuthnot's eyes narrow with curiosity briefly. 'And how is your mother, dear? We miss her dreadfully at the Women's Institute. Will you let her know?'

'We will pass on the message,' Grace says a little more firmly as Mrs Arbuthnot tries to peer past her to get a better look at the house. Grace moves her body slightly to block the view, and Mrs Arbuthnot looks disgruntled for a moment before correcting her features.

'Very well. I'd best be getting on to the other houses,' she says sniffily. 'Do think long and hard about signing up, won't you? I know my Archie would if he were still living on this street.' And with that, she turns on her heel, potters down the path and takes off up the street again.

There is silence for a moment as Grace closes the door, then turns slowly to face me with a look of concern. 'Clem, what did you do?' she asks slowly.

'I love how you assume this has something to do with me!' I retort hotly, feeling my cheeks blaze scarlet.

Grace gives me a long hard look, but I refuse to come clean, so she sighs and makes for the stairs. 'I suppose I had better give this to Mother.'

An hour later, I am in the midst of the most horrible task of de-cobwebbing the ceilings, when the door knocks a second time and I am convinced that the game is up. Perhaps Mrs Arbuthnot's neighbourhood lookout has already sniffed me out. Grace has left for work, and I contemplate not opening the door at all, but I fear that they will keep knocking and wake Mother. Between a visit from the police and the wrath of my mother, I choose arrest. I wonder if they will let me continue practising ballet in my cell, and I hope that they will let Grace and Rudi visit at least once per week. I pause with my hand on the door and take one last breath of freedom as I pull it open; but I don't find a policeman on the other side. Instead, I am greeted by a pair of startlingly green eyes, only now they are not hidden behind a mass of hair and beard. The man before me is clean shaven, his dark-blonde hair swept back beneath a grey fedora hat. He looks much younger than he did last night, perhaps in his mid-twenties, with a broad chest and shoulders, but he looks a bit hollowed out in the cheeks and there are dark shadows under his eyes. I recall Mrs Arbuthnot saying he had been unwell after some exotic expedition, which would explain the groaning I heard last night, I suppose. I take a step back, half in surprise, half in case whatever he had is still infectious.

'Ah! Just the person I was hoping to see,' he drawls, his chin held high as he removes his hat with a wide smile that reveals a row of perfectly white, straight teeth. 'I believe I have something that belongs to you.' His accent is peculiar, not as strong as I had expected from the way Mrs Arbuthnot had described, but not quite British either. There is a strange lilt to his speech, a bouncy rhythm that exudes confidence and energy. He reaches into the pocket of his suit jacket and hands me something small, smooth and pink. I grasp at the ballet shoe and tuck it quickly into my own pocket. 'Don't worry,' he says, 'I won't be telling anyone about our little mishap. This shall be one mystery the neighbourhood brigade shall not solve.' His eyes sparkle as he speaks and he barely manages to conceal his smile. Something tells me I am going to like our new neighbour.

'That's very kind of you, Mr Draper,' I say politely. 'I would appreciate that incident staying between the two of us . . . and, for what it's worth, I am terribly sorry about last night.'

'Why, not at all. For which part though? Breaking into my house or throwing your shoe at me?' He grins and I blush deep crimson. 'And please don't call me Mr Draper, that makes me sound downright ancient. My name is August. A pleasure to properly make your acquaintance, Miss . . . ?'

'Harrington,' I reply, offering him my hand. 'Clementine Harrington.'

He shakes it and I notice how small my hand is in his. His arms are incredibly tanned, and his palms are rough with callouses. 'Clementine? That's a peculiar name,' he muses as he lets go.

'No more peculiar than August,' I quip and he throws back

34

his head and laughs as I slap my hand across my mouth. 'Sorry,' I mumble from behind my fingers. 'That was very rude. My name is a bit of a point of contention.'

'No, you're quite right. In fact, it is worse than you think, Miss Harrington.' He looks around him, then leans in closer so that I can smell the bergamot notes in his cologne. 'My mother was fascinated with Ancient Rome when she was pregnant, and my full name is actually Augustus, but you must swear never to tell anyone. I don't think I could live it down.'

'I'll take it to the grave,' I swear solemnly. I don't know what I was expecting from our new neighbour, but it was not this. The man before me is so incredibly charming that I find myself at ease with him almost at once.

'Well, there you go then. We both have a secret of each other's to protect.' He nods, and the corners of my lips tug up into a smile as a little ember of warmth glows in my chest. There is something about sharing secrets that instantly connects two people.

'Now, Clementine, I would love to shoot the breeze with you all morning, but I did come here with a mission,' he says, interrupting my thoughts. 'Tell me, is your father home?'

'Oh,' I say abruptly. 'No, he's dead.'

His green eyes widen in shock at the blunder. 'Oh gosh, I am sorry.'

'It's OK, it was a long time ago.' I shrug.

'Nevertheless, it never gets much easier, does it? Both my parents passed away when I was fifteen, and I still miss them every day . . .' His eyes lose focus for a moment and I feel a pang of sympathy for him. I wonder if he is terribly lonely in that big house all on his own, but before I can say anything, he snaps out of it and smiles widely again. 'What about your mother, is she around?'

I let out a humourless chuckle and cross my arms, leaning against the door jamb. 'You haven't been told much about our family yet, have you?' I reply with a stoic smile. 'I'm surprised Mrs Arbuthnot hasn't given you a ring binder with the detailed history of all your neighbours. She must be slipping in her old age.'

'Ah, yes . . .' he says uncomfortably. 'Interesting woman, Mrs Arbuthnot. Very involved in the community, I gather.'

'Involved is one word for it,' I mutter and his green eyes twinkle mischievously. 'Mother isn't well,' I say, bringing him up to speed. 'She's rather infirm and doesn't leave the house much.'

'I'm sorry to hear that,' he says politely, but he can't hide the intrigue on his face. 'In which case, Clementine, may I leave it to you to pass on the message that I am planning a dinner party to introduce myself to the neighbourhood this Friday, and I would be delighted if your family could attend.'

My pulse quickens at the thought of a dinner party, and I think once again of the cupboard stuffed full of food in August Draper's kitchen. 'That's very kind of you. I will pass on the message,' I reply, and he nods then takes off back down the steps. He stops on the pathway and turns back around just as I am about to close the door.

'Oh, and Miss Harrington, I do hope you didn't mistake my calling your name peculiar as an insult. I think it is rather beautiful.'

I feel my face flush with colour as he places his hat back on his head, opens the gate, and takes off up the street.

Chapter 6

'You actually met Mr Draper?' Grace interrogates me for the third time on the bus home from the library.

She is far more excited about it than Rudi was when I tried telling him about my midnight excursion after ballet class. He was surprisingly cross with me for having been so reckless, and while I was touched that he cared, it really rather put a dampener on the rest of the story. He showed little to no interest in the exact shade of August Draper's eyes, or that he had travelled the world, discovering new species of plants, and he seemed positively affronted that I was considering returning to the Draper house for dinner.

'What did you talk about?' Grace asks impatiently, stirring me from my thoughts.

'He introduced himself properly and asked a bit about our family, then . . .'

'What do you mean introduced himself *properly*?' she interrupts shrewdly. 'Have you seen him before?'

'Oh . . . no,' I stumble, feeling my cheeks burn, 'I just meant . . . it was a proper introduction.'

Grace narrows her eyes suspiciously at me, so I change the subject hastily. 'Anyway, you interrupted me before the most important part! He invited us over for dinner this Friday.'

'Oh gosh . . .' she murmurs, looking out of the window at the grey street. 'Just us or the whole street?'

'He'd certainly spoken to Mrs Arbuthnot,' I reply with a look, and Grace's lips twitch into a smile. 'I think he said there would be others. Will Mother let us go?'

'I don't know . . .' she murmurs, her nose wrinkling with

concentration. 'I'll see what I can do.' She makes to get off the bus and I look at her in confusion.

'Where are you going?' I ask her. 'We are still ten minutes away from home.'

'I thought you needed new ballet shoes? The shop is just up this road, isn't it?'

'Oh, I had another look at them and they really aren't so bad,' I lie, feeling awfully guilty. Grace and I have always been honest and open with one another, and now my one act of deceit seems to be snowballing.

When we arrive home, Grace immediately tramps up the stairs to our mother's bedroom. I linger on the staircase, listening intently to the soft murmurs that drift through the crack in the open door. I can only pick up the occasional word. 'Draper . . . dinner . . . good impression.' Grace is trying her best to convince Mother, I can tell. I just hope her curiosity is piqued enough to bite. I sit down mid-way up the flight of stairs, and roll my neck back and forth. The muscles are stiff and aching from today's ballet practice, and it feels good to elongate them, relieving the tension. I hear Mother's door close softly and spin round a little too quickly, pulling my neck once more with a painful twinge. Grace is standing at the top of the stairs, her fingers placed delicately on the banister. She stares at them for a moment as if she is lost in contemplation.

'Well?' I whisper, and her eyes meet mine with a look of confusion, as if she had forgotten what she was doing.

Her bow lips spread into a smile and she gives me a short sharp nod as she descends the stairs and sits beside me on the step.

'We can go?' I ask excitedly.

'Yes, she says we *must* go,' she replies, almost heavy heartedly.

I glance up at her beneath my eyelashes. 'Well, that's good news, isn't it? This is what we wanted.'

'Yes, of course it is, Clem,' she says with a reassuring

smile, but I can't help feeling that she is holding something back from me.

The next morning, I rise with the sun and begin my ballet exercises. I bend, fold and stretch my body every which way, relishing the feeling of my muscles lengthening, the power that ripples just below my skin, the control I have over every inch of my body.

By the time I have finished, there is a film of sweat on my chest and my brow, and my heart is beating rapidly. I sit on the edge of my bed as I slip off my ballet shoes and stuff them deep into my duffel bag. I take my time in the bathroom, washing my hair and rinsing the sweat from my skin. The water runs sporadically hot then cold, and it sputters occasionally as if it is going to give out altogether, but it keeps on, almost as if it knows we can't afford to get the pipes examined. Sometimes, I feel like this old house is alive, like it has a spirit of its own. Sure, it needs an awful lot of attention – the wallpaper is peeling, the roof is leaking, the floorboards are in desperate need of a varnish, the springs in the mattresses have entirely given up the ghost, and if you sit in the wrong place on the sofa, it swallows you whole . . . just like Grace and me, the house is barely holding it together but it never, never gives up entirely. Everything works just enough for us to get by, and for that, I am eternally grateful. I pat the side of the bath tub affectionately as I step out and wrap myself in a scratchy towel.

I pad down the hallway, leaving a trail of wet footprints behind me, but stop suddenly before I reach my bedroom. My ears prick at the sound of voices coming from downstairs. I recognise Grace's soft, dulcet tones immediately, but the other voice is a mystery. It is strangely familiar, but I simply can't place it. Whoever it is, they are speaking most animatedly to Grace, and from what I can gather, she seems far less enthused, but is trying her best to appease the person. That's when it hits me. I whip around and gaze down the hallway to where Mother's bedroom door is wide open. Sunlight is pouring through the open curtains, curtains that haven't been opened for almost ten years. My feet appear to be glued to the spot, but I will myself to walk towards her room, one arduous step at a time, as if I were walking through clay. I peer round the door jamb. The counterpane has been thrown back from the sheets, the faint smell of lilac perfume lingers, the room is empty.

I fly down the stairs, clutching my towel to my body, and halt in front of the sitting room. Though I am seeing it with my own eyes, I can't believe that my mother is stood by the fireplace. She is dressed in a long, black skirt and matching black, high-necked blouse, a cameo pin at her throat. Her hair has been washed and is coiled into a neat bun at the nape of her neck. Her skin still has that sallow look, but there is nothing to be done about that after years of being trapped indoors. Her bony fingers are wrapped tightly around an old cane. I haven't seen that cane in years . . . it used to belong to our father. It is a rich russet brown stick with a highly polished finish, and an ornate brass handle in the shape of a bowing eagle, each tiny feather painstakingly carved into the metal. Father didn't always walk with a cane, only when his war injuries were playing up. Though relatively unscathed (physically, at least) from the war, he did take a bit of shrapnel to his knee and this would often give him grief in the colder, damp months. That was when he would use the cane my mother's scrawny hand is now grasped around. I remember sitting on his lap and admiring the shiny brass eagle. He would bounce me up and down and make the eagle fly around the room for me. He always said, if he must walk with a cane, he wanted it to be a thing of beauty and it truly is.

'Clementine!' Mother barks, shaking me from the memory and bringing me back to the present situation. 'What on earth are you doing downstairs in nothing but a towel? Go upstairs and get dressed immediately.'

I balk and turn on my heel at once, charging back up the stairs to get dressed as quickly as possible. I slip a long-sleeved yellow floral dress over my head, which Grace made for me out of a pair of old curtains. It is slightly too short for me now, but acceptable enough with a pair of thick woollen tights. I stuff my feet into a pair, and rush back downstairs where Mother is now speaking animatedly to Grace.

'This place is a state,' she grumbles, casting her eyes around the hallway. She is right of course. The wallpaper is peeling away from damp spots on the wall, there are chips in the floor tiles and the high ceilings are crowded with the cobwebs that I couldn't quite reach.

'We have been trying our best, Mother, but we had to let the last maid go last year.'

'Has your brother not been sending money?' she asks sharply.

Grace and I share a look. As soon as he turned eighteen, our older brother Edmund flew the nest, and then flew on as far as he could to join a cattle ranch in America. He sends a letter once a year at Christmas, but there has never been any money to accompany his well wishes.

'Typical of the men in this family,' Mother scoffs. 'It would appear he has grown up to be just as much of a disappointment as your useless father.'

I bow my head and bite my tongue. It is hardly Father's fault that he died, but I daren't rock the boat by saying as much to Mother.

'All a woman can count on in this world is herself,' Mother continues, then her eyes fall on Grace with a rare look of benevolence which she never spares for me.

'Now, we must discuss this dinner party . . . You will need something head-turning to wear, darling,' she says affectionately, and I feel a stab of envy in my chest as I watch from the shadows.

'I have plenty of nice dresses, Mother,' Grace tries to insist. 'We don't need to waste money on something so frivolous as a new outfit.'

'Nonsense!' Mother interrupts. 'I still have a little money

tucked away for such occasions. Besides, you are a young woman now, you should be dressing accordingly. How will you ever find a husband in all these hand-me-down outfits?'

Mother insists that we call down a black cab to take us to Bond Street. Grace tries to suggest that she should take it easy, as she has barely left her bed in years, and from the way she clutches our father's cane, it is clear she is struggling more than she lets on, but she is adamant that we must go shopping. We drive past plenty of beautiful shops with the most magnificent outfits in the windows but Mother tells the driver to keep going until finally she commands him to stop outside a rather tired-looking boutique. It has a dusty pink awning with the word 'Archambeau' painted across it in peeling gold letters. The mannequins in the window look down on us in their cocktail finery, and I glance at Grace dubiously.

'We are certain to find something here,' Mother instructs, gingerly making her way out of the car. She rings the doorbell and an austere woman with a short, sharp bob, peppered with streaks of silver, comes pottering towards the door. Her face lights up in surprise when she spots our mother.

'Madame Harrington!' she exclaims, enveloping her in a hug and kissing her on each cheek. 'It has been so long, I thought you were . . .'

'Thought I was what?' Mother asks shrewdly, and the old woman seems to shrink a little, but her face breaks into a warm, crinkly smile.

'Nothing, nothing . . .' she murmurs and ushers us into her shop. 'Your account is, of course, still open. What can I help you with today?'

'My daughters and I are going to a dinner party this Friday. We are in need of some new garments.'

I look at Grace in surprise. I am not sure what I had expected, but I certainly didn't think Mother would be joining us at Mr Draper's. It will be the first time she has left the house in years; all our neighbours will be there and they will have so many questions. I try waving my hand to catch Grace's attention, but she is adamantly avoiding looking at me. I guess she knew all along when she made the deal to get us to go.

Mother turns to look at me, her face twisted in a snarl. 'What are you doing, flailing your arms around, silly girl? Be still for once and behave.'

I feel the blood rush to my cheeks as I mumble an apology and make something up about a fly buzzing around. Grace finally looks my way and gives me a sympathetic smile, which I now choose to ignore in turn.

'New clothes, very well. For all three ladies?' the woman asks as she leads us into a back room. I don't dare to look at Mother, but I hold my breath, wishing and hoping there will be a new dress for me.

'Just the eldest,' she says plainly, forcing Grace forward as my heart sinks.

Unlike the front of the shop, there are no gilded rails of dresses, no tables bedecked with satin clutch bags and strings of pearls. There don't seem to be any clothes on display at all, just a beaten-up chaise longue, an empty podium and a desk covered in swathes of material, pins, scissors and chalks. Mother limps towards the chaise longue and sinks down into it with a sigh of relief, resting her pale hands on Father's eagle-headed cane. She beckons for Grace to join her, while I stand awkwardly by the desk, trying to stifle the urge to reach out and touch the fluffy mass of tulle fabric draped over it. This material would make such a beautiful skirt to dance in. I can imagine how it would float around me like wisps of cloud as I spin across the stage.

'Can I get you anything to drink?' the dressmaker calls from another room. 'Some tea, perhaps? Or champagne, since it is a special occasion?'

'Tea will suffice,' Mother replies, and I watch Grace fiddle with her fingers in her lap, her tawny head bowed.

The dressmaker returns with a golden trolley laden with a large teapot, three delicate floral teacups, and a plate of chocolate-dipped biscuits. Mother speaks with her for a while about what she is looking for, and the dressmaker jumps up with the spryness of a woman twenty years her junior and comes back moments later with a rail of outfits and an assistant.

'Up you get, Mademoiselle,' she instructs Grace, gesturing to the podium. 'And strip down to your slip.'

Grace looks up at last, her blue eyes wide and nervous, like a doe caught in headlights. The assistant comes towards her with a measuring tape, so she quickly does as she is told and stands awkwardly in her threadbare slip while the assistant wraps the tape around her waist, her bust, up her legs and down her arms, writing it all down on a notepad with a pencil. The dressmaker stands with her arms folded, tapping her finger on her chin and studying Grace, as if she were a complex puzzle.

'Let's start with evening wear,' she says, clapping her hands. The assistant disappears between the rails and pulls out a powder-blue, silk dress with a pleated halterneck and wide sash band.

'Arms up!' she orders and Grace does so without a second thought as the assistant slips the dress over her. It looks luscious and smooth to the touch, and Grace is instantly transformed. I finally see what Mother has been saying. I don't know when it happened, but Grace is indeed a woman now. Her body curves in and out at all the right places, her delicate collarbones jutting out from the neckline of the dress. Her legs are long and lithe, and in this dress, she carries herself differently, transforming herself from the Grace I have seen every day of my life, to the glamorous woman before me now. She looks daring and different, and I almost don't recognise her at all.

'Spin,' the seamstress commands, and Grace does as she is told, snapping her head round to keep her eyes on her reflection, as if she can't quite believe what she is seeing either. The assistant sticks some pins in the dress here and there, raising the hemline, pulling in the sides slightly and nipping in the waist, then she pairs the dress with a white and gold ombré cape and the look is complete.

'Perfect!' she declares, whipping it all off and casting the clothes to the assistant's waiting arms. 'Now, shall we look at some daywear?' She reaches for a shell-pink linen dress with short sleeves and an embroidered scalloped detailing on the bust.

On and on the performance goes, the pile of clothes in the assistant's hands growing ever larger as Grace is fitted in new dresses, skirts, blouses and matching accessories. But the more and more clothes that she tries on, the sadder her eyes become. I can't understand it. Here she is, being showered with material things and getting Mother's full attention and glowing praise, but it seems to be bringing her nothing but discomfort.

Once all of Grace's alterations have been noted down, the seamstress turns to me. 'Now, are you sure we can't do something for this one? It looks like you are in need of some new clothes too,' she remarks, noticing how my dress is creeping up to knee-length.

'She won't be needing anything. We can alter her sister's clothes to fit her, I'm sure,' Mother says, without even casting a glance my way, and I feel my heart plummet. I wasn't expecting anything, but even so, it is hard not to feel envious when surrounded by so many beautiful clothes and having to sit back and watch them all bestowed upon my sister. Even if Grace had one less dress, it wouldn't make any difference to her now overflowing wardrobe, and I could have something new. Grace shoots me an apologetic glance as we make our way to the front of the shop while Mother is fitted for some new outfits too; it appears everyone will be leaving the shop with something, except for me. My eyes cast around the boutique, breathing in the heavily perfumed floral air and gazing lustfully at the beautiful garments I shall never own. There is a small display of cosmetics on the counter, lipsticks in gleaming gold cases, glittering palettes of eyeshadow, and beautiful velvet pouches to store them in. I read the sign above it: *La Belle Rose*. The most glamorous woman I have ever seen stares back at me from the sign, brown eyes like chestnuts beneath a set of voluminous lashes. Her blonde hair is short and neatly crimped around her heart-shaped face; the perfect advocate for the beauty range, and suddenly I want it all. My fingers reach out all by themselves and take one of the lipsticks from the display. I pop the lid and twist it to reveal a stick of dusky pink lipstick just as the seamstress returns from the backroom to get some catalogues. She catches sight of what I am doing, and I put it back quickly before she can tell me off, but she smiles, her eyes softening, and she stops before me.

'A tricky customer, your mother,' she winks. 'Always has been. I see the years have not changed her.'

'No, I suppose they have not,' I agree, my eyes falling on the make-up display once again. I cannot look away.

There is a pregnant pause and when I look up, I find the seamstress is looking at me with a torn expression, somewhere between pity and wishing not to overstep her position.

'Would you like the lipstick?' she asks benevolently, and my eyes widen with surprise. She plucks the lipstick from the display and hands it to me. 'Everyone deserves a little treat every now and then.' And without another word, she returns to the back room where Mother is waiting for her.

I pocket the lipstick quickly, not wanting to be accused of theft, and join Grace over by the sofa where she is glancing out of the window, looking unusually glum while I can barely contain my joy at my secret gift.

'What has got into you?' I ask, collapsing down on the chaise longue beside her. 'You have been treated to a whole new wardrobe, yet you look as if you have been sent to purgatory.'

'Oh, Clem, you don't get it, do you?' she sighs, breaking her silence and turning her gaze to me. 'This was not a treat. She has basically purchased my trousseau.'

'Why on earth would you need a trousseau?' I ask, my nose wrinkling. 'You're not getting married.'

'Not yet, but you should have seen the look on her face when she heard that Mr Draper is looking for a bride,' Grace replies grimly. 'If she gets her way, she will have me married by the end of the year. I will have to move out, and you will be alone in that decrepit old house with Mother, and that will be the end of our happy times together.'

'Mr Draper is looking for a *bride*?' I inquire. 'Do you think he hopes to scope out potentials at the dinner party?'

'Yes, I expect so,' Grace muses, then wrinkles her nose at me. 'But why do you look so excited by the prospect? Did you not hear what I just said about the end of our happy times?'

My mind is travelling a million miles a minute. Truth be told, I can think of nothing worse than the end of mine and Grace's companionship, but an idea has occurred to me, and now I can't let it go.

What if I were to marry Mr Draper? There would be no more concern for my dance career, and that looming countdown to my eighteenth birthday wouldn't be a problem anymore. And to top it all off, he is fond of travelling, so I am sure he would see no problem at all in me dancing my way around Europe and beyond.

'Clem?' Grace's voice shakes me out of my daydream. 'What on earth are you thinking about?'

Before I can answer, Mother returns and settles our bill. It is all I can do to pick up my feet and follow her into the taxi, dumbstruck by the sudden, yet – now that I think about it – obvious turnaround in her behaviour. Of course she wants to marry Grace off. I cannot imagine living without her. She is the only thing that still makes our house feel like a home. And what will this mean for Mother and I? The two of us rattling around the empty rooms, she unable to hide her disdain for my very existence. Now that her confinement has ended she will be on at me to find a job and pay my way, and my ballet dreams will be in tatters. And Grace . . . Poor Grace forced to play housewife, alone in some great big house. It doesn't bear thinking about, I *can't* think about it.

Chapter 7

On Friday evening, Grace stands appraisingly in front of the mirror in one of her new dresses, twisting this way and that. Her tawny hair falls around her shoulders in loose ringlets as she leans forward to apply a little lipstick. Neutral Rose. It was what our mother always wore when Father was still alive. Now there is barely anything left on the stick and Grace tries to scrape out a tiny amount with a brush and apply it to her lips.

'Why don't you use this?' I say, withdrawing the pink lipstick from my pocket and handing it to her.

'Oh, Clem, that is *your* special lipstick. I can't take that.'

'I insist,' I reply, pressing it into her hands. 'What good is it, having nice things, if you can't share them with your loved ones?'

'Well, that is a very nice way of looking at it,' she says, plucking off the lid and unscrewing the stick. 'How about I put some on you too?' She brushes the colour across her lips, looking so lovely in her new dress. She deserves something nice, she spends all her own money on us.

Once she is done, she sits me down in the chair in front of the mirror. The only time I ever wear make-up is for the stage, and that is usually heavy greasepaint to make my features stand out to the audience from a distance. I watch now as Grace delicately brushes powders and smoothes ointments across my face, subtly enhancing my features.

'You have such lovely eyes, Clem,' she says, brushing an eyeshadow across my eyelids. 'This shade will really bring out their pretty brown colour.'

'How did you learn all this?' I ask, turning my face this way and that to admire her handiwork. She has somehow managed to enhance my cheekbones so they look fuller, and she is right, my eyes are sparkling in a way I have never seen before. They look a dark tobacco colour, rather than dull hazel brown.

'Oh, you pick these things up after a while.' She shrugs. 'I can teach you.'

'I would like that,' I say softly, clasping her hand, and she smiles down at me.

I can't stop thinking about what she said in Archambeau's earlier in the week . . . Is Mother really planning to marry her off to the first eligible bachelor she finds? At least no one has any plans for me to marry. I am perfectly happy to continue keeping a low profile until I can finally make my escape to the Vic-Wells Ballet Company. Once I am out from under my mother's rule, I will never have to answer to anyone ever again. The only adoration that interests me is that of my audience. I tug at the hem of my slightly too short navy dress absently, and Grace furrows her brow.

'I think we can do a bit better than that dress too, Clem,' she says kindly, taking my hand and coaxing me over to her wardrobe. She rattles through the hangers, now dripping with new garments, freshly delivered from Archambeau's.

She pulls out an old, dark green dress and holds it up for me to admire. It is quite simple, but always looks so elegant on Grace. It is the dress she wears when she knows important scholars are coming to the library and she wants to be taken seriously.

'I can't wear that,' I dismiss. 'It won't fit me properly and I'll just look like I'm playing dress-up.'

'Nonsense!' she says, holding the dress up against me. 'Fashion is all about confidence, Clem. This dress has never failed me before and tonight I guarantee it will come through for you too.'

I try to object but she thrusts the dress towards me more vigorously.

'Just start by trying it on,' she urges, so I do, even if only to shut her up. I shrug out of the short navy dress and slip the green dress over my head. It instantly drowns me like a big-top tent and I huff exasperatedly.

'I told you it wouldn't fit,' I cry. 'I bet I look ridiculous.'

I try to make a move towards the mirror, but she grabs me, needle in hand. 'Don't look yet,' she commands, as she cinches in the waist and begins sewing me into the dress.

'Grace, you can't, you'll ruin it!'

'Oh, it will be fine.' She dismisses me brusquely and works in silence for a few minutes, methodically threading the needle through the fine material and tightening it here and there. She finally stands up and rolls her neck. 'There, now you can look.'

I walk slowly towards the mirror with trepidation, not quite sure what I am expecting to find, and stop dead in front of my reflection. Somehow, she has weaved magic with her needle and the dress doesn't look anywhere near as awful as I had expected. I turn to face her and she is smiling smugly.

'You are wasted in that library,' I say honestly, and she chuckles.

'I *like* the library. Anyway, what do you think? Will it do?'

'Will it do?' I exclaim. 'It's perfect. I don't know how you did it, but I actually look . . . quite nice.' I paint my lips pink with my new lipstick, and before I know it, I am swaying in front of the mirror just as Grace had been.

'You always look nice, Clem,' she insists, coming to stand beside me. 'Now, come on, we had better be going or we will be late.'

Mother is waiting for us in the sitting room. It is still so strange to see her out of her bedroom after so many years, and despite her frail physique, the sight of her momentarily cows me. I bow my head but I am not quick enough. She pulls herself up with her cane, her face creasing in discomfort, and stomps towards me. She may have been confined to her room for many years, but she is still surprisingly fast. I know she didn't spend all her time in bed; I would often hear her pacing around her room late at night when she thought everyone was asleep. Her hand is at my chin in seconds, her bony fingers digging into my flesh.

'What is that you have on your face?' she sneers, her eyes scanning every inch of me as I wilt beneath her touch.

'Nothing, it is just a bit of lipstick!' I protest, finding my voice at last and resolving to meet her steely gaze.

'Where did it come from? Did you steal it?' she demands.

'No, of course not!' I cry, trying to wriggle free from her grasp. 'It was a gift. Please, Mother, you're hurting me.'

'Go and wipe it off immediately,' she sneers. 'You look like a common strumpet.'

I dash from the sitting room to the bathroom, tears threatening to overspill from my eyes. I manage to hold it together until I reach the bathroom and turn the tap, the water gushing and sputtering from the faucet loud enough to drown the small cry that escapes my throat. I look at my reflection in the mirror: my eyes are red and puffy, my cheeks blotchy, making the pink lipstick clash horribly with my skin. I can't believe I actually thought I looked pretty. How foolishly vain I was to think one of Grace's dresses and a bit of make-up could transform me into something else. I snatch a wad of tissue from the roll and begin furiously trying to wipe it off. I splash my face with cold water and take a few deep breaths, waiting for my skin tone to even out a little, then make my way back down the hall with what I hope is a calm composure. As I draw closer to the sitting room, I catch the tail end of a conversation between Grace and Mother.

'That dress was a good choice, Grace, darling. Perhaps tonight's little soirée may introduce you to some eligible bachelors. Men of stature.'

Once again, my stomach drops at the thought of losing

Grace and having to live alone in this rotten old house, just Mother and I.

'You can't marry her off!' I cry before I can stop myself, and Grace's eyes widen as she looks back at me, but Mother's narrow as she takes me in for the first time.

'Oh, can't I?' she scoffs. 'And why is that?'

'Well, she is just . . . twenty-one is still so young, that's all. What's the hurry?' I mumble, my gaze dropping to the floor.

'Look around you, child!' she says angrily, stomping her cane on the cracked tile floor. 'This house is falling apart, we need money and we need it now. Your father's measly pension is as good as gone. The only savings we have left, your father tied up to serve as dowries!' She turns her attention back to Grace, her expression softening as she rests a bony hand upon her cheek. 'Darling, you were blessed with good looks. Let us not squander them. We shall find you a good Christian husband who has no need for a dowry.'

'Christian?' Grace echoes, speaking up for the first time, and I wonder why that is the part of Mother's statement that has her the most flustered.

'Yes, of course,' Mother says, looking nonplussed.

Grace nods, trying to contort her expression into a smile, but it ends up looking more like a grimace. 'We should go,' she says at last. 'We don't want to be late.'

There is a cool chill to the evening that marks the start of autumn. The air has that smell of bonfire and decaying leaves as we cross the street and make our way towards the Draper house. The curtains are drawn, but there is a flicker of warming light coming through the cracks, and as we approach the front door, the sound of rising laughter and bubbling voices can be heard from inside the house. I take a deep breath, trying to still the unsteady beating of my heart as Mother rings the doorbell.

August Draper swings open the door with a pleasant smile. He is dressed in a tailored three-piece suit with fine pinstripes, his dark-blonde hair swept off his face with a neat side parting, and his vivid green eyes seem to sparkle as they meet mine.

'Welcome!' he says warmly over the sound of the voices from further inside the house. 'Mrs Harrington, I presume?' He reaches for Mother's hand and gently places his lips upon her bony knuckles. For a moment I could swear I notice her visibly thaw. 'I am so glad you could join us this evening.' He then turns his attention towards Grace and me. 'And these must be your lovely daughters. Of course, I have met your younger daughter already, but it is a pleasure to have you all in my home. Come in and let me take your coats.'

He helps Mother first, his manners impeccable as he slides her out of her moth-eaten fur, then moves on to Grace. 'I don't believe I have made your acquaintance yet, Miss Harrington,' he says, taking Grace's cape.

'For that, I must apologise, Mr Draper,' Grace says demurely, almost curtseying in her nervousness. 'My name is Grace.'

I take a step forward, but August's eyes are still fixed on Grace. 'Please, call me August, if you will, Miss Harrington. I can't bear to be called Mr Draper.'

Grace's eyes flit to Mother's for approval and she gives a curt nod.

'Very well . . . August. Thank you for inviting us to dinner this evening.' She turns her attention to me. 'Clementine, why don't you give August your coat?'

August's eyes dart to mine and he gives me a small, secret smile that almost takes my breath away, then sweeps into a low bow, winking at me as he rises and reaches for my coat. 'My apologies, Miss Harrington, I almost forgot you were there.'

I can't deny the rush of disappointment I feel to have been forgotten so easily in the presence of Grace, but when he looks at me the feeling dissipates. I gaze into his verdant green eyes and I feel myself relax, safe in the knowledge I am in the company of an ally, joined together by our shared secrets. He alone knows about the night I snuck into this very house, and in return he entrusted me with his true name. *Augustus* . . . I breathe the word as he takes the coat from my outstretched hand. Mother is looking at August too, but with a different look, one of hunger and opportunity, before her face quickly slips into a more neutral expression as August whips around and offers to escort her through to the sitting room.

'Oh, I am quite alright with my stick,' she insists. 'But Grace has hurt her ankle, poor dear. Would you be so kind as to lend her your arm.'

'Of course!' August exclaims, turning his attention to Grace and offering her his arm.

Grace and I share a split-second look. This is the first I have heard about her ankle, and by the look on Grace's face, it is the first she is hearing of it too. I open my mouth, not entirely sure what I am going to say, but before I can find the words, Mother subtly raps me on the shin with her stick and the instant throbbing pain that it sends up my leg stops the words dead in my mouth.

'Stand back and let them go ahead,' she mutters under her breath, and the two of us watch as August leads Grace away before we follow after them.

The sitting room looks rather different from the last time I was here. The mass of blankets has been extricated from the velvet sofa and the piles of books have been painstakingly alphabetised and placed on the shelves. A lively jazz tune is playing on low from the turntable and the room is full of dancing light from a newly installed crystal chandelier. Mrs Arbuthnot is seated in a squashy velvet armchair with a glass of sherry in her hand, talking the ear off our elderly neighbours Mr and Mrs Duval. Mr Duval was once a famous pianist, and he travelled the world with his wife, performing in some of the biggest concert halls and rubbing shoulders with high society, but now he is snoozing on the sofa, no doubt as a result of Mrs Arbuthnot's latest tale of her son Archie.

I spy Grace and August over by the turntable, making polite conversation, and I take a step towards them when Mrs Arbuthnot cries out.

'Good gracious, Helena!'

Mother's back stiffens a little as Mrs Arbuthnot shuffles towards us. She looks genuinely pleased to see our mother up and about, but the shine in her wide eyes is due to nothing other than voyeurism. 'How long has it been?' she exclaims as she comes to a stop and places a kiss on Mother's hollow cheek. 'Gosh, you *do* look well.'

'Regina, what a pleasure to see you,' Mother replies, as if it had only been a few weeks rather than ten years.

The two of them begin exchanging pleasantries and I find my eyes wandering across the room to the turntable where August is laughing at something Grace said, his brilliant white teeth a stark contrast against his golden tanned face. Grace catches my eye and gestures for me to join her. I almost do, just as I catch the tail end of Mother's conversation with Mrs Arbuthnot.

'Well, while I appreciate I haven't been able to worship in church myself, I have always ensured that my girls still attend mass,' Mother says haughtily, and I feel all the colour drain from my face as Mrs Arbuthnot casts a suspicious gaze my way. For the first few years after our father's passing, Grace and I certainly kept up appearances at church, but after a while, other responsibilities got in the way . . . From the age of fourteen, once I was finished with school, I began helping Madame Lebedev teach ballet classes, one of which is on a Sunday. And Grace has been working at the library to keep the roof over our heads.

'Is that so?' Mrs Arbuthnot says slowly. 'Every Sunday?'

'Gosh, I'm awfully thirsty!' I interrupt loudly, desperate to change the subject and avoid a conflict.

August must have overheard me, because he finally looks up from his conversation with Grace and waltzes over. 'I am terribly sorry,' he says, 'where are my manners? Far too much time spent in the jungle and not enough spent in polite company. Can I offer you some wine?' He grins sheepishly and Mrs Arbuthnot visibly fawns over him. Even Mother cracks a seldom seen smile.

'Just a soda water for me,' she says. 'My daughter will have the same.'

'Couldn't I perhaps have a small glass?' I ask almost pleadingly but she shoots me down.

'Wine is not for children.'

I feel my cheeks flood deep crimson and the top of my ears burn hot as I bow my head.

'Oh, Mother, she is almost eighteen,' Grace says imploringly, coming to stand beside me. 'Perhaps a small glass with dinner wouldn't hurt.'

Mother looks set to crumble under the pressure of an audience, so I take my moment to look up at her beseechingly. She purses her lips in distaste.

'Very well,' she admits defeat. 'But at the first sign of silliness, you will be sent straight home.'

'Speaking of dinner, it must nearly be ready,' August says, extricating himself from the group. 'I'd best go check in with my housekeeper and I'll be right back with your drinks.'

Mother's eyes light up at the mention of professional help, then I watch as her eyes survey the sitting room properly and she takes in all its splendour. I can almost see her totting up the value of our lavish surroundings. A gong sounds in the hallway, causing me to jolt, and Mr Duval to awake suddenly from his slumber. August Draper appears moments later with the mallet in his hand.

'A thousand apologies,' he says to the startled pianist, in his warm American accent. 'It's an old relic I picked up on my travels and I do rather like an excuse to use it. Now, ladies and gentleman, if you will follow me to the dining room, dinner is ready.'

The dining room is panelled in a dark mahogany and hung with paintings of exotic fruits. The wide window is draped with velvet curtains in a shade of deep-plum, tied with golden tassels, and an ornate glass-cut lampshade hangs from the ceiling, creating a spotlight on the table. Everything in August's house is new, from the fine crockery, painted with a border of intricate vines, to the crystal-cut glasses and decanters, to the glimmering brass cutlery. The long table is festooned with vases of freshly cut flowers and dotted with candlesticks, their flickering orange light casting dancing shadows across the room. We all sit down in a hum of anticipation: this is by far the most extravagant event that has taken place on our street in a good many years. August travels around the table and begins to pour wine from a decanter into each of our glasses. I catch a waft of his cologne as he leans over me, the floral, heady scent of bergamot, and I close my eyes for a moment, feeling a little light-headed. He lingers a little longer over Grace's glass, his eyes fixed firmly upon her as she stares resolutely down at her plate, coy as always. Something like jealousy spasms in my chest and it takes all my willpower to keep it from surging forth until he moves on. I lift my glass to my lips, but no sooner have I taken a sip when Mother flashes another warning my way.

'I mean it, Clementine,' she says sharply. 'Any silliness and that glass shall be taken off you.'

I blush as deep a red as the wine in my glass and set it down again just as August takes his place at the head of the table and his housekeeper comes in with a trolley.

'Thank you, Mrs Darnton.' August beams, leaping to his feet once again to help her. 'Mrs Darnton has been a lifesaver for me,' he tells us all as he helps her hand out bowls of pea soup. 'I cannot cook to save my life, and I have never been much of a housekeeper either. I am very lucky to have her in charge.'

Mrs Darnton smiles beatifically, clearly as susceptible to August Draper's charms as the rest of us.

'So, tell us, Mr Draper, how goes things at the Royal Botanic

Gardens?' Mr Duval asks as we all tuck into our soup. 'I hear you are the new Assistant Director. Is that correct?'

'Indeed, it is.' August smiles modestly. 'It is certainly a new experience for me to be based in one place after so many years of travelling the world, but they assure me that I will still get plenty of chances to explore.'

'But are you not interested in settling down and finding a wife?' Mrs Duval pipes up, and I notice my mother's spoon hovering mid-way to her mouth as she awaits his answer.

August sighs, a deep exhale and looks down at his bowl. 'I would very much like to settle down, Mrs Duval, but I have been rather unlucky in love so far.'

'Must be those American girls,' Mrs Arbuthnot assures him, patting his hand as if he were her precious Archie. 'I am sure we can help find you a nice, sensible English wife.'

'Well, as it happens, that is one of the reasons I have chosen to settle in one place,' he replies, taking a sip of wine. 'I am hoping to find a companion.'

My eyes shoot up towards August, but his gaze is fixed on Grace. I can feel what is going to happen. He is already enamoured with her, and if she feels the same way, it will be the end of our happy twosome. I glance at Grace. She doesn't seem remotely interested in him as she sips daintily at her soup, her head down. I breathe a happy sigh of relief. As far as I can tell, Grace has always been far more interested in fictional men than real ones, and unless Mr Darcy himself leaps from the pages of *Pride and Prejudice*, I am fairly confident she will keep her head. Perhaps I should have told her about my first meeting with August, that night when we collided in this very house.

'It is a rather peculiar name,' I hear Mrs Duval remark to Mother, and it stirs me from my thoughts. I know without being told that they are talking about me. 'What made you choose it, Helena?'

'I played no part in it,' Mother responds curtly, placing her soup spoon down with some force and gaining everyone's attention. 'If I had had my way, she would have been named Verity. I believe girls should be named after virtues in order to instil them, just like Grace.'

'There is no denying you are very graceful,' August says quietly, leaning towards my sister with a lopsided smile. 'I have never seen someone move with such ease on an injured ankle.'

Grace blushes, knowing she has been caught out in Mother's lie. 'And you are clearly very astute, Mr Draper.'

'Your secret is safe with me,' he murmurs and I feel a stab of jealousy run right through my chest. Did he not say the very same thing to me?

'So, why was she called Clementine in that case?' Mrs Arbuthnot asks Mother, and I turn my head back to the conversation at hand, taking a larger gulp of wine as I watch them discuss me as if I were not there.

'It was her father's doing,' Mother sniffs. 'He simply came back with her birth certificate and declared he had looked into her eyes and had a change of heart.'

'He always was a romantic soul,' Mrs Arbuthnot sighs. 'Well, I am sure he had his reasons, whatever they may have been.'

'Oh, he had his reasons alright,' Mother mutters, her voice laced with malice now. 'And though romance certainly played a part in it, I would not say it was down to the nature of his soul.'

I look up at her, my spoon mid-air. I had no idea that she knew the reason why Father chose to change my name at the last moment. I catch Grace's eye and she is looking back at me, as perplexed as I feel.

'What were they?' I ask, unable to contain my curiosity. 'His reasons?'

Everyone around the table is looking at Mother now, the pea soup growing gelatinous and long forgotten. Only Mother is still eating, swirling the spoon round her bowl before popping it into her mouth, swallowing thoughtfully.

'I discovered the truth shortly after my husband's passing when I was sorting through his belongings,' she says matter-of-factly. 'I found a series of letters in his study. It would appear he took a liking to the name while he was stationed in France during the war.'

Everyone waits in anticipation for her to divulge more information, especially me. My heart is in my throat. I know that she is relishing the attention, but I can't look away, I am desperate to know.

'The letters were quite damning . . . Shall we say he was less than faithful to the sanctity of our marriage while he was away.' She finally looks at me, her eyes cold but her expression victorious. 'Clementine was the name of your father's French mistress.'

'Mother, really!' Grace gasps in horror as the table falls silent, but Mother is not looking at Grace.

Her eyes are still firmly set on mine. She doesn't seem to care that she may have ruined Grace's chances with August; she doesn't even care what our neighbours might think. What this could do for our social standing, our reputation. She will take any opportunity to tear me down. She is daring me to create a scene. I can sense her waiting for me to finally grow a backbone and stand up for myself, but I can't do it . . . I feel sick and the room is spinning. Father would never have had a mistress, *never*! He doted on our whole family. He used to tell me nothing was more important to him than his three special ladies: Mother, Grace and me.

But now that I think about it, did he ever specify that he meant Mother? It was always very clear how much he loved Grace and me, but I can't remember a single moment of intimacy between my parents . . . The borders of my vision are growing fuzzy and it has nothing to do with the wine. I can feel everyone's eyes on me, their pitying glances. I drop my napkin and excuse myself from the table, rushing from the dining room as quickly as I can without running.

Out in the hall, I take a deep, gasping breath. I can feel

my chest rising and falling but I don't feel any better. I lean against the wall, listening to the muffled conversation in the dining room.

'Should someone see if Clementine is alright?' Mrs Arbuthnot asks, and for the first time in my life I feel a grateful surge of warmth for her.

'She'll be fine, she is simply being dramatic. I did say she was too young for wine,' Mother scoffs. 'Grace, sit down. Please do not be as rude towards our host as your sister.'

I hear the scuffing of chair legs against the wooden floor as Grace tucks her chair back in. I flush with embarrassment and anger. How has Mother managed to paint *me* as the one who has been inappropriate? How many years has she sat on this piece of information, and she chose now to reveal it. What must August have thought? And what am I to think?

Even in my daze I know I can't go back in there and sit down to the rest of the meal. I resign myself to the fact that I must go home. I tiptoe down the hallway, grab my coat from the hook, and am just about to leave when I hear footsteps approaching.

'Clementine?' the voice says quietly, a smooth American voice.

I turn, my eyes still brimming with tears, to find August standing in the hallway. His green eyes look at me kindly, but they are full of pity and I can't bear to look at him. 'You must think me awfully rude,' I say, turning away. 'I am sorry to up and leave in the middle of your party but I fear my presence will only make things more uncomfortable for your guests.'

'Clementine, please,' he says softly, taking a step towards me. He cups my face in his hands and wipes a tear from my cheek as my heart starts to race. 'What your mother said back there . . . it's – it's inexcusable. Please don't cry. You are such a sweet girl.'

I look up at him, barely able to conceal my disappointment.

A *girl*? So that's how he sees me. I brush his hand away from my cheek. 'I thank you for inviting me this evening, Mr Draper, and for your hospitality, but I really must go.'

He steps back, a bemused look upon his face, and I take the opportunity to make a break for it.

Our house feels colder and darker, having left the warming glow of August Draper's home behind me. I close the door and the silence engulfs me for a moment. I feel small in this house, like I never quite grew up. Maybe I am still just a girl. I am about to climb the staircase to my bedroom, when I stop outside Father's study. I remember now, after his funeral, how Mother spent hours every night locked away in here. Grace and I used to watch the flickering light pool out from the crack beneath the door until one of us would fall asleep on the stairs and the other would inevitably drag them upstairs. When Father was still alive, Grace and I used to sit in the study whenever we pleased. Grace would read a book aloud, curled up in her favourite green leather armchair, while I lay on the sheepskin rug by the fire and listened. Sometimes Father would be there too. I can picture him at his desk, a smile growing beneath his moustache. If Grace struggled with a word, she would sit on his lap and he would teach her to spell it out phonetically.

After he died, the study remained locked to everyone except Mother. Then, one day, she came out. Grace and I were sat on the stairs as usual, wondering what Mother was doing in there, when the door was flung open, causing us both to start in surprise. We thought we would be in trouble, but she didn't even seem to see us. Her eyes were dark and hollow like two holes, crescent-moonlike shadows hung beneath them. Her skin seemed to sag around her bones and her hair was unkempt as if she had been running her fingers through it over and over. She locked the door behind her and slipped the key on a chain around her neck. Then she sloped up the stairs, straight past us, to bed. And she didn't get out of that bed again until last week.

I come back around from the memory and find my hand clutching the brass doorknob. I look down at it in surprise. I hadn't noticed myself reach out and grasp it. The metal is cold beneath my hand, and I try to turn it but it is still firmly locked. My heart sinks with disappointment and I trudge upstairs to my bedroom. I unzip my borrowed dress and slip back into my leotard and ballet shoes, ready for one final round of stretches before calling it a night. I limber up by the window where I can still see the glowing lights of the Draper house. I watch shadows pass by the windows; it looks like they are dancing, or maybe it is my imagination. I can't take my eyes off the house as I practise my barre exercises. I should be there, I should be a part of the merrymaking going on inside, but Mother ruined it. Tonight, even ballet cannot distract me from my misery. I change into my nightdress, unable to watch the party from across the street a moment longer, and climb into bed.

'*Clem!*'

I open my eyes to find Grace sitting on the side of my bed. She is swaying from side to side a little and her eyes look slightly glassy in the darkness.

'You're drunk,' I comment.

'I am *not*.'

'Why are you swaying so much then?' I ask, pulling myself up into a seated position and plumping my pillow.

'Never mind that,' she dismisses. 'I came to see if you are alright.'

'I've been better,' I tell her truthfully. 'Oh, Grace, do you think it's true? Do you really think Father had a mistress during the war?'

Her nose wrinkles in the manner it always does when she is concentrating. 'I don't know, Clem,' she answers truthfully. 'We were so young when he died, but it doesn't seem right, does it? I just keep thinking that doesn't seem like something he would do. But then the war was hard on everyone . . . How can we possibly understand what he went through?'

'So you *do* think it's true!' I needle and she rolls her eyes with exasperation.

'I didn't say that, I said I don't know,' she replies diplomatically. 'But I can't imagine Father ever being so callous as to name one of his children after his mistress – it just doesn't make sense.'

'This is why Mother hates me, isn't it?'

'She doesn't hate you, Clem.'

'She has a funny way of showing it,' I reply, rolling away from her to face the wall.

'I think Father's death hit her a lot harder than we perhaps understood as children, that's all.'

'Well, she seems to have made a spectacular recovery now that August Draper has moved across the street,' I respond. 'How was the rest of the evening?'

'Not as much fun without you there,' she says earnestly. 'I am so sorry I didn't come after you, Clem. I wanted to, I really did, I stood up to dash after you but Mother forbade me to leave. August was really worried too. I could tell he was unhappy to see you like that.'

'You two seemed very cosy,' I remark, glancing at her out of the corner of my eye, and I notice a small blush appear at her cheeks.

'Yes, he was certainly very charming,' she replies, trying to feign nonchalance. Then she catches my eye and whatever she is trying to keep bottled up inside bursts forth. 'Oh, Clem, Mother thinks he may make a potential suitor. Can you imagine?'

'You?' I splutter. 'And August?'

'Yes, I must admit he isn't exactly the type of man I had imagined myself settling down with . . .' she murmurs.

'I imagine he would always be galivanting off on expeditions, leaving you at home to look after the children.' I yawn, and a peculiar expression crosses her face.

'Yes, I suppose he would,' she mutters, then she brightens. 'But just think about what it could mean for *us*! No more scraping by, no more cold winters and empty pantries. We would be set for life; he is incredibly wealthy. And the best part is, I wouldn't have to move far away, I would be just across the street, Clem. It would almost be as if nothing had changed!'

'You mean to say you plan to ensnare him for his money?' I retort, ignoring her justifications and growing more outraged by the moment.

'That seems like a rather cut-throat way of describing it.' She recoils, nettled. 'But yes, I certainly would consider a proposal for the good of our family. You heard what Mother said: we barely have two pennies to rub together.'

I flop back down in bed and pull the duvet over my head in a fury.

'Clem, what is the matter?' she asks in surprise.

'I'm tired and I wish to go back to sleep,' I reply bluntly from under the covers. 'I was sleeping soundly until you came and disturbed me.'

'Oh,' she says, her soft voice brimming with disappointment. 'Well, goodnight then.'

I don't reply as I feel her lift herself off the bed. My heart is hammering in my chest. It feels like it is trying to escape and force its way up my throat. My mind is swimming with images of Grace and August, the way his hand lingered on her arm, how his eyes followed her around the room. I picture Grace and August married . . . Grace alone at home with their children . . . Would she be happy? I think of what she told me at the boutique, and her face at the dinner table tonight . . . Is she doing this for us? Or herself? And then I see myself in this crumbling old house with Mother. The spinster aunt, named after her father's mistress. What about my ballet? If it were me in Grace's position, August and I could travel the world together. I could dance on all the international stages I have ever dreamed of, and he could travel with me, exploring countries far and wide, discovering new plants and writing papers along the way.

Mother's plans for Grace to marry August make no sense at all. She would be miserable, at home on her own all the time. And I would be miserable too, stuck at home with Mother. If anyone is to marry August, it should be me. That way, Grace is free to live as she pleases and I am free to dance. I know it makes more sense that way. I just have to make them see it.

Chapter 8

Rudi is waiting for me outside Anna's family bakery on Thursday. It is the first day of October, and the air has that rich, almost metallic, smoky quality to it, as if someone has lit a bonfire nearby. The sun is bright and there isn't a cloud in the blue sky, but it is rather chilly and I shove my hands deep into my coat pockets as I approach. Rudi is leaning against a lamp post, his feet perfectly turned out and his sharp nose deep in a book. He doesn't see me until I am almost upon him, when he suddenly looks up, his face cracking into a wide smile that stretches from one ear to the other.

'You made it!' He grins, snapping the book shut and stowing it away in his rucksack.

'I promised I would,' I remind him. It has been a long time since Rudi has been interested in a girl for long enough for me to make her acquaintance, so I know this must be important to him.

'Come on, let's go,' he says, rubbing his hands together then wrapping an arm around my shoulders. 'I just know you're going to like her, Clem.'

He leads me inside the small bakery and I am hit by a waft of warmth and the sweet, buttery smell of freshly baked pastries. A beautiful girl with flame-red hair and a face wreathed in freckles has her elbows propped up on the counter, her chin resting in her hands. She looks up expectantly as the two of us walk in.

'Rudolf!' she exclaims, her face brightening at the sight of him. She rushes around the counter and envelops him in an embrace, and I watch, a little enviously, as he brushes his cheek against the top of her head. What I wouldn't give for someone to cherish me in that way. The closest I have ever come to such intimacy is when Rudi and I are acting out our roles on the stage. Anna pulls back, her hands still clasping on to Rudi's as she looks at me. 'You must be Clementine!' She beams. 'I have heard so much about you. It is so lovely to meet you.'

'Nothing too bad, I hope!' I half-chuckle as she pulls me into an unexpected hug.

'Quite the contrary,' she insists. 'It's a good thing I'm not the jealous type as it's always "Clem said this" and "Clem did that".'

Rudi rolls his eyes lazily and smirks. 'Don't make me regret introducing the two of you.'

'Well, you've done it now, and who knows, perhaps I will prefer Clementine's company to your own,' she teases, sticking her tongue out playfully. 'How much time do you have before ballet?'

'We are on our way now, but I couldn't resist picking up some more *sharlotka*,' he replies, and her face drops. 'But I will be back after class,' he reassures her, lifting her soft chin and gazing intently into her eyes.

I watch her visibly melt under the effects of the famous Rudolf Lebedev charm, and I find it almost unbearable. They may not have known each other long, but there is an intimacy between them that makes me feel like an intruder. I ignore the ache it produces in my chest and peruse the shelves of baked goods while they share a private moment. The shelves are lined with beautiful cakes, piped with pastel-coloured buttercream ruffles and flowers. I gaze hungrily at them, but they look far too good to eat. My eyes scan the rest of the offerings, and I spy Rudi's special *sharlotka* cake, pink iced buns, sugar-crusted doughnuts and Bakewell tarts with big fat glacé cherries nestled in soft beds of fondant. A forgotten memory suddenly comes back to me. I see my father and I walking hand-in-hand. I can't see his face because I am too small, but I know it is him. We are on our way back from the bank; he used to take me with him every Friday. Then, as a treat, we would stop at a bakery on the way home and he would buy a Bakewell tart for us to share. We would sit on a park bench and he would split it in two, pigeons inching nearer as crumbs of pastry spilled everywhere. He would always give me the half with the cherry. I can almost taste it, that sickly sweet jam and pastry with a hint of bitterness.

'What do you want then?' Rudi asks, making me jump as he comes to stand beside me, his hands in his pockets. 'Are you alright?' he frowns. 'Sorry, I didn't mean to surprise you.'

'It's not your fault. I was deep in an old memory,' I reply wistfully, gazing at the Bakewell tarts.

Rudi's gaze follows mine, then he looks up at Anna who has returned to the counter. 'Can we get a slice of the *sharlotka* and one of these tarts with the cherries on top please, Anna?'

I feel a little glowing ember of warmth for Rudi in the pit of my stomach. He always knows exactly what I am thinking without ever having to ask. Anna scoops the tart into a brown paper bag and hands it to me with a warm smile. 'It was so lovely to meet you, Clementine. I do hope I get to see you again soon.'

'Thank you, Anna.' I blush, clutching at my paper bag. 'And the same to you too.'

Rudi hands her some money and takes his own paper bag from her grasp in exchange for a kiss on the cheek. 'I'll see you in a few hours,' he promises, as he holds the door open for me and we make our way back out onto the street.

'So, are you going to tell me what you were thinking about?' he asks as we make our way towards Montpelier Mews and Madame Lebedev's studio.

I tilt my head and squint up at him. 'I thought you would be more interested to know what I thought of Anna.'

'I'm not worried about that.' He shrugs. 'Anna is a peach. What's not to like?'

'She does seem very lovely, Rudi. Try not to mess this one up.'

His mouth stretches into a lopsided smile as he glances down at me, his bronze curls falling into his eyes. 'Excellent deflection, Clem, but we were talking about you, not me.'

'Those Bakewell tarts, they reminded me of my father,' I tell him, and I feel him straighten a little beside me.

'Ah, I'm sorry, Clem,' he murmurs.

'No, it's alright. It was a good memory,' I insist. 'Something I had completely forgotten about. He used to love Bakewell tarts and he would always share one with me.'

He looks at the brown paper bag in my hand. 'What's so good about them?' he asks curiously. 'I've never tried one.'

'Then we must remedy that,' I reply. 'Here, let's sit down a while. We've still got plenty of time until class.'

We spy an empty park bench and sit down, watching people rush by, and pigeons picking aimlessly at crumbs in between their feet. Rudi reaches his arm around me and I rest my head on his shoulder, breathing in his familiar scent. I reach into the grease-spotted paper bag and pull out the Bakewell tart, tearing it in two and gazing down at the pieces for a moment, before handing the half with the cherry on top to Rudi.

We are the first two to reach the studio on Montpelier Mews, and as we make our way inside, Madame Lebedev is pinning up the role sheet for *Giselle*.

'Ah, there you are!' She grins. 'How are my two principal dancers feeling this afternoon? Limber, I hope.'

I glide towards the role sheet and there are our names at the top. I am to play Giselle and he will be Count Albrecht.

'You can't really be surprised,' he mutters, coming to stand beside me. 'She as good as told you the part was yours.'

'I know, I know,' I murmur, trying to fight the anxious feeling in my stomach. 'And I'm thrilled, naturally, but it is going to be a difficult afternoon.' My gaze wanders towards the door and I can almost picture Alice Blakely swanning in, spying the sheet and then frothing with fury when she realises she has been bested once again.

'If you want to dance professionally, you are going to have to get used to the likes of Alice Blakely,' Rudi reminds me, reading my thoughts once again.

We make our way down the hall to the studio and begin our stretches. As I bend down to touch my toes, I hear an almost strangled scream. Moments later Alice waltzes into the studio with a look of well-practised calm composure.

'Madame, may I have a word?' she asks sweetly, completely ignoring Rudi and me as we share a conspiratorial glance.

'Of course, Alice darling, is everything alright?' Madame ushers her to a corner of the studio and I watch out of the corner of my eye as Alice whispers to her in heated undertones. I don't catch what she is saying but I have a good idea.

'But darling, Myrtha is the perfect part for you,' Madame replies. 'She is the Queen of the Wilis – girls who died from betrayal and broken hearts, she is incredibly proud and powerful. You did such a marvellous job as Odile in last year's *Swan Lake*, it seemed obvious to me that you would be a natural fit for Myrtha.' Madame's flattery seems to be working its trick, and as I practise my pliés at the bar, I notice Alice's shoulders soften a little. 'You wouldn't really want to play Giselle, would you?' she coos, gently coaxing out Alice's ego. 'A peasant girl with a weak heart?'

I know the comment is not supposed to be directed at me, but I wince at Madame's words, and Alice looks back over her shoulder at me and smiles a wicked little smirk. 'You're right, Madame,' she says more loudly. 'Now that I think about it, you have cast the roles perfectly.'

'I am glad you think so, Miss Blakely,' Madame replies, flashing me a warning from her cool grey eyes to bite my tongue. 'Now, girls, please take your place at the barre so we can begin.'

We begin our pliés and I soon forget all about Alice's cutting remarks as the music begins to play. I focus intently as all the muscles in my body begin to align and Madame's voice talks us through the movements.

'Now bend for two, and stretch, and open into second. Don't turn your shoulders, Marianne. *Demi-plié*, *demi-plié* and now all the way down into the *grand plié*. Keep your arms strong, Rudolf.'

The barre exercises continue like this for half an hour as our bodies warm up to the tune of the piano music and the soothing instructions of Madame Lebedev's voice, until we make our way to the floor and begin what will be our first piece of choreography for *Giselle*.

'We shall start with act two,' Madame calls to us as we take our place in the centre of the studio. 'Act two is the main heart of *Giselle*. The most important thing is that you Wilis are all in sync with one another. You must know who you are in line with, who to follow; you must know the patterns of every piece of choreography like the back of your hand. As such, I will be pairing each of you with a partner so that you can guide and support each other through the process. As I call your names, please partner up.'

She starts listing off names and I wait anxiously to see who she will pair me with. I know I won't be with Rudi this time as he is not one of the Wilis, but there are certain partners who I would be comfortable with and others who would be catastrophic. I fidget from foot to foot as I wait, until finally there are only two of us left.

'And that leaves Clementine and Alice,' Madame finishes as my heart sinks. 'Seeing as you two will both have slightly different roles from the rest of the Wilis, it makes sense to put you together.'

'Or maybe we don't need a partner at all?' I suggest desperately, cradling my arms.

'Yes, Madame, I really don't think it's necessary,' Alice

chimes in, agreeing with me for once. She looks just as unhappy at the prospect of our partnering as I feel.

'My decision is final,' Madame says, her voice sharp, her eyes narrowed and deadly.

We fall silent and accept our fate.

'You will meet with your partners once a week to practise outside of class,' she continues. 'Now, let's get started.'

She begins to map out the choreography, and we shadow her movements. I love watching Madame Lebedev dance; it is like looking into a magic mirror from the past. I can picture how beautifully she must have twirled across the stages of Russia's finest theatres; how princes, captains and aristocrats fell at her feet with adoration night after night. I know she was gifted many precious trinkets and jewels in her time at the Bolshoi, but now they are all gone, sold off one by one to ensure safe passage for her and her family out of Russia. It may seem strange but there are a lot of similarities between my family and the Lebedevs: we have both fallen from riches to rags, letting go of our prized possessions to keep afloat, but never our pride. The only difference is, Madame Lebedev never let the experience change or embitter her; sadly, I cannot say the same for my own mother.

'The hardest part of *Giselle*,' she instructs, lifting her leg into an arabesque as we follow suit, 'is the marriage of feeling and the technical feats you must undergo. The Wilis you are playing are the tormented ghosts of women who died of heartache, women who hate all men and who are seeking vengeance. You must be terrifying but vulnerable, bold yet soft.'

My head is all jumbled with different instructions as I try to take on Madame Lebedev's instruction while also following the moves. We mark it out over and over until I feel as if I can't possibly do it again, then we do it one more time.

'Good!' Madame Lebedev exclaims. 'Everyone take a break.'

I collapse on the floor, wiping my face with a towel from

my bag as Rudi sidles over and sits down beside me, chewing on a banana.

'Gosh, you must be exhausted from all that watching,' I joke a little sarcastically, and his lips spread into a wide smile, his eyes closed.

'Don't you worry, my time is coming,' he reassures me.

'Yes, but I am also in your dances!' I laugh, leaning back and relishing the feel of the cool studio floor against my hot, prickly skin.

'That is the downfall of landing the titular role.' He nods, taking another bite. 'So, how was the dinner party on Friday night? I am surprised you haven't filled me in on all the details yet.'

'Oh, it was fine,' I mumble, a heavy sensation settling in the pit of my stomach as I remember the way Mother orchestrated her plan to push Grace and August together so meticulously, the way she belittled and embarrassed me . . . the things she said about my father . . . But that wasn't even the worst part. I am still feeling resentful towards Grace for playing along with Mother's plan to coerce August into a proposal. It is so out of character that I feel I barely know her right now. Is it really what she wants?

Rudi raises his eyebrows so high that they disappear beneath his crown of bronze curls. 'That is all you have to say for yourself? Come on, Clem, you were practically bouncing with excitement last week.'

I look up at him. 'Things have developed somewhat since my mother left her bed . . .' I sigh. Rudi was, of course, the first person I told about Mother's very sudden change in health. 'She has discovered that our neighbour Mr Draper, is on the hunt for a bride, and she wants Grace to be the one to charm him. She spent the entire evening pushing the two of them together, while taking every opportunity to ridicule me. She-she—' I pause, a lump forming in my throat. 'She embarrassed me and bad-mouthed my father in front of everyone. She said my father took a mistress during the war and that he chose to name me after her.' I can feel the heat rising in my cheeks and I hide my head in my hands with shame.

'Oh, *solnyshko* . . .' he murmurs tenderly, pulling me closer to him and wrapping me in a warm embrace. 'After everything you have told me about your father, I don't believe for one second that this is true.'

'But what if it is?' I mumble into his chest.

'If it is . . . it doesn't change how much he loved you.' He looks down at me, a quizzical look on his face. 'But that's not all that's bothering you, is it, Clem?'

'How do you know?' I ask, looking up and meeting his gaze.

'I always know,' he replies mystically, releasing me from his arms with a smug look on his face. 'So, what else happened?'

'Well, it's just, August, the gentleman my mother wishes to set Grace up with, he's . . . he's not right for her at all. He won't make her happy, they are completely incompatible. Grace is going along with it for all the wrong reasons, and . . . and . . .'

'And *you* like him,' Rudi interjects astutely, casting his gaze away from me, his thick eyebrows knitting together.

'Y-yes . . .' I stammer. 'How did you know?'

He smiles wanly. 'I have known you for a very long time, Clem. I pick up on these things.'

'Well, now August is going to fall in love with Grace – because, why wouldn't he? And Grace is already saying she will accept a proposal if he offers!' I exclaim. 'He only sees *me* as a child. But if I were to marry August instead, Grace would be free to find a man she truly loves, and I wouldn't have to worry about turning eighteen and giving up ballet. I know he would support my dream. He has to travel for his work so it would be perfect. I think we could be happy together, if only he could see me as an adult. Everything has spun out of control so quickly, Rudi . . . I don't know what to do.'

'Well, making him see you as an adult, and what's more, a desirable one, seems quite simple to me,' he replies pointedly, inspecting his fingernails with a grating air of nonchalance. His eyes meet mine. They are shining, more silver than grey, and his mouth twists into a lopsided smile. 'Make this August fellow jealous. Let him see what he is missing.'

'And how exactly will I do that?' I sigh. 'I am not beautiful like Grace, and I certainly don't have men lining up at my door, clamouring for my hand.'

'You *are* beautiful, *solnyshko*. Never say that about yourself.' He frowns. 'And as for your need of a man . . .' He bows his head, his hands outstretched, then looks back up at me and winks.

'Oh, don't be ridiculous!' I scoff. 'Who would ever believe that we were a couple?'

'Half the girls in this class already do.' He shrugs, and there, I must admit, he has a point. I cast my eyes around the studio and I notice several of them are trying to watch us as inconspicuously as possible.

'But what about Anna?' I counter, and he rolls his eyes.

'It wouldn't be a real relationship, Clem. We'll just act like we normally do, maybe I put my arm around you from time to time, bring you flowers and bestow you with some special treatment. Let's see if he pays more attention to you. No one gets hurt.'

'I don't know . . .' I contemplate it for a moment, but it feels strange, the thought of Rudi and me pretending to be in love with one another.

'Well, the offer is there if you wish to take it,' he says plainly, climbing back to his feet. 'But, Clem, you always shine as a principal when you dance. When are you going to start acting like the main character of your own story off the stage?'

Without another word, he turns and walks back towards his mother, leaving me to contemplate his suggestion. I just can't picture it, Rudi and me, but maybe he is right.

Maybe this is the way I can get August to see me as a grown woman . . . and Grace will be free to find someone who will make her happy. She deserves better than to be left at home alone, months at a time, single-handedly raising a family while her husband explores the world. If nobody will get hurt, what could I possibly have to lose?

Chapter 9

Begrudgingly, Alice and I agreed to meet to begin practising the Dance of the Wilis together. I don't know what Madame Lebedev was thinking; pairing us together is a disaster waiting to happen. Alice tried to suggest that we meet at her house but I absolutely refused to meet her on her own territory. However, there was no way we could meet at my house either, so we settled on the neutral ground of the library. Grace assured me there would be a private room we could use without disturbing anyone.

I arrive at the library early, not wanting Alice to get a jump on me. I am surprised to find August there, leaning against the counter. I hear him before I see him, his intoxicating laugh fills the echoing hall and I feel its reverberations deep in the pit of my stomach. My footsteps pick up, eager to reach him, my heart skipping in my chest. His head is bent low, and I wonder what he is reading to produce such a reaction. I am almost upon him when he looks up and says, 'Oh, Grace, I haven't laughed like that in years.'

I stop dead in my tracks; it feels like ice is dripping down my back, and I stare open mouthed as Grace straightens from behind the counter, a look of coy pleasure on her face.

'Who is this schmuck?' a disgruntled voice says from behind me, and I turn to find Jacob glaring at the back of August's head.

'Jacob!' I breathe, and smile up at him.

He tears his eyes away from August and looks down at me, his mouth spreading into a smile, though his chestnut eyes are missing their usual sparkle. 'Hello, Clem. How are you doing?'

'I was having quite a good day, but now I'm feeling a little nauseous,' I grumble as I watch August lean over the counter and whisper something in Grace's ear. She giggles then shakes her head as she picks up a pile of books to return to their shelves.

'I feel the same,' Jacob replies. 'That Draper fellow has been sat there all morning, flirting with Gracie . . . Doesn't he realise we have work to do?'

'Well, Grace could have asked him to leave if he was bothering her,' I huff, folding my arms. 'If you ask me, she seems to be enjoying the attention.'

'Do you think she likes him?' he asks, raising an eyebrow.

'I think she likes what he has to offer.' I sniff. 'Whether or not she likes him seems to have very little to do with that.'

'You can't mean to say she's after his money?' he laughs, but the jovial expression dies on his face as he sees I am not joking. 'She wouldn't,' he scoffs. 'Grace isn't like that.'

'I thought so too,' I say, watching Grace giggle at another of August's jokes.

Jacob narrows his eyes at me, his thick eyebrows knitting together. 'What's wrong, Clem? It's not like you to side against Grace.'

'Why? Has she said something?' I say sharply.

'No, of course not. I can't get a word in edgeways with this guy around.' He nods his head stiffly towards August. 'But I know you two, it's not like you to say anything bad against your sister. You always have each other's backs.'

I feel a jolt of guilt at this comment. Jacob is right; Grace and I never fall out. We bicker on occasion perhaps, but we made a promise to one another that we would always stick together. However, since she told me that she would encourage a proposal from August in order to improve our family's standing, things feel so different between us, and I can't help but harbour a secret resentment towards her.

'It's nothing,' I lie, folding my arms across my chest.

Jacob looks at me suspiciously, but before he can press the matter any further, Grace spots me and dashes over.

'Clem! How long have you been here?' she says, wrapping her arms around me.

'Long enough,' I mutter, stiffening a little, and she has the decency to look chagrined.

'August popped by to look at some of our books on botany. Why don't you go over and say hello?' she says, then turns her attention to Jacob. 'And what's got you looking so down in the dumps?'

'Nothing, I'm just tired,' he sighs, then takes off towards the poetry section.

Grace watches him go, then turns back to me. 'Did he say anything to you? He's been in a foul mood all afternoon.'

'Perhaps you should spend more time helping him and less time seeing to Mr Draper's needs,' I comment sniffily and she snorts with laughter.

'Is that what *he* said?' She folds her arms. 'Well, it is my job to help people find the books they need, and if Jacob has something to say about it, he can say it to my face!' she mutters through gritted teeth, then marches after him, leaving me alone with August.

I pull up a seat beside him and he looks up, beaming. 'Clementine! What a pleasant surprise.' His eyes skim over my hair, still scraped back in a bun, and the duffel bag slung over my shoulder. 'Just back from ballet class, I take it?'

'Actually, I have come here to rehearse in one of the private study rooms. We have a show coming up in a few months.'

'And what part are you dancing?' he asks, leaning over, his green eyes gleaming with genuine interest.

His gaze is so captivating, I almost forget to reply. 'Giselle,' I utter at last, hoping to see a glimmer of pride, anything, but his face remains blank. Pleasant, but blank. 'She's the main character,' I start to explain, and finally see a glimmer of admiration on his face that causes me to beam uncontrollably. 'She's a peasant girl who falls in love with a count, only to be deceived and end up dying from a broken heart.'

'Golly,' he laughs. 'It all sounds rather intense. Congratulations, though, that is really wonderful news. It is nice to see you smiling again after . . .' He trails off and takes my hand. It is entirely engulfed by his. 'Well, it is just good to see you so cheerful. And, may I take this moment to apologise if I caused you any further upset or distress the other night. It wasn't my intention.'

'Th-thank you,' I stammer, looking down at my hand, still cradled in his. It feels as if it is on fire, and the sensation is running up my arm and coursing through my chest. He lets go and fishes in his pocket for a packet of cigarettes, but the tingling sensation remains, bubbling away beneath my skin.

'You must be really rather good,' he says, striking a match and holding it to the cigarette in his puckered lips, and for a moment, I have no idea what he means and I blush uncontrollably. Then he adds, 'At dancing. I would love to see you dance one day.'

'Boasting again, Harrington?'

It feels like someone has tipped a bucket of ice water over me as I hear Alice's snide voice. She sidles up towards me, her face contorted into its usual sneer, her blonde hair scraped back into a high bun on top of her head.

'One of your friends?' August asks light-heartedly, and I begin to feel a little sick.

'Oh, Clementine and I are more than just friends,' Alice assures him with a falsely bright voice. 'We're dance partners, isn't that right, Clem?'

She has never called me Clem in her life and it sounds strange on her tongue. She must have picked it up from Rudi.

'Yes, something like that,' I murmur, eager to create some space between my nemesis and August. I grab her hand and she almost recoils in horror. 'Come on, *friend*, let's go and rehearse.'

The moment we are out of sight, I drop her hand as if it were poisonous, and she takes a step away from me, her arms crossed. 'This is ridiculous,' she huffs.

'That is something we can both agree on,' I murmur under my breath. 'For once.'

I push open the door to the private study room that Grace has set aside for us and Alice waltzes in behind me, casting her gaze around in assessment. 'So, why couldn't we meet at your house?'

'I assumed you wouldn't want to,' I lie, and she raises an eyebrow.

'But your sister's place of work is far more neutral,' she replies sarcastically.

'Look, it is just better for everyone this way,' I snap, not in the mood to deal with Alice Blakely's little irritations today.

'Fine!' she replies haughtily. 'Let's just begin our practice so we can get this over and done with.'

We run through the choreography for the Dance of the Wilis over and over. Alice loses no opportunity to snipe at me if she thinks I am out of time. I breathe deeply, refusing to let her get under my skin, and finally she stops trying to rile me and we actually begin to dance in unison as Madame had wished. On our fifth run-through, we begin to become more in sync with one another's movements, adding in small touches with our arms to embellish the story. We finish as one in twin poses, catching one another's eye with surprise. For a split second, Alice looks annoyed, like she thinks I have copied her. My chest constricts, ready for another argument, but then she giggles and, once she starts, so do I, the laughter washing over us both like relief. We drop our stance, relaxing at last, both reaching for a much-needed glass of water.

'You're far less insufferable outside of class,' Alice says between sips, wiping the sweat from her gleaming brow.

'And you're a far better dancer when you're not pining after Rudolf,' I smirk from behind my own glass.

Her head shoots up in surprise, and once again, I think

she is going to start a fight, but instead her face contorts into a frown. 'What's the deal with you two? Is it true that you are involved?'

'If we were, I certainly wouldn't tell you,' I remark, folding my arms. 'But, for your information, we are just good friends.'

'Well, now I don't know what to believe.' She smiles, a mischievous glint in her eye.

'Believe what you will, I have no time for idle gossip,' I reply and she rolls your eyes.

'That is your problem, Clementine, you never know how to have any fun.'

'I'm not here to have fun,' I say simply, carefully placing my glass back down. 'I am here to forge a career.'

'You're not the only one who wants to make a career out of dancing, you know,' she retorts hotly. 'It's not easy for the rest of us when Madame gives all the best parts to you.'

'She gives me the best parts because I am the best dancer.' I shrug. I don't mean it to sound arrogant, but I hear how it sounds and the look on Alice's face tells me that is how she has taken it.

'And that is why none of the girls in our class like you, Clementine,' she says stiffly, picking up her bag and shrugging it over her shoulder.

'I only meant that I want it more,' I try to justify myself, but I can tell I am digging a hole. 'I do so many extra hours—'

'Spare me the inspirational speech,' she interrupts and turns on her heel, pushing the door to the private study room open with significant force. It swings shut behind her with a loud bang and I flinch. I should have kept my mouth shut. That is the closest Alice and I have ever got to a civil conversation but I let my ego get in the way.

I wait a few minutes for Alice to leave before picking up my things and returning to the main hall of the library. August is still propped up at the desk, smoking a cigarette and chatting away to Grace as she loads books onto her trolley, ready to return to the shelves. She looks a bit harried.

She keeps rubbing the back of her neck as if it is causing her discomfort and looking over her shoulder every few minutes. She hurries off with the cart before I can reach her. I watch August for a while as he peruses the book in front of him, flinching slightly as he carelessly flicks ash onto the pages. I am about to step forward and say something when Jacob rounds the corner, his usually boyish face filled with thunder.

'Hey, there's no smoking in here!' he yells, his words echoing around the library as he shoves an ashtray under August's nose.

August recoils slightly, startled by Jacob's aggression, and quickly stubs the cigarette out. 'Sorry, pal, there weren't any signs.'

'Yes, well most people can work it out for themselves,' Jacob growls. 'Books are rather flammable, you see.'

Grace reappears behind him. Her eyes are red and puffy, and she looks as if she's been crying, but when she sees August and me, she smiles and rolls her eyes like this is just another of Jacob's amusing antics.

'There you are, Clem. All done with your rehearsal? It's time we were getting home. If we leave now, we will make the next bus.'

'Never mind the bus, I'll drive you,' August interjects, sliding off his stool and clutching the book beneath his arm. 'I think I had better go.'

'You can't take that with you.' Jacob nods sharply at the book. 'You're not a member.'

'I said he could borrow it,' Grace interjects quietly, looking up at Jacob beseechingly. I watch some of the anger leave his eyes as he returns her gaze, only to be replaced with something else that I can't quite place. He almost looks forlorn.

'Fine,' he says bluntly, returning to his place behind the desk. 'Take it.'

Grace looks torn. Her eyes flit between August and Jacob for a moment, then she nods curtly. 'Thank you for offering to drive us, Mr Draper. If you are sure it's no trouble, let's go.'

She ushers me out of the library without another word. I look back over my shoulder as we leave, worried about Jacob. I don't think I have ever seen him lose his temper before. His elbows are resting on the counter and his head of floppy brown hair is cradled in his hands. I want to call out to him, to go back and see if he is alright, but Grace is marching ahead. She looks back at the last moment to see why I am dawdling; she must see Jacob, but her expression is entirely inscrutable.

'Come on, Clem,' she snaps, as the door of the library closes behind her.

I remain silent in the back seat of August's car while he and Grace chat to one another. He is regaling her with stories from his latest trip to Peru, and she asks questions and exclaims in all the right places.

'Have you ever travelled abroad, Grace?' he asks her, his eyes upon her, rather than the road ahead.

'No, I am afraid I have lived a rather dull life compared to yours.' She smiles. 'I am far more interested in escaping through my books than travelling. It's Clementine you must speak to about travel. She is desperate to see the world, aren't you, Clem?'

She turns around and nods encouragingly at me, and I open my mouth to speak. It is true, one of the reasons I want to join a prestigious ballet company is to see more of the world. I want to dance on stages in Vienna, Paris, Rome, perhaps even travel to South America and farther afield like August has. I am about to tell him as much when he interjects, moving the conversation along, and I settle back down into silence.

'What is your favourite book?' he asks her.

'Oh, that's an easy one. *The Secret Garden* by Frances Hodgson Burnett. It is so . . . magical, the way the garden seems to have a personality of its own, how it brings the characters together. I think it's perfect.'

'Ah, so we may make a botany enthusiast out of you yet, Miss Harrington.' He nods approvingly, then finally looks back at me, his green eyes flashing in the dappled sunlight. 'The two of you should come to Kew Gardens, I could give you a guided tour.'

'Oh, that would be wonderful, wouldn't it, Clem?' Grace exclaims, and even my slightly sour mood is lifted by the thought of a visit to the Royal Botanic Gardens.

'Marvellous, I shall see you there tomorrow morning. We'll make a day of it.'

Chapter 10

When Grace and I arrive at the grand gates of Kew Gardens, August is already waiting for us. He is leaning against the twelve-foot brick wall that encircles the entire park, shielding whatever delights await inside from view. He looks effortlessly handsome as always in a pair of stone-coloured trousers, a light blue shirt tucked in loosely at his waist, the top button open to reveal a tantalising triangle of sun-browned skin. He looks up as we approach, his face splitting into a wide grin.

'Good morning, ladies. I hope you are ready for an adventure.'

'Most definitely,' Grace replies. 'I think Clem is just about ready to burst with excitement.'

'I am *not*,' I reply, trying to sound nonchalant. 'Not to say I am not excited,' I add to August, 'only that I have the appropriate amount of eagerness. I am not some child who cannot control her emotions.'

August laughs, 'Well, I shall take that as a personal challenge to leave you entirely enthralled.' He gestures for us to enter the gates ahead of him. 'I thought we would start with the greenhouses, if you don't mind? That is where I spend most of my working hours, and I do have a few things to attend to as we tour the grounds.'

'Of course,' Grace replies modestly. 'We don't want to disturb your plans. We are simply grateful for the opportunity to have a look around, aren't we, Clem?'

I nod in agreement. Personally, the thought of seeing the famous Kew Gardens greenhouses sounds riveting and I am more than satisfied at the thought of watching August at work. He leads us down the boardwalk, past ancient trees so tall that their boughs stretch high, high up above our heads as if they were reaching for the clouds. As we walk, he regales us with stories.

'Across the water, you will see the famous Palm House,' he tells us as we walk around the lake. 'It is home to some of the rarest specimens in the world and was the first glasshouse ever to be built to such a large scale. We'll take a look inside later, but I would like to save it for the end.'

I gaze across the still water at the magnificent structure. The domed glass roof gleams in the sunlight, an ethereal glow emanates through the misted glass and I can spy the shadows of gigantic plants, their monstrous leaves clamouring to burst free from their enclosure.

'Clementine?' Grace calls, and I realise I have stopped in my tracks, struck by the sheer marvel of it. I am desperate to get inside and have a proper look around, but I run to catch up with them, eager not to be left behind.

August is already marching on. I suppose he gets to see these views every day, and while still special, the magic must start to wear off after a while. We wander on beneath a shady canopy of oak trees and birches, following a winding path to the nursery.

'Here it is!' August calls, pointing straight ahead towards a glass building with a gabled roof. 'This is where we grow and cultivate all our new specimens. Some of the cuttings I brought back from Peru are currently housed in here. I must check on their progress.' He stops at the door to the nursery before holding it open for us. 'I must ask that you don't touch anything in here, it is all rather delicate.'

We nod solemnly and make our way into the stifling heat of the nursery. There are several rows of long, worn wooden tables all laden with trays containing sprouts and saplings of various ages. August makes a beeline for the end table, swiping a pair of secateurs on his way. Grace stands a little awkwardly by the door, taking August's warning not to touch anything very seriously, but I am eager to explore. I wander down the aisles between tables, reading all the little tags affixed to each tray and inspecting the specimens within. I linger by a sapling with strange, fan-shaped leaves. They are beautiful, like the full skirts of a tutu.

'That is a ginkgo sapling,' August remarks from behind me, causing me to start in surprise. 'The ginkgo tree hails from China. It is also known as the maidenhair tree. In the fall, the leaves turn a beautiful golden colour, resembling the flowing locks of a fair maiden. However, despite their delicate appearance, they are incredibly hardy trees, perfect for urban environments like London.'

As I turn to acknowledge him, his shining eyes are the same shade of green as the ginkgo in the shafts of sunlight that stream through the greenhouse. 'The leaves are quite beautiful,' I reply, finding my voice at last.

'You have a keen eye for botany, Miss Harrington.' He smiles, and a small petal of delight unfurls in my chest. 'Tell me,' he continues, 'what must I do to inspire the same fascination in your sister?'

The feeling dies almost instantly as my gaze lifts to where Grace is still standing by the doorway. 'If you wish to inspire my sister, you must reach her through her own passions,' I reply bleakly.

He looks thoughtful for a moment, then utterly lost.

'Through literature,' I intone and a dawning realisation rises upon his face.

'Ah, of course,' he sighs, snapping his fingers. 'Thank you, Clementine. I know just where we must go next.'

Without another word, he glides towards Grace and takes her arm. 'Come, my dear, I have something to show you that will excite you far beyond the mundanities of the nursery.'

'The gardens were founded in 1759 by King George III's mother, Princess Augusta,' he tells us as we wander down a winding path through a grove of magnificent late-blooming rhododendrons in shades of shocking pink, blood red, orange and yellow that climb abundantly over one another, their vines intertwining to create a floral rainbow.

'Are you a namesake of hers, by any chance?' Grace enquires, stopping to smell one of the large bell-shaped flowers.

'Ha! Not quite,' he chuckles, sharing a secret look with me that causes my heart to flutter like the wings of the small brown birds darting across the path.

I drop his gaze and attempt to slow my breathing, as well as my racing heart, as we walk on. Eventually we come to an abrupt standstill outside a magnificent red-brick building. Grace and I glance at August expectantly as he casts an admiring gaze over the building.

'This,' he proclaims, 'is the Kew Gardens library.'

Grace gasps and August's smile widens victoriously as he gives me a conspiratorial wink, but I can feel my brow knitting into a frown. I have set myself up. I told August exactly what to do to woo Grace. What was I thinking?

He ushers us forwards, bowing slightly as he holds open the door, and shows us into the library. There are rows beyond rows of bookcases, their shelves bowing under the weight of hundreds of leather-bound books. I look back at Grace and her eyes are wide and shining with awe.

'Feel free to run wild,' August says with a lopsided smile, his green eyes sparkling. 'There is no one else here at the moment.'

The words are barely out of his mouth before Grace dashes past the two of us and begins running her fingers across the gilt spines. I hang back. Books have always been Grace's passion rather than mine, but even I am entranced by the ancient volumes before us.

'Don't be shy, Clementine,' August bends forward and whispers, his warm breath tickling my ear, sending a shiver down my back. 'I am sure you can find something to suit your own curiosities too.'

A wide, albeit reluctant, smile spreads across my face, and I am not sure if it is the result of his closeness or the opportunity to explore. Personally, I am more interested in the building itself. The walls are panelled with oak and the bookcases are all carved with intricate filigrees. Hefty tomes lie open on plinths atop polished wooden worktops, displaying intricate hand-drawn illustrations of fruits, fungi, leaves and exotic flowers. They look just like the framed illustrations in August's sitting room. I lean over one of the ancient books and breathe in the sweet, musty smell of decaying paper. I wander off, deeper into the depths of the library, my footsteps echoing loudly against the polished floor. I find a wrought-iron spiral staircase, and when I look up, I realise there are many more floors of treasures to discover. I climb the staircase eagerly, taking the steps two at a time, and when I reach the top, I hang over the railing looking down at the floor below. I make to call out to Grace, but I don't see her at first. I scan the aisles, looking for a curl of tawny hair or her slender arms trying to drag an almighty volume off the shelves. It is August I spot first, his golden hair catching the light like a halo. He is leaning over something and muttering, his voice low. I tiptoe along the balcony for a better angle and lean a little further over the railing, then nearly lose my footing. It is no wonder I couldn't find Grace. He is towering over her, one hand resting on the bookshelf beside her head, the other under her chin. My heart is hammering in my ears and I can barely hear what they are saying, but I manage to catch the final few words of August's plea.

'Please tell me you'll consider it, Grace.'

She looks up at him from her large blue eyes, her expression torn as if she is fighting some internal battle. 'I'll . . . I'll have to ask my mother,' she says at last, then as if she can feel my gaze burning into her, she looks up, her eyes finding mine instantly. I stumble backwards, mortified to have been caught snooping, but my mind is racing. What could he possibly have asked her to consider? Surely not a proposal already . . . She looked so uneasy, my poor Grace. I cannot allow this to happen. My stomach twists and I feel for a moment as if I am going to be sick. It is as if all the air has been sucked out of the stuffy, old library and I cannot breathe.

'Clementine!' Grace calls, but I don't answer, my hand on my chest as it rises and falls rapidly. The rushing in my ears grows louder until I cannot hear a thing, then everything goes black.

I open my eyes to find Grace looming over me, and am acutely aware of a blinding pain in my head.

'Oh, thank goodness!' she breathes, leaning away. 'What on earth happened, Clem? There was an almighty crash and then we found you crumpled on the floor with your eyes closed.'

'Almighty seems like a bit of an overstatement,' I grumble, and her face relaxes.

'Well, I see the fall didn't knock the sarcasm out of you.' She grins.

I sit up a little, cradling my head. I have a throbbing headache and there is a bump sticking out of my forehead.

'You must have hit your head quite hard, Clem. Maybe you should stay lying down.'

'Where's August?' I ask, ignoring her advice and looking around.

'He's gone to get the car,' she replies, blushing at the mention of his name. 'He's going to drive us home.'

'You don't have to leave early on my account. You didn't get to see the palm house,' I say, sitting up straighter, and then instantly regretting the words as I speak them. The last thing I want is for Grace to be left alone with August, coerced into making the wrong decision.

'Don't be silly. I'm not going to leave you,' Grace insists to my relief. 'Besides, I would like to go home . . .' she trails off, her eyes glazing over. They seem to do that a lot these days. There was once a time when I knew everything Grace was thinking, but now it seems her head is so full of secrets I barely know her. Then again, I suppose mine is too. I reach out instinctively to grab her hand and she looks at me in surprise.

'I love you so much, Grace,' I say urgently. 'You do know that, don't you?'

'Yes, of course I do.' She smiles, squeezing my fingers. 'It's you and me against the world. It always has been.'

'And always will be?' I press.

A small crease forms between her eyebrows. She opens her mouth to speak. I wonder if she is going to tell me what August was asking her earlier, but before she gets the chance, he reappears.

'Oh, thank goodness,' he cries. 'Back in the land of the living. You gave us quite a scare, Clementine.'

'I'm fine, honestly!' I exclaim, leaping to my feet. All the blood rushes to my head and I almost topple once more.

'Come on,' Grace says, grabbing my arm. 'Let's get you home.'

I sit quietly in the back of the car with my eyes closed, hoping that August and Grace will continue the conversation I had eavesdropped on earlier. To my disappointment, they both remain silent for the duration of the journey home. It is strange; though no one is speaking, there is such an atmosphere that I can almost hear Grace's brain buzzing with thoughts. I wonder if she is thinking about August's proposal or if there is something else on her mind. I never did get to the bottom of Jacob's peculiar behaviour at the library. I feel as if I have accidentally wandered into snippets of a story I am not privy to.

I must have actually dozed off because when I open my eyes again, August is standing on the pavement and holding the door open for me. Grace stands a few feet behind him, her arms wrapped tightly around her woollen coat.

'Thank you,' I murmur as I climb out of the back seat and he nods, tipping his hat towards me.

The moment I am out of the car, Grace turns on her heel and begins trotting up the front steps.

'Oh, Miss Harrington?' August calls, and we both turn, but he is talking to Grace, of course. 'You will ask your mother about next Friday, won't you?'

I look back at Grace and she nods curtly, then continues up the steps. She has the key in the door before I can get through the gate but I rush after her. 'What is happening next Friday?'

'Oh, it's nothing, it's just a party,' she mutters, shrugging out of her coat and hanging it in the hall.

'A party?' I exclaim, my eyes lighting up as she rolls her eyes. A party invitation is a far cry from a proposal. It is also another opportunity for me to put a stop to the latter ever happening.

'This is precisely why I didn't want to tell you,' she sighs. 'I don't even know if Mother will allow *me* to attend, let alone you.'

My heart drops. She is right. Mother has plenty of reasons to let Grace go to a party at August's, anything that will push them closer together will be a win in her eyes. However, she has no reason at all to let me go. In fact, if anything, she will probably see my attending as a hindrance in her scheming. I realise that Grace is still talking and tune back into the tail end of whatever she is saying.

'Then there is the matter of a costume . . . What on earth would I wear?'

'Wait, it's a costume party?' I interrupt and Grace looks a little perturbed.

'Yes. Weren't you listening?'

'Of course, I was.' I blush. 'I'm just feeling rather slow after my knock on the head,' I add, rubbing the raised lump. I then feel instantly terrible as her face twists in concern. It really doesn't hurt so much anymore.

'You should get straight to bed, Clem,' she insists, chivvying me towards the stairs. 'I'll speak to Mother about the party, then I will come and check on you.'

I do as I am told and change into my nightdress, not even stretching before bed as I have done every night for the last ten years.

I don't know how long I have been lying awake when Grace quietly pushes open the door, carrying a flickering candle, her bare feet padding across the floor.

'Are you still awake, Clem?' she whispers.

'No,' I mumble with my eyes closed.

'Oh, that's a shame . . .' she replies. 'I had hoped to share the news with you tonight.'

'What news?' I ask, sitting bolt upright.

'Be careful!' she chides, gently pushing me back down onto my pillow. 'You'll make yourself faint again if you keep on like that.'

'What news?' I repeat. 'Is it about the party?'

'Mother says we can both go.' She smiles, her face awash with the warm glow of the candle.

'Really?' I ask, astounded.

'Really.'

'How in heaven's name did you convince her?'

'That,' she responds mysteriously, 'is confidential. All you need to worry about is your costume.'

PART TWO

'A person has rights to discover her own mistakes,
to make her own way, to grow and blossom
in her own particular soil.'

– Olive Higgins Prouty, *Now, Voyager*

Chapter 11

'You failed to mention it was a fancy dress party,' Rudi says disparagingly as we warm up in Madame Lebedev's studio. It is true that when I first asked Rudi to join me at August Draper's party, I conveniently left out the dress code requirement until after he had agreed to come.

'Don't we spend enough of our lives in costume?' he continues with a look of despair.

'Oh, come on,' I needle, nudging his arm. 'It will be fun! Costume parties are exciting. You can pretend to be someone completely different for the evening.' The thought of masquerading as a different character fills me with anticipation. Perhaps it will be an opportunity for August to finally see me in a different light.

Rudi scrutinises me, his eyes steely, then sighs as he looks to the heavens. 'Fine,' he says grumpily. 'If it means that much to you, I will go. I suppose it was my idea to trick the American in the first place . . .'

'You can't make me go to this thing alone,' I protest. 'It will be torturous.'

'I thought you said it would be fun?' he shoots back, his eyes narrowing.

'Well, it will be with you there.' I smile sweetly.

'And I suppose you want to raid Ma's costume cupboard for an outfit too?' he says, watching my reflection in the mirror as he stretches his leg over the barre and begins to limber up.

'Do you think she would let us?' I ask excitedly.

'I am sure she would allow it for you.'

'Oh, Rudi! That would be amazing,' I exclaim. 'I honestly hadn't even thought about costumes yet.' I sit on my hands in an attempt to stop myself fidgeting, the urge to dive deep into the costume cupboard is tantalisingly tempting.

I catch Rudi's eye in the mirror again and he sighs. 'You want to look now, don't you?'

'No, it's fine. Finish warming up,' I insist, but he brings his long muscular leg down slowly from the barre.

'I don't need to be limber to try on a costume, Clem, not most of them anyway . . .' he adds thoughtfully. 'Come on, let's have a look and then you can stop thinking about it.'

The possibility of me not thinking about the party seems unlikely, but I don't tell Rudi that as he leads me towards Madame Lebedev's closely guarded costume room. The door is locked, but he has a key, and as he slowly swings the door open, the sweet smell of mothballs and faded perfume drifts out to greet us. The room is not large, just big enough for the two of us to fit inside. A long, brass rail sweeps round the walls, with all the costumes Madame Lebedev has collected over the decades hung up and meticulously labelled. The colours are magnificent, even though some have faded from their original glory. I run my fingers across emerald velvet sleeves, sparkling golden brocade, blush-pink netted tutus, and ivory silk shirts. I pull a white cotton dress from the rail, and read the tag, though I can already tell this is Clara's nightdress from *The Nutcracker*. I remember Alice swanning around in it in last year's performance. She made a big song and dance about landing the 'lead', though everyone knows that the Sugar Plum Fairy is the most technical and sought-after role.

'Perhaps turning up in nightwear will send the wrong message,' Rudi suggests with a wicked grin.

'I also don't need August to think I am any more of a child than he already does,' I add in agreement. 'No, Clara is not the right outfit for me.' I continue to browse, my fingers brushing against delicate skirts of chiffon and satin bodices.

'What about a costume from *Les Sylphides*?' Rudi asks, pulling a white dress from the rail with delicate puffed sleeves, a heart-shaped neckline and the most intricate tiny wings.

I pull a face at the large puffy white skirt. 'I don't know . . . I love *Les Sylphides*, but will I look too much like a debutante out of context?'

'A debutante with wings?' he asks, raising an eyebrow.

'This is trickier than I thought,' I sigh. 'Why don't we focus on you. What about Prince Charming?'

'Well, I wouldn't need a costume for that.' He grins as I roll my eyes. 'No, it's bad enough that you're making me go to this party, I'm not turning up in a tunic and a pair of tights.'

'That doesn't leave you with many options in a cupboard full of ballet costumes . . .' I point out, but he reaches into the rail and pulls out a blousy white shirt with large bell sleeves from *Romeo and Juliet*.

'This will do,' he says with a tone that suggests he couldn't care less what he wears. 'With a pair of black leggings, I can almost pass it off as a normal outfit.'

'Romeo?' I giggle. 'Gosh, you do think highly of yourself, don't you?'

'Only to counterbalance the torrent of abuse I receive from you,' he retorts, his eyes narrowing as he slips the shirt over his clothes. 'There. What say you, ma'am?'

I must admit that it looks better than I expected. He could easily tempt a hundred girls down from their balconies dressed like that.

'Why don't you go as Juliet?' he suggests, pulling out one of her many dresses for me to try. 'That would certainly get the American's attention if we turned up in matching outfits.'

'A couple of star-crossed lovers?' I scoff. 'It's already going to be difficult enough to pretend that we are courting. Please don't make it any more nausea inducing than it needs to be.'

'God forbid,' he mutters loftily, and I shoot him a look, but he has already turned back to the rail. He stops, his fingers lingering over a particular costume, but I can't see what he has found. He deliberates for a moment, then pulls it from the rail and reads the tag. 'Ahh, I thought so . . .' he murmurs to himself.

'What? What is it?' I pester, trying to get a better look. He spins around and holds up a Grecian-style tunic in a delicate shade of ivory with elaborate drapery that droops around the hips like wilting petals, then falls elegantly to about ankle height. The bust is secured with a bronze swathe of silk ribbon, and the neckline plunges into a wide V with beautiful blousy puffed sleeves that rest right on the edge of the shoulders. A brooch of oak leaves and acorns is fastened to the bust, and a matching headdress intertwined with gold ribbons is dangling from the hanger.

'Is that a costume from *The Dryad*?' I ask in a hushed whisper. It is not a part I have ever played, and I can tell the costume is very old, but I know the story well enough. *The Dryad* is the story of a nymph who is trapped inside an oak tree, and only released once every ten years.

'Yes, I think it was my mother's from before she joined the Bolshoi,' he says as he glances down at the costume with a faraway look. I wonder if he is thinking of home and I almost reach out to take his hand, but something holds me back. My fingers hang limply in the space between us, but before I can make up my mind, he thrusts the dress towards me. 'This is the perfect costume,' he says, his winning smile reappearing and lighting up his handsome face.

'She would never let me wear it,' I sigh, caressing the light material with my fingers. 'And rightly so. It is too special.'

'She wouldn't have to know . . .' he says pointedly.

'Rudi, I can't steal from my ballet mistress! That must be one of the most disrespectful things a student can do,' I insist, turning my back on the beautiful dress and continuing to search the rails.

'No, but as her wayward son, I could quite easily take it . . .' he says decisively. 'Come on, Clem, I saw the way your face lit up when you saw it. You should wear it! What good will it do leaving it in this cupboard to be eaten to bits by moths?'

'What about a snowflake from *The Nutcracker*?' I ask, ignoring his attempts to sway me. 'I'll blend in nicely with the weather.'

'Why on earth would you want to *blend in*, Clem?' he asks despairingly, coming to lean on the rail beside me. He looks down at me, a loose curl dropping into his unyielding eyes. 'If you insist on *The Nutcracker*, at least go for the Snow Queen. You aren't supporting role material and it's time this American knew that.'

'Fine, the Snow Queen it is,' I say, lifting my chin to meet his gaze. But no matter how beautiful the Snow Queen costume may be, all I can think about is the nymph.

We take our costumes from the cupboard and lock the door behind us as Madame Lebedev hurries into the studio. She looks a little harried, her hair which is usually so neatly swept back looks slightly flyaway, and there are shadows beneath her eyes. She looks at us both suspiciously, her gaze lingering on the costumes in our hands.

'What have you been up to?'

'Just borrowing a couple of costumes for a party, Ma, nothing for you to worry about,' Rudi replies nonchalantly, taking the two costumes and hanging them from one of the barres.

'Very well, so long as they return in good condition,' she says brusquely. 'I hope you have both been limbering up. We have a lot of work to do this afternoon. I want to finish setting the choreography for the meeting of Count Albrecht and Giselle. Let's go from the start of the opening *pas de deux* in act one,' she instructs, as I take my place on the marker, ready to perform, Rudi moves to the edge of the studio ahead of his entrance.

I begin, my steps light and airy to symbolise Giselle's joy and love for dancing. This part is easy for me and the smile on my face comes naturally. I step into an *arabesque* on pointe as Rudi steps in and we begin our *pas de deux*. I love this sequence. It is fun and full of push and pull between Giselle and Count Albrecht. It should be a breeze for Rudi, who already embraces the charm of Albrecht, but he looks unusually nervous as he approaches me.

'Smile, Rudi!' Madame calls from the corner of the studio. 'You are supposed to be falling in love. Save the attitude for the Dance of the Wilis.'

He readjusts his face into a pleasing smile, his grey eyes locking on to mine, then he finally begins to enjoy himself. I turn away from him and he takes my arm, reaching for my hand and bending to kiss it as I snatch it away at the last moment and spring into a set of *jetés*, skipping from one foot to the other.

'More grace, Clementine,' Madame Lebedev cries. 'You must be weightless.'

We continue. I reach for a flower prop and pluck the petals one by one. He loves me, he loves me not, he loves me, he loves me not . . . I drop the flower and skip across the studio away from him, but he retrieves it and bounds after me.

'Higher, Rudi, jump higher!' Madame Lebedev seems tense, like a string on a violin pulled too taut.

I stop dancing and watch him. He is already flying as high as I have ever seen him, his muscular legs flexing with the effort.

'If I go any higher, I won't make it back down in time for the music!' he declares with a huff as he lands, his cheeks flushed from the exertion.

'Then you must come down faster,' she demands and he looks at me in exasperation. 'Take it back to the beginning of the flower sequence.'

'Maybe we should take a break,' I suggest, bending to collect the loose petals off the floor, but Madame glares at me.

'Do you think the Vic-Wells Ballet would allow you a break?' she exclaims. 'That is what you both want, is it not?'

I nod enthusiastically, but Rudi merely folds his arms with a sullen look at his mother which she chooses to ignore.

'I have received word that a scout will attend the opening performance of this ballet. This is your chance.'

The words settle in my chest, and I feel a tingling sensation spreading through my body to the tips of my fingers and the ends of my toes. A scout for the Vic-Wells Ballet! I glance at Rudi. This is what we have dreamed of for years, but when I look at him now, I can't see the same excitement on his face that I feel. He bows his head in defeat and nods.

'Right, then let's get back to work,' Madame says with finality.

We repeat the sequence with the flower once again. Now that I know how much is resting on this performance, I find I have a new sense of determination, and Rudi does indeed jump higher than before as he chases after me. He comes to a standstill before me, plucks the last petal dramatically, and holds it towards me as a declaration. He loves me. He bends down on one knee and looks up at me once more, his eyes earnest with intent, and for a moment something passes between us. It is like a current of electricity. It crackles in the air and my skin feels hot, scorched by his gaze. I almost lose my balance. His eyes widen, he is ready to catch me, but I steady myself, my heart racing, and as the music dies, it is replaced with applause.

I turn in surprise, as if waking from a dream, to find Grace and August watching us from the hallway. My cheeks flood with colour and I take a step back from Rudi as he unfolds himself from the floor.

'Hold the applause!' Madame says crossly. 'What happened, Clementine? You were doing so well, then you lost your balance!' She marches towards me and places her hands on my stomach and my spine. 'Now, rise back onto pointe and hold your core muscles.'

'She knows how to balance, *Mamasha*.' Rudi leaps to my defence. 'She is just tired. We both are.'

'No, really, I'm fine,' I insist. I think again of the Vic-Wells Ballet, of my need to perfect this performance, and then that feeling when Rudi looked at me. It was surely a fluke, a moment of light-headedness, and I must master it. 'Let's do it again.'

Rudi sighs and throws his hands in the air in frustration before bringing them back down to rest on his hips.

'Perhaps I am pushing you too hard,' Madame muses. 'Gosh, look at the time. We should have finished up half an hour ago.'

'Precisely,' Rudi replies icily, and I wonder if he has plans with Anna as a little knot forms in my stomach.

'What is wrong with you?' I hiss at him, surprised by my own annoyance. 'This is everything we have worked for.'

'There is more to life than performing, Clem.'

'In other words, you have plans tonight?' I reply, crossing my arms and raising an eyebrow. 'I am glad you have finally found whatever it is that you have been chasing all these years, Rudi, but I hope it won't distract you from our dream. This could be our big chance.'

I lower my heels to the ground, my aching feet screaming for rest, and make my way over to Grace and August. 'What are you doing here?' I whisper, folding my arms across my chest.

'Don't try that prima ballerina attitude with me, Madame.' Grace grins. 'I finished at the library early, and August was with me, so we came to catch the end of your rehearsal.'

'I hope you don't mind,' August says courteously, bowing his golden head but keeping his green eyes fixed on mine. 'I begged your sister to allow me to tag along. You dance beautifully, Clementine.'

'Didn't I tell you that she and Rudolf have such perfect chemistry?' Grace says proudly, glancing up at August as Rudi comes over to join us.

'Oh yes.' I nod eagerly. 'I am so lucky that he is my partner. You can't fake that kind of dance chemistry.'

'Hello, Grace,' Rudi says, slipping his arm around my waist, a convivial gesture he has probably made a thousand times before, but now I notice how both Grace and August's eyes linger on our emtwined bodies. 'Who is this?' he asks stiffly, nodding at August.

'This is our neighbour, Mr Draper,' I reply candidly, stepping away and letting Rudi's arm fall to his side. There is a fine line between making our romance believable and making sure Grace doesn't stop us spending time together unchaperoned. He looks at me, half confused, half hurt, then glances at August who offers him his hand.

'August Draper. I recently moved in across the street from the Harringtons. You must be the famous Rudi Lebedev I have heard so much about.'

Rudi looks down at August's outstretched hand, leaving it hanging there for a moment. It must only be a second or two, but it feels like an excruciatingly long time before he finally shakes it.

'Rudolf,' he says at last, and August's eyes widen bashfully.

'My apologies,' he starts, but I cut him off.

'Don't listen to him. He is just in a bad mood because our practice has overrun,' I scoff, and Rudi gives me a long look, his grey eyes challenging.

'She's right,' he shrugs eventually, 'I have somewhere else to be.' Then he grabs his bag and shoulders his way past August and Grace without another word. I watch him go, wondering again if he has plans with Anna, my stomach hardening at the thought.

'Charming,' August says quietly as he looks back over his shoulder at Rudi.

'I'm sorry,' I reply nervously. 'He's not usually like that. I think he's just tired. It was quite a gruelling rehearsal.'

I dash across the studio to collect my things, unlace my ribbons as quickly as I can and stuff my pointe shoes back in the bag before cramming my feet back into my plimsolls. I stop at Madame Lebedev and thank her again for the lesson, then rush out into the corridor where Grace and August are waiting for me.

'It's no wonder he was upset,' I overhear Grace saying as I leave the studio. 'I'm not joking about the chemistry. If you ask me, they are perfect for each other.'

'Yes,' August replies. 'The boy clearly has feelings for her. I suppose they're not so young after all . . .'

A grin spreads across my face. Despite the altercation with Rudi, the plan is beginning to work! Now that August sees me as a grown-up, all Rudi and I have to do is keep up the façade and convince him to fall in love with me. Then both Grace and I will be free to follow our dreams.

Chapter 12

It is raining by the time we arrive back on our street, so August stops the car outside our house and lets us make a run for cover. Rudi is waiting for me, seemingly unfazed by the rain and gazing down the tree-lined road towards the heath. His hair is soaked and his curls hang looser than usual around his angular face.

'You want to be careful,' I say as I approach, my coat pulled over my head for cover. 'Our neighbourhood lookout is terribly vigilant and you look like you're up to no good.'

He grins, a Cheshire Cat smile that reveals all of his teeth. There is a glint of mischief in his eyes. 'I'm always up to no good, Clem. That's why you like me.'

'I thought you had plans with Anna,' I say, lifting my chin sharply to scrutinise him. 'You couldn't wait to get away earlier.'

'I never said I was seeing Anna.' He raises an eyebrow sceptically. 'I simply said I had somewhere I needed to be. I have been there, and now I am here.' He spreads his arms open, a smug smile spreading across his face and I fight every urge in my body to stick my tongue out at him. Grace is still waiting for me by the front door, shielded from the rain by the porch awning. Rudi glances in her direction. 'Can you get away for a bit?'

'Wait here a moment,' I tell him and I skitter up the front path to where my sister is patiently waiting with a small smile upon her face.

'Is it alright if Rudi and I go for a walk?' I ask. 'We just need to talk through this afternoon's rehearsal—' I start, but her smile widens and she shakes her head a little, as if she is privy to some inside information that I know nothing about.

'Whatever the two of you are up to, I don't want to know,' she replies, then looks towards Rudi who is now waiting by the gate. 'Just keep my sister out of trouble please, Rudolf.'

'Always,' he responds solemnly, sweeping into a low bow, the rivulets of rain dripping from his hair.

'Don't be too late, Clementine,' Grace warns as she opens the front door. 'And I would recommend you take a brolly.' She hands it to me and waves goodbye, closing the door behind her.

I look at Rudi suspiciously. 'So, why are you here?' I ask, but before I can question him further, he takes me by the hand and begins dragging me back down the street.

'You ask too many questions, *solnyshko*. Just follow me.'

I pester Rudi for clues on the bus, but he won't give me an inch until we reach Covent Garden. The rain has stopped, thankfully, but the wet cobbled streets glisten like silver as we pass over them.

'Come on.' He stands abruptly. 'This is our stop.'

I follow him off the bus, past public houses full to bursting with drunken patrons. He draws closer to me as a man with red cheeks and a swaying gait lunges across the street, singing merrily to himself at the top of his lungs.

'Stay close, Clem,' he murmurs, taking my hand in his, then looking down at me with a jovial smirk. 'I don't want to get in trouble with your sister.'

He leads us down a cobbled street, then takes a left and stops in front of the Royal Opera House.

'What are we doing here?' I ask, gazing up at the grand limestone structure with its domed glass conservatory.

'A friend of mine works here as an usher,' he says, reaching into his pocket for a ring of keys and waving them in front of me. 'He owed me a favour.'

'You can't be serious!' I hiss. 'Rudi, we can't break into the Royal Opera House. What if we get caught?'

'Stop worrying, Clementine, it will be fine,' he insists, trying each key in the lock until finally it clicks. He raises his eyebrows and smirks, pushing the door open and ushering me inside.

'What about the security guards?' I whisper as he closes the door softly behind us, engulfing the hallway in darkness.

'I have conveniently timed our excursion with the shift changeover,' he replies, striking a match on the wall and cupping it with his hand as he searches for the light switch. 'Ah, here we go.'

He flicks the switch and I shield my eyes as they adjust to the light.

'Come on,' he says, striding ahead. 'This way.'

I hurry after him, eager not to be left behind as we wander down corridor after corridor. I have no idea where he is taking me until he makes a sudden stop outside a door to our right.

'Are you ready?' he asks.

'I don't know!' I whisper. 'I have no idea what I am supposed to be ready for.'

His face cracks into a lopsided smile and he pushes the door open.

'After you.'

I take a deep breath and cross the precipice into the unknown.

'Close your eyes,' he instructs and I do as I am told. I hear him flick on the lights, then his hands are on my shoulders and he is gently pushing me forwards. 'Keep them closed. There's a step here, and another.' I feel the surface change beneath my feet from carpet to something hard and springy, a surface I know well. It feels like a stage. 'OK,' he murmurs, releasing me from his grasp. 'Now open them.'

My vision is blurry at first. All I can see is the warm glow of a hundred lights, and colours, so many colours. Deep velvet red, glimmering gold and duck-egg blue, like the first September skies. Slowly the details come into focus and I realise where I am. This is the stage of the Royal Opera House. Row upon row of red chairs surround me in a horseshoe shape, rising up into the rafters. There must be well over a thousand seats, each section separated by Corinthian columns of cream, decorated with rich gold leaf. Every box is surrounded by gilded oak wreaths and acorns, connected by a continuous stream of overflowing roses and other flowers. I spy cupids, their tiny wings aflutter, and the heads of satyrs, boys with harps, and large festoons of fruit and foliage. I lift my head towards the domed ceiling and my jaw almost hits the floor. It is like standing in the bow of the most magnificent ship, and my heart swells in my chest with excitement. This is it! This is my dream.

'Rudi . . .' I murmur, awestruck. 'It's-It's-'

'There aren't quite words for it, are there?' He smiles, gazing up at the Renaissance-styled panels. 'This is the home of so many musical memories. The operas, the symphonies, the ballets that have been performed here . . .' He crosses the stage. 'This very stage has been danced upon by Nijinsky and Pavlova.'

I can picture them gliding past us, their glittering costumes of tulle and brocade catching the light and glistening like stars. I can almost hear the ghost of the applause. This room has a magic to it, like it has stored up all the beauty, the power, the passion of every performance and absorbed it into its splendour. I shake my head, returning to the real world as Rudi strides across the stage into the wings.

'Where are you going?' I call, my voice echoing around the cavernous theatre.

He returns moments later, dragging a gramophone onto the stage. 'It is time to make your dream a reality, Clementine,' he says, placing the needle down on the record as the opening notes of our *pas de deux* begin to play.

'You are letting the pressure of this talent scout get to you, when really, this is where you belong. Now, are you ready to perform?'

I grin, pulling my pointe shoes from my bag and taking great effort to carefully tie the ribbons in place. I straighten my back and take my place on the stage. This time, when we dance, it is effortless. We are not dancing for an audience, for Madame Lebedev, for a scout from Vic-Wells, we are dancing for each other, for the sheer joy of it. I laugh as we play out the scene, plucking the petals from the flower. I feel weightless, and every movement comes easily. Despite how tired my legs must be, I simply don't feel it. My whole body is coursing with adrenaline as Rudi and I dance side by side. We kick our legs out in perfect unison, bringing them back in with tempered control, then he spins to face me, his hands on my waist once more and he leans in, ready to kiss my cheek. For one moment, I think he is going to actually kiss me, and my heart stutters in my chest. He draws in so close that I can smell the scent of cloves on his neck. My skin bristles, almost as if it is clamouring for his touch, but his lips never quite touch. I feel his breath like the whisper of a kiss and then he retreats. My breath hitches momentarily, and my chest grows tight as he skips back across the stage and blows me one last ardent kiss before disappearing into the wings as the music dwindles.

He reappears a second later, clapping his hands together and with a huge grin on his face. 'We did it, Clem!' He rushes towards me and picks me up with ease, spinning on the spot as the lights blur in a kaleidoscope of colour. 'We danced on the stage at the Royal Opera House, and it was the best we have ever danced! Don't you think so?'

I nod enthusiastically, my face wreathed in smiles, fighting back tears. I don't know why I feel like crying. Perhaps it is the adrenaline, perhaps I am just overtired from rehearsing too much. A single tear rolls down my cheek and Rudi stops spinning instantly and places me gently back down on the ground.

'Are you OK, *solnyshko*?' he asks softly, wiping the tear away with one slender finger.

'Yes!' I croak. 'Honestly, I'm fine. I don't know what came over me . . . Thank you, Rudi, this was wonderful, utterly wonderful!'

His hand is still resting on my cheek. I can feel his heartbeat in his fingertips. It is beating like the wings of a hummingbird, just like my own.

'Clementine, I—'

'Hey!' Someone calls from the back of the theatre and our heads snap in the direction of the sound. An old security guard is hobbling towards the stage as quickly as he can, weaving between the red velvet seats.

Rudi looks at me, his eyes wide. 'Run!'

He drops his hand from my cheek and grabs my arm, pulling me behind him as he sprints from the stage. He runs so fast that my feet fly out behind me in my attempt to keep up with him. He smashes through the door where we entered as the guard calls for us to stop. Then we are rushing down the darkened corridors once again, past the changing rooms and costume cupboards, weaving out of the way of abandoned rails as we hear more voices and the sound of footsteps catching up with us. We make it to the stage door and Rudi pushes it open with all his might, practically flinging me out onto the cobbled street. He doesn't bother to close the door behind him, but grabs my hand once more and again we are flying as fast our feet will carry us down the empty streets, the leather soles of my ballet shoes slipping on the slick cobbles. Rudi's maniacal laughter echoes off the buildings as we run. I don't know how he has the breath for it, my own lungs are burning with the exertion.

We finally stop running when we reach the river. Sharp, shooting pains are running up my shins and I bend over to rub them as Rudi climbs onto the wall and dangles his legs over the side. I straighten up and join him on the wall, looking out at the inky black water.

'I much prefer the Thames at night,' he says. 'You can't see how murky it is. With all the lights and the moon shining on the surface, it almost looks inviting.'

'I think we've had enough excitement for one evening without taking a dip in the river,' I breathe, rolling my neck back and forth.

I feel him turn to look at me. 'Would you say it was worth it though?'

'Absolutely.' I grin, facing him. As I meet his eyes, I am reminded of that moment, right before the guard caught us. His hand was resting on my cheek and he wore such an earnest expression. 'What were you going to say earlier?' I ask. 'Before the guard caught us.'

'Oh, that,' he says, looking back to the water. 'Nothing really, I was just going to ask how things were going with the American.'

'I wish you wouldn't call him that,' I reprove.

'And I wish he wouldn't call me Rudi.' He shrugs.

'Well, at least that is your name—'

'It's what my friends call me,' he interjects, his eyes narrowing. 'That man is not my friend.'

'Why not?'

'I just don't like him,' he replies, growing standoffish. 'He's foolish if he can't see how great you are, and I have no time for fools.'

I feel my cheeks flush with heat and I duck my head, letting my hair fall in front of my face so he won't see. 'That's a shame . . .'

'Why?' He sits a little straighter.

'Because August wants us to join him and Grace at The Midnight Nest on Friday. It's a jazz bar in Soho apparently.'

'I know what The Midnight Nest is, Clem,' he replies with an eyeroll and a small smile.

'Well, I don't!' I exclaim in a flap. 'I don't know the first thing about jazz music. How does one even dance to it?'

'It's easy.' He shrugs nonchalantly. 'You just move to the music, as you would in ballet.'

There is no way it is that easy. Ballet isn't simply free-flowing movement, it is a discipline, and it takes years of training to be able to do what we do and make it look easy. If his justification was meant to soothe my nerves, it has had quite the opposite effect.

'Well, if it's that easy, you won't mind accompanying me then?' I challenge him.

'I don't know, Clem, maybe this isn't such a good idea,' he says cautiously.

'Going to the jazz bar or you coming with me?' I ask, leaning forward to look at the water below and trying to mask my disappointment.

He is silent for a beat too long and I wonder what he could possibly be thinking. 'Maybe all of it,' he says at last, and my heart sinks.

'But the plan is starting to work!' I insist. 'When we left our rehearsal this afternoon, I overheard Grace say she thought you loved me – isn't that funny? – and August actually said we are not *children* anymore. I don't want to force you into anything you don't want to do, Rudi,' I continue, trying to keep my tone light and jovial. 'But I shall certainly be going.'

'It's not that I don't want to go dancing with you, Clem, it's just . . . don't you think you're focusing on the wrong goal?' He takes my hands in his and coerces me to meet his gaze. 'We've got *Giselle* to focus on. There's going to be a talent scout at the opening night. This could be everything we ever wanted! Why are you so fixated on The Amer—on August Draper?'

'Why does it have to be one or the other?' I shoot back. 'I haven't asked you to choose between dancing and Anna.' He doesn't understand; without the financial stability of someone like August, there will be no dancing in my future.

'That's different,' he replies uncomfortably, rubbing the back of his neck.

'How is it?' I press him.

He sighs and clasps his hands. 'Well, I'm more . . .' He circles his hand in the air, searching for the right word. 'Experienced than you. You are still very naïve in these matters.'

It feels like a punch in the gut.

'You are such a pig, Rudolf Lebedev.' I scowl, pulling my legs back up onto the wall and dropping down onto the pavement with a thud.

'Clementine!' he calls, following after me with a look of exasperation. 'I didn't mean it like that, I simply meant—'

'I know precisely what you meant,' I interrupt, placing my hands on my hips. 'You think that because I haven't left a string of broken hearts in my past, I can't possibly know what I am getting myself into. Is that why you offered to help me woo August, because you think I need your assistance?'

'No, of course not!' he insists, frowning.

'It's so *easy* for you, Rudolf, you get to do whatever you please, and pick and choose whichever woman takes your fancy. You don't have to worry about marriage, because you are a man. Everything will just fall into place for you, and one day, when you *finally* decide to grow up and stop using women like objects instead of beings with feelings and hearts, you can simply choose to marry because you *want* to. Not because your freedom and your livelihood depend on it.'

Before he can say another word, I stomp up the street and hail the approaching night bus to take me home. I flop down in my seat, sparing one singular glance back at Rudi who is standing in the middle of the pavement a little forlornly. I am still seething with anger, but perhaps there was some truth in what he said. I *am* inexperienced in real-life situations. I have always preferred to watch from the wings, rather than put myself out there. It is different when I am dancing, I can pretend to be someone else. I am whichever character the audience requires me to be. But when it comes to being myself, I still have a lot to learn about taking centre stage. It is time for me to take my place in the spotlight, and The Midnight Nest is just the place to do so.

Chapter 13

'There is absolutely no way I will allow you to go to The Midnight Nest,' Mother says over breakfast the next morning.

She still eats her usual breakfast of porridge. Only now, we have the displeasure of her company at the dining table.

'It is one thing for your sister to go, accompanied by a respected chaperone, but for you? You are only a child and there is no one to take you.' She drones on, but I stop listening. I am awfully tired from last night's excursion with Rudi.

At the thought of our argument last night, my chest tightens into a knot. It was horrible to hear him speak about me in such a way, to hear that he thinks that I am naïve . . . And maybe I spoke out of turn too. I was quite harsh in my assessment of his romantic pursuits. Is that really how I feel, or was it more that I was envious of his freedom and how he chooses to use it?

'Clementine, are you listening to me?' Mother's sharp tongue cuts through my thoughts and draws me back to the rather grey and unappetising bowl of porridge in front of me.

My eyes meet Mother's as they narrow to slits.

'Foolish girl, your head is always in the clouds,' she chastises. 'It will do you no good there.'

Grace, who has been looking nervously between the two of us, opens her mouth to speak but I catch her eye and give my head the barest inch of a shake. There is no point arguing my case with Mother, it will only result in Grace losing her own privileges.

* * *

I spend the rest of the afternoon in my bedroom, practising my stretches. My legs are spread in a forward split across the wooden floor when Grace calls for me from the landing.

'Clementine, would you mind giving me a little help with the fastening on this dress please?'

I huff, folding my legs and rising to standing once more. It feels rather heartless of Grace to ask my help when she knows I cannot join her, but I put my petty feelings of jealousy aside and dash to my sister's aid.

When I reach her on the landing of the third floor, she is already dressed in a black silk crepe dress with embroidered pearls, one of her many new outfits from Archambeau's. I open my mouth to speak, but she instantly hushes me and drags me into her bedroom.

'Grace, what is going on?' I ask, the moment she closes the door behind us.

'Keep your voice down!' she hisses. 'There is no way I am leaving you behind tonight, Clem. I promised you that you could come with me, and I am not going to break that promise simply because Mother does not wish it.'

'And how do you propose we get past her?' I ask, folding my arms across my middle.

'It's simple. She takes a sleeping pill around seven o'clock. She will be out like a light by eight. I'll head over to August's around half past seven, then you come and call for us at eight, once Mother is definitely asleep.'

She looks at me from wide, shining eyes as if it were the most brilliant plan.

'What if she wakes up?' I ask.

'She won't.'

'What if the neighbours see me leave? What if Mrs Arbuthnot sees? We all know she can't keep a secret, and now she's got the excuse of the neighbourhood lookout to spy on us at her leisure.'

'Oh, what if, what if, *what if*!' Grace sighs exasperatedly.

'Clem, do you want to come or not? You can't live your life worrying about what *might* happen and miss everything that *could* await you if you just took a risk.'

This strikes me as a very un-Grace thing to say. She never takes a risk. Everything she does is calculated and rational. She must really want me to come with her tonight. I take a deep breath and close my eyes. I picture myself in a Soho jazz bar . . . it is difficult as I have never been to one, but the image in my mind is dark, sumptuous and smoky . . . couples dance close together, swaying to a lively piano tune. Rudi's face appears before my eyelids and I feel my heart jolt in surprise. I feel a tug of regret in my chest as I open my eyes again. I wish I hadn't told him not to come. Grace is looking at me expectantly.

'Well . . . ?' she asks impatiently, practically dancing from foot to foot.

'OK, let's do it.' I grimace as she whoops and flings her arms around me. 'What happened to keeping the noise down?' I remind her, and she turns bashful.

'Sorry, I'm just so excited. It will be like old times, Clem. You and me, on an adventure. The inseparable sisters!'

I offer her a weak smile and squeeze her hands. Now I can tell how much this means to her, I suddenly feel like I have been quite awful to her recently. Too wrapped up in my own envy to realise that perhaps the thing that has been missing recently, the reason I feel so restless and out of sorts, is because I have missed the nearness of my dear sister.

As Grace predicted, Mother takes her sleeping pill at seven o'clock. Grace checks in on her at quarter past the hour before heading to August's. She stops by my bedroom before she leaves and pokes her head around the door.

'She could barely keep her eyes open!' she whispers to me. 'She will be fast asleep in ten minutes, but perhaps still wait until eight, just to be sure.'

A momentary flare of jealousy threatens to lash out for a

second. I can't help thinking that she wants to keep August all to herself for as long as possible before I join them, but then I remember how happy she had been at the prospect of me coming out tonight, and I feel immediately guilty. I swallow the bubble of envy and give her a nod as I smile encouragingly.

'I'll see you very shortly,' I whisper back and she grins before closing the door softly behind her.

The moment she is gone, I begin rifling through my wardrobe for something to wear. Most of my clothes are unsuitable for any evening affair, as I'd never had the opportunity to go to anything even remotely formal until August's sudden appearance in our lives. I push the hangers back and forth, feeling thoroughly uninspired. I pull out the same black dress three times, then huff and replace it in the wardrobe. It is a hand-me-down of Grace's; she wore it to our great aunt Nora's funeral a few years ago, which is what is putting me off wearing it tonight. However, it really looks as if I have no other options. I could make it look a little less mournful with the addition of some jewellery. I slip the dress over my head and zip up the back. It is a trifle too short for me these days, the hem falling just below my knees, no matter how much I tug at it. It doesn't look as awful as I had expected though. I spin slowly in front of the mirror and run my hands over the rayon material to smooth the creases. I creep upstairs to Grace's room in search of some jewellery to pilfer. She has a box of costume jewellery atop her chest of drawers, and I am sure she won't mind if I borrow something for tonight, considering she is already dressed and waiting for me.

I rifle through the kaleidoscope of gems, picking out different necklaces and holding them up to the dress, but none of them look quite right. My fingers linger on a string of fake pearls; I don't think I have ever seen Grace wear them. Perhaps they were a gift that she wasn't so keen on, in which case I am sure she won't mind me borrowing them. I unhook the clasp and loop them around my neck, wincing slightly at the chill against my neck. They transform the dress from dowdy to sophisticated. As I am already feeling quite reckless, I recover my hidden Belle Rose lipstick and paint my lips in the lovely pink colour, then slip out of the front door as quietly as I can.

August opens the front door with a welcoming smile. 'Good evening, Clementine. I am so glad you could join us tonight.'

He sounds sincere and I feel the heat rising in my cheeks as I bow my head and enter the hallway as Grace appears. 'Oh, Clementine, you made it!' She beams, giving me a hug and then taking a step backwards. 'You look beautiful . . . Oh, is that my necklace?' she asks, looking slightly affronted.

'Y-yes, sorry,' I stammer. 'I didn't think you would mind. I can take it off.'

I start to fiddle with the clasp, and she looks conflicted. 'No, it's fine.' She smiles tightly. 'I wasn't wearing it anyway.'

'Good, now that's decided, shall we get going?' August says, grabbing Grace's coat off the hook and passing it to her.

She nods and smiles convincingly enough for August, but I cannot shake the feeling that something about the pearl necklace has upset her.

By the time we arrive at The Midnight Nest, my nerves are in tatters. I wish I hadn't agreed to come. What use is it me being here if I simply watch August woo Grace all evening while she pretends to be enthralled. I don't know what led me to make such an irrational decision. If Mother finds out I snuck out without her permission, the punishment will be severe. And what will it all have been for? Then I remember how desperately Grace had wanted me to come. I want to be a better sister to her. Half the reason I am doing this is to save her from a fate she does not deserve. I tug at the hem of my dress, my head hung low, as we join the queue of excited people, all dressed in their finery and fizzing with anticipation to enter the club.

'Clem, I feel awful for dragging you out,' Grace mutters beside me, squeezing my fingers. 'I thought you would enjoy it! You should have said if you didn't want to come.'

'I do, honestly!' I insist, perking up in a bid to not disappoint her. 'We are going to have such a fun evening, just you wait.'

Her gaze lifts over my shoulder and her expression brightens. 'I think *you* certainly are.' She grins, nodding in the direction of the doorway.

I turn around to see what she is talking about. Rudi is leaning against the brick wall, one leg crossed over the other as he smokes a cigarette and passes the time of day with the bouncer. My heart lifts. Despite how cross I was with him the last time we spoke, and no matter how much I swore I didn't need him tonight, I am beyond relieved to see his face. He must feel my eyes upon him because he turns and looks directly at me, his lips spreading into a repentant smile. He drops the cigarette, crushing it underfoot, and waltzes down the queue to meet us.

'*Solnyshko*,' he murmurs, taking my hand and kissing me on the cheek. 'I am sorry for what I said last time we saw one another. Will you please forgive me and accept me as your chaperone for the evening?'

'I would be delighted,' I say, grinning from ear to ear.

'*Solnyshko*?' August interjects, and for the first time I find his American accent quite grating. 'What does that mean?'

'Little sunshine,' Rudi says, his eyes still glued to mine. 'For that is what she is.' He finally looks at the others. 'Come on, there's no need to queue. I befriended the bouncer while I was waiting for you and he'll let us jump ahead.'

We bundle past a few disgruntled people in the queue and I smile apologetically over my shoulder as Rudi parades to the entrance. After a few words of Russian, the bouncer lifts the rope, allowing us instant access to the club. It is so dark inside, it takes a moment for my eyes to adjust, and my nose prickles at the thick haze of smoke that twists its way through the air. Girls in short dresses bustle by on their way to the stage, the tassels of their fringed costumes swishing as they swan a sultry trail through the dance floor. The back wall is taken up with a long, polished bar, six or seven waiters dashing to and fro behind it, attempting to keep up with the waves of punters, all clamouring for a drink.

'What does everyone want?' August asks, gesturing towards the bar. 'Champagne?'

I have never had champagne before. Champagne is a luxury that our family hasn't been able to afford for far longer than I have been allowed to drink it. I look to Grace imploringly, but there is no need, she looks as excited at the prospect as I do, a wide grin spreading all the way to her gleaming eyes.

'That would be lovely, thank you, August,' she says, smoothing down her dress in an attempt to compose herself.

'Rudolf?' August asks, pasting on a smile. 'Something stronger for the gentlemen?'

'Vodka,' Rudi replies, then his features contort into a more pleasant expression that looks like it possibly pains him. 'Please.'

August nods and disappears in the direction of the bar as we file through the crowds, looking for a seat.

'Who comes to a place like this to sit down?' Rudi scoffs, his eyes wandering towards the dancers.

'Play nice,' I murmur in his ear and he readjusts his scowl into something more neutral.

We find a table and sit, waiting for August to reappear with refreshments. It isn't long before he finds us, holding a tray of glasses and a metal bucket. He pours out two glasses of champagne for Grace and me, then hands the tumbler of vodka to Rudi.

'Cheers to good company!' he yells over the music, lifting his own glass of bourbon to meet ours.

'*Za nas!*' Rudi replies in his mother tongue and chucks the contents of his glass back in one.

I take a sip of champagne, and it is not what I expected. I had always thought it looked so enticing, like bubbling liquid gold, but the taste is sharp. I wrinkle my nose in distaste and put the glass back down.

'Do you not like it?' Grace asks beside me, and August looks my way, a slight frown marring his typically smooth brow.

'Oh, no, it's lovely!' I lie, eager not to disappoint them. 'I just want to savour it.'

'Come on,' Rudi says, rising to his feet. 'You can "savour" your champagne later, let's get on the dance floor.'

August leaps to his feet in agreement and bows to offer Grace his hand. She accepts and the two of them melt into the crowd almost instantly. I feel a pang of envy. I am completely out of my depth here, and no matter how much I would love for August to offer me his hand in such a way, I would not know what to do with the offer.

'I don't know how to dance to music like this,' I say to Rudi, my shoulders sagging.

He offers me his hand and an encouraging smile. 'I'll teach you,' he says simply, and I am so grateful to him for not taking the opportunity to recall how emphatically I had told him I didn't need his help. He leads me towards the dance floor where Grace and August are already waltzing. My heart starts nervously hammering in my chest. I don't want to make a fool of myself. My head turns this way and that, watching the couples all around us dancing with ease. I am sure none of them could land a *pirouette*, but this, they make look so easy. Rudi places a slender hand on my cheek and turns my attention back to him.

'Don't look at anyone else, *solnyshko*,' he instructs, his hooded grey eyes steady and sincere. 'Focus on me and you will forget your nerves, just like ballet.'

'I have no idea what I am doing!' I hiss as he places his hand on my waist.

'Just listen to the music and follow my footsteps.'

I nod and begin to trace his movements, allowing him to lead me around the floor.

'This feels so strange!' I giggle and he tips his head to one side.

'How so?' he asks.

'Well, usually you are the one to chase after me when we dance. I am not used to following you.'

'I'll try not to let it go to my head.' He grins, lowering his gaze, his bronze curls gleaming beneath the dim lights of the club.

I smile, feeling safe in the arms of my best friend, and I stop worrying about onlookers and simply let my feet move to the rhythm of the music as Rudi guides me.

'So, is all forgiven?' he asks, glancing down at me.

I screw up my nose in response.

'That is a "no" then, I take it?' He smiles placidly as he lifts his arm and spins me on the spot, then pulls me closer to him, so close that he is all I can see, and I begin to feel a little dizzy.

I almost forget why I am mad as I breathe in his intoxicating scent, but I come to my senses at last. 'You called me naïve for wishing to follow my dreams, Rudi,' I remind him.

'Your *dream* is to join the Vic-Wells Ballet Company, Clem,' he replies slightly sternly. 'Not to chase some gentleman who cares more about plants or wooing your sister than you.'

'And what if I don't make it before I turn eighteen?' I ask, my voice catching in my throat. It is something I have lived with the fear of for so long, but never dared to speak aloud to Rudi. Perhaps the champagne has loosened my tongue.

'What do you mean?' he asks, almost forgetting his steps.

'As soon as I turn eighteen, I will be expected to get a full-time job to provide an income. I won't have time for ballet anymore. If I don't marry August, I will either have to make it into the Vic-Wells Ballet in the next six months, or give up my dream forever.'

'Why does it have to be August?'

'Who else could it be? He's wealthy, he's looking to marry now, he would allow me to follow my dreams . . .'

'I see . . .' he muses, a far-off look in his eye. 'But, Clem, you really don't know this gentleman all that well. You have only just met him, you don't know that he would allow you to continue your career. What if he refuses? Then you will be stuck with him.'

'I don't have a lot of other options.' I swallow. 'It's a risk I must take.'

He looks down at me, perturbed, then gently lifts my chin. 'I am not going to tell you it will be easy, *solnyshko*, but we will do everything in our power to win over that talent scout for the Vic-Wells Ballet. This performance of *Giselle* will be our best yet, our crowning glory. You don't need a husband to achieve your dreams, you can do it yourself, with me of course.'

I suppose he is right, and I feel foolish for having never thought of it before. But it is more complicated than that. What about Grace? I can't allow her to throw away her future with this marriage of convenience. It is my turn to make a sacrifice for her for once. My eyes linger on Rudi's neck, and I find myself wondering how it would feel to rest my head on his shoulder, to feel his soft skin against my cheek as I breathe in his comforting scent. I must have laid my head on him a hundred times before without giving the action two thoughts, only now I am fixated, almost magnetised towards him.

When I don't respond, his eyes meet mine, and my breath catches in my throat for a second.

'Are you alright, Clem?' he asks, his expression concerned.

'I'm fine,' I reply unsteadily, my heart faltering in my chest. 'I just—'

'Excuse me.' A young, blonde girl taps Rudi on the shoulder. 'Are you free for the next dance?'

Rudi's posture stiffens a little. 'I'm actually dancing with my friend at the moment,' he says politely. 'Perhaps later.'

'No, please go ahead!' I interject, eager to put some space between the two of us before I do anything silly.

I notice his lips press together slightly, but if he is disappointed he does not say so. The blonde girl is still waiting to see if Rudi will dance with her. I drop his hand and wind my way back to the table, picking up the glass of foul, fizzing liquid and gulping it down as I watch Rudi offer his hand to her.

I rise from my seat abruptly, tired of watching, and wander off in search of the bathroom. I push my way through the throngs of people; the air is so thick and hot, I am finding it hard to breathe. I finally make it out into the hallway and join the queue for the bathroom. It is cooler and quieter out here, just a couple of girls chattering in the queue ahead of me. Someone is crying in the corner, like her life depends on it, while her friend rubs her back, and a couple look like they are in a heated argument by the stairs. And then I do a double take; the arguing couple are in fact Grace and Jacob. I relinquish my place in the bathroom queue and sidle a little nearer to try and make out what they are saying.

'What did you expect, Grace?' he says with an air of frustration. 'Did you think I would just wait around forever in case you change your mind? My parents have expectations of me too.'

'No, of course I didn't!' she insists. I can't see her face but there is a desperation in her voice. 'Jacob, please can we not argue again?'

It strikes me as an odd thing to say. I have never seen Grace and Jacob argue; they have always got on so well. Sure, they squabble and pick at each other from time to time, but their relationship has always seemed so easy and comfortable, like mine and Rudi's. I know I shouldn't be listening in but I find myself clamouring for more information. I take another step towards them, but it is one too many. Jacob spots me and his expression immediately changes to something more jovial.

'Clem!' he says my name loudly, purposefully, and Grace turns around, her eyes are watery and wide with shock, but she still smiles.

I wave innocently and take a step towards them. 'I thought it was you, Jacob,' I say, trying to keep my voice from shaking. 'What brings you here?'

His eyes linger on the pearls around my neck. 'Nice necklace,' he adds stiffly, his mouth drawing into a thin line. I do not understand the response these pearls bring about in people, but I shall never borrow them again. 'I was here with a friend,' he continues. 'But I'm just leaving.'

'Jacob, no,' Grace pleads so quietly, I only just hear her above the music. 'You don't have to leave.'

'Actually, I do,' he says sincerely, holding her gaze.

I watch the way they look at each other, and much like when Rudi took me to the bakery to meet Anna, I feel like I am interrupting a moment so intimate that I should not be privy to it. I am about to shrink back into the shadows of the club, when Jacob breaks away from her at last, and returns his attention to me.

'See you around, Clem.' He smiles, though there is a resignation in his eyes. 'Grace,' he adds, with a curt nod in her direction, and then he is gone.

The moment he disappears, Grace seems to collapse in on herself a little, her head drooping, her arms loose at her sides. I take her hand in mine and she looks down at our interlaced fingers.

'Grace, what is going on?' I ask her, but she plasters a smile back on her face and squeezes my hand comfortingly.

'Nothing, Clem,' she tries to reassure me. 'I think I am ready to go home though. Are you?'

I turn my attention back towards the dance floor where Rudi is now dancing energetically with a willowy girl with short, blonde hair. I glance around him, watching all the girls spin by with their partners, eager to be next in line for a dance with Rudi and I feel another rush of sickness. I wonder what Anna would think if she could see him now; it is evident that settling down couldn't be further from Rudi's mind.

'Yes, I think so,' I reply. 'I feel a little nauseous. I'll go and say goodbye.'

I push my way through the throngs of dancers towards Rudi. There are still several girls keeping a keen eye on him as they sway past with their partners. I tap him on the shoulder and he stops spinning for a second; the girl who was in his arms moments ago crosses her arms in annoyance.

'Clementine!' His face stretches into a huge smile. 'Where did you go?'

'I'm leaving,' I say abruptly, and his face drops.

'But we just got here.'

'Well, I'm not having much fun, and Grace isn't feeling well,' I reply stiffly.

His sharp nose wrinkles. 'Have I done something wrong?'

'No, not at all. Though how I am supposed to make August jealous when my partner is dancing with every girl in the club, I do not know.'

'You were the one who left the dance floor!' he protests, looking affronted. 'I thought we were having a nice time and then you ran off.'

'We were not here to have a nice time, as you well know!' I snap. He recoils, making me feel instantly guilty.

'My apologies,' he says formally, his eyes turning cold and hard like stone. 'I have clearly allowed myself to get carried away into believing that not everything we do together revolves around August Draper.'

'That was always the plan, Rudi. *Your* plan, might I add.'

'You're right, Clem.' He nods, gazing into the distance just over my shoulder. 'I suppose I allowed my own feelings to get in the way.'

My heart skips a beat. Feelings? Does Rudi have feelings for me? He can't do; he is with Anna. Besides, he has known me since we were children. He has only ever seen me as a friend. That's the only way anyone ever sees me.

I open my mouth to speak, but before I can say anything Grace appears and grabs my hand. 'Come on, Clem. August has our coats. It's time to go.'

I look back at Rudi, he is now standing alone. 'Your dance partner has disappeared,' I remark, and he shrugs indifferently.

'I am sure I'll find another.'

I don't know why this bothers me so much, but it does, and I instantly feel foolish for even considering that Rudi might have been insinuating any romantic interest in me. I roll my eyes and turn away from him, following after Grace without looking back.

Chapter 14

The next morning, I begin my usual morning routine, changing into my leotard and ballet shoes before beginning my stretches; however, this time my mind is plagued with memories of last night. I can't stop thinking about my argument with Rudi, and what he had meant when he said he had allowed his feelings to get in the way. I must have been practising for twenty minutes or so, mulling all this over and getting no nearer to a solution, when my attention is brought to the sound of voices downstairs.

I change quickly out of my ballet clothes and make my way into the sitting room to see who has come to visit. I am barely halfway down the stairs when I hear a voice that makes my eyes roll.

'My Archie loves dancing. I've never understood it myself, but he always used to go out at the weekends. Every girl wanted to dance with Archie when he still lived on this street. Oh, they were always calling for him . . . I'm sure they still do wherever he is now.'

I am about to turn and creep back to my bedroom, when Mrs Arbuthnot spots me.

'Oh, Clementine! I have just been hearing all about your lovely evening at The Midnight Nest from Mr Draper. I do hope you were well behaved! Though I am sure you were, in the charge of your sister.'

I sidle into the sitting room, lingering as close to the door as possible. Grace is sat by the fireplace, her head bowed and her face a little flushed. I have a strong suspicion that she has been crying again. My eyes flit to Mother. Her face is immovable but she is emanating an aura of unfiltered rage. I can feel it rippling off her and notice the small signs – the way the whites of her knuckles show how tightly she is gripping the arm of her chair, how her lips are pursed into a line so thin that they have almost entirely disappeared. Mrs Arbuthnot seems completely unaware and sips merrily on her tea as the silence draws on. Grace keeps her head bowed, refusing to make eye contact with anyone. She knows trouble is brewing as well as I do. I should have known; there is always a price to pay for a moment's pleasure.

Mrs Arbuthnot finishes her tea and places her cup down with a satisfied sigh. 'Right, I must be off,' she says, rising to her feet with a little difficulty. 'I have a list of errands as long my arm to see to today. Helena, it was so lovely to see you up and about. Please do pop by mine any time.' She turns to Grace and me. 'And, you girls, be sure to take good care of your mother. You can't spend every evening out in jazz bars, or all that debauchery will rub off on you!'

The moment Mrs Arbuthnot closes the door behind her, Mother turns on us.

'Grace, go to your room.'

'Mother, please, I—'

'Go,' she commands, and Grace bows her head as she leaves, lifting her eyes to offer me a look of moral support on her way out.

I swallow, waiting for the onslaught.

'I expressly forbade you from going to that club and you went anyway.' Mother doesn't raise her voice but her tone is icy. 'You have always been insolent, Clementine. I hoped it was a phase you would grow out of, but I realise now that was foolish of me.'

'Mother, I'm sorry, I didn't mean to disobey—'

'Do not lie to me, child!' she hisses, her eyes narrowing to slits as she finally looks at me. 'Of course you made a choice to disobey. You are selfish, Clementine, and you are a liar, just like your rotten father.'

'He was *not* rotten!' I yell back. 'And I am not selfish. I'm just not the person you want me to be. I'm not Grace.'

'I don't want another Grace,' she sneers, then her lips curl and her eyes glint maliciously. 'I certainly didn't want another daughter.'

I stumble backwards as her words hit me. I don't know why it takes me by surprise, why it feels like she has reached into my chest and torn out my heart. I have always known it to be true. She never wanted me, but I suppose I never expected her to say it out loud. It was fine when Father was still alive. I knew how much he loved me, how I was cherished, the apple of his eye. I didn't need my mother's love when my father was my everything. When he died, it just became something that Mother and I both knew but never spoke of, like a tacit agreement – she didn't want me and I didn't particularly want her either. Only now, she has broken the pact, tearing Pandora's Box wide open, and there is no way we can put all the hurtful feelings back inside.

'You will not go to Mr Draper's costume party.' Her words are faint over the rushing sound in my ears, but I nod in submission, blinking back the tears in my eyes. 'Now, get out of my sight,' she barks, and I flee from the room.

Chapter 15

The evening of August's costume party comes around quickly. Too quickly. The whole street is abuzz with excitement, and caterers, decorators and all sorts of vehicles have been coming and going from August's house all week. Whisperings on the street have suggested that tonight could be Mr Draper's attempt to finally choose his new bride. Everyone will be there, everyone that is but me.

'One day,' I tell myself, gazing forlornly out of the window as I watch August's costumed guests begin to arrive, 'I will be far away from here, and I will wear beaded gowns until I am sick of them. I will go to parties every night of the week, straight from the stage to wherever the night takes me.'

I close the curtains and don my leotard once more. Ballet is the only thing that keeps me sane, the only time I feel fully in control. All this practice will bring me that much closer to my dream of freedom. I begin warming up, then start to practise my half of the first *pas de deux* from *Giselle*. I mark it out as best I can in my small bedroom, not daring to perform any of the leaps in case I attract Mother's attention. Already I can feel my anger at being left behind tonight subsiding. It melts away from me like the beads of sweat that gather and roll down my skin. While I dance, I try to picture the life I want for myself. I think of August and I strolling arm in arm along the River Seine in Paris. It is winter and the reflections of a hundred twinkly gold lights are shimmering on the black surface of the water. I am wrapped in a big fur coat and August pulls me closer to keep me warm. Only when I look up at him, I realise it is not August at all, it is

Rudi. I stumble out of my *pirouette*, catching myself just in time to avoid an injury.

I flop down on the bed, rubbing my ankle and stretching it out to avoid any swelling. I cannot think what made me picture Rudi's face, but then again, wherever we go, we will be going together. I can't imagine dancing without Rudi. We have had the same pact for years now – when the time comes, we shall audition for the Vic-Wells Ballet, then we shall make company, and dance the rest of our days together until our legs give out. Even now, when I am feeling so disheartened after our argument at The Midnight Nest, the image of our future together brings a smile to my face.

A knock at the door soon wipes it from my face, and I spring from the bed in surprise. I whip my ballet shoes off and thrust them under the bed before flinging a dressing gown over my leotard.

'Come in!' I call a little squeakily, then Grace's face peers around the door and I breathe a sigh of relief as I fall back onto the bed. 'You gave me a fright! I thought you were Mother.'

'Sorry!' she giggles as she sits beside me. 'Gosh, your face was a picture.'

'Your apology would be more believable if you hadn't laughed through it,' I remark, raising an eyebrow at her.

'You're cross with me, aren't you, Clem?' she says, glancing at me guiltily.

'I am not cross,' I insist, taking her hand and desperately trying to ignore the clawing envy in my chest.

'I so wish you could come tonight,' she exclaims. 'It isn't fair!'

'No, it isn't fair,' I grumble.

'See, I *knew* you were cross!' she remarks, slapping my leg playfully. 'You know Mother is only allowing me to go because she doesn't want to scupper her plans to convince August to propose to me. She's got it in her head that tonight is the night he will be choosing his future wife. It sounds like everyone on our street has been discussing it.' She rolls her eyes. 'It won't be any fun without you there. I wish I didn't have to go.'

'Then don't!' I say eagerly, leaning towards her. 'Why don't we just stay in tonight and spend the evening together like we used to. We could do each other's hair, I could teach you a dance routine. We haven't done that in such a long time! I can't remember the last time we had fun, just the two of us . . .'

She looks tempted, but then she sighs and bows her head. 'I can't, Clem. I must go to the party. I have a duty to our family to try and secure a proposal from August.'

I look away, hoping she won't see the disappointment in my eyes, but she must sense it because she takes my hand in hers.

'When did everything become so complicated?' she murmurs. 'Remember when we used to make up stories about the Drapers to make life more interesting?'

'Well, at least *your* life has become more interesting,' I moan. 'You get to go to the party. I'll be stuck in my room all night.'

'Trust me, Clem, I would give anything for a completely boring life.' She sighs, closing her eyes. 'I'm not looking for excitement, not like you. I just want to be content.' She is quiet for a moment, then she stands and looks out of the window, across the street to the Draper house. 'I can't promise anything, but I will do everything in my power to get you to that party, Clem.'

An hour later, I hear the front door open and close as Grace makes her way to the party. I gaze out of the window and watch her scurry across the road in a blue dress and white apron, her hair tied with a white ribbon. I wish I could understand what is going on in her head. We used to know each other's thoughts inside out, but it seems like the connection between us is weakening. She didn't seem remotely excited about the party tonight, and I still don't understand what her argument with Jacob was about at The Midnight Nest. I wonder if she feels the same way about me. She has no idea how I feel about August, and I still haven't told her about the Vic-Wells Ballet scout who will be attending the performance of *Giselle*. How can I? The outcome would be everything I want, but it would leave her all alone, or worse . . . married to August, whom she does not love, and all for nothing. I try not to think about it, eagerly reaching for my ballet shoes in my determination not to waste the evening moping.

I mark out my steps for my *pas de deux* with Rudi once more. I practise again and again, remembering all Madame's points about improving my grace and being lighter on my feet. I need this performance to be the best I have ever given. I am about to start again for the fourth time, when a scuffling sound outside draws my attention and I turn my head to see what is causing the commotion. I nearly get the fright of my life when Rudi's curly head appears on the other side of the window.

'Rudi!' I hiss, crossing the room and lifting the window open with haste. 'What on earth are you doing?'

I lean out over the windowsill to discover he is clinging to the drainpipe, dressed in his Romeo costume beneath a thick, grey overcoat.

'How did I know you would be rehearsing?' he responds, ignoring my question with a smirk. 'If you wouldn't mind, Clem, could you please move out of the way before I fall to my death?'

'Sorry!' I whisper, ducking my head back inside as he clambers into the room. 'Now you are in a slightly less perilous position, I must ask again. What are you doing here?'

'I'm here to take you to the party.' He grins, his grey eyes shining with mischief.

'I can't, Rudi,' I reply monotonously, collapsing back

onto my bed. 'My mother found out that I snuck out to The Midnight Nest, and she has forbade me from attending tonight.'

'Clem,' he says soothingly, perching on the edge of the bed. 'You can do as your mother says and stay here, feeling sorry for yourself, or you can get off that bed and come to the party with me. Remember how excited you were? This is your chance to shine.'

I turn my head slowly to look at him. 'I don't have anything to wear. I was supposed to come by the studio this afternoon to pick up my costume.'

'Never fear.' He winks, then reaches into his rucksack and pulls out a carefully wrapped bundle of satin and a crown of oak leaves.

My eyes widen.

'You didn't . . .'

'I did,' he replies, passing me his mother's nymph costume from *The Dryad*. 'Why don't you just try it on and see how you feel?'

I reach out one tentative hand and run my fingers across the smooth material. It ripples beneath my caress like liquid.

'It's rather poetic, don't you think?' he coerces me. 'A girl who is only allowed out for one night of freedom. This costume was made for you, *solnyshko*.'

I sit up and take the dress from him. 'Close your eyes.'

He does as he is told and lies back on the bed with his hands over his eyes while I get up, wriggle out of my leotard and slip into the nymph costume.

'OK, you can look now,' I say nervously, pulling at the skirt of my dress. When I look up, he is staring at me, eyes agog. 'Do I look alright?' I ask uncertainly.

'Alright?' he echoes, standing and taking a step towards me, the laurel of oak leaves in his hand. 'You look magnificent.'

I feel the heat rise in my cheeks as he places the laurel upon my head. His hand lingers by my cheek, a mere fraction of an inch from my skin. I can feel all my nerve endings crying out for him to touch me. He is so close that I can smell the familiar scent of cloves that clings to his skin. It reminds me of safety, of home, for that is what Rudi is to me. A shiver runs through my body and I come to my senses.

'If you are trying to put your famous Lebedev charm to work, it won't have any effect on me,' I smirk, taking a step back and adjusting the crown of oak leaves.

His eyes widen ever so slightly, a look of confusion flashes across his face, and then he settles into his old familiar smile. 'I wasn't trying a thing, Clem. Perhaps my charms are more powerful than you think.'

I laugh, feeling flustered. 'But how are we going to sneak out of here without my mother hearing us?'

'I figured we would exit the same way I entered.' He shrugs, looking back towards the open window.

'You must be joking?' I exclaim. 'You want me to shimmy down the gutter in your mother's stolen dress?'

'It seems rather in keeping with your character for tonight, don't you think?' I feel a knot of anxiety begin to tighten in my stomach.

'Maybe this isn't such a good idea—' I begin, but he cuts me off.

'No backing out now, Clem,' he says, striding towards the window and arching one leg over the sill. He extends his hand towards me, looking more like Romeo than ever before, and I take a deep breath and grasp it.

When we arrive, the party is already in full swing. Guests, dressed in their costumed finery, are spilling out of the house, and the sound of chatter and raucous laughter carries on the night air. I run my hands down the fabric of my tunic, smoothing out the creases in the ivory folds, then shoot a glance at Rudi. He looks cool and calm as ever, and his lips break into a casual smile as he looks down at me.

'Relax, Clem. Everything is going to be fine.'

I nod stiffly, then cross the perimeter into the house. Jazz music is hopping through the air, drifting between the snippets of conversation I pick up as we make our way further into the house.

'Do you really think the King might abdicate the throne for this Wallis Simpson?' I overhear a man dressed as a medieval knight ask a woman who appears to be dressed as a mermaid.

I look back over my shoulder but I don't hear the mermaid's response. The potential abdication seems to be all anyone can talk about: though the British media has kept tight-lipped of any such plans of the King's, it is all over the American gossip magazines and word from overseas spreads far easier than one might think.

Rudi takes my hand, his palm cool against my own which appears to be on fire. He leads us through to the sitting room which is milling with even more people, and makes a beeline for the bar. He pours himself a glass of red wine, then looks at me questioningly.

'I'd better not. I don't want to spill anything down your mother's dress,' I reply anxiously.

He nods, then turns back to the bar and pours a measure of gin into an ice-cold glass, tops it off with tonic water and drops a wedge of lime into the glass, then hands it to me.

'Drink it slowly, or it will go straight to your head,' he instructs, taking a sip of wine and casting his eyes around the room. 'Do you know any of these people?'

I follow his gaze around the sitting room. It is hard to tell when everyone is in costume. I spot several Cleopatras with thick eyeliner and blunt fringes, their arms wrapped tightly with gold, snake-headed bangles. I spy a bald friar, a knight of the round table in fake chainmail and even a fairy godmother with a glittering tiara nestled in her curly blonde hair, but I don't recognise any of the people beneath the make-up.

'I don't think so,' I say at last. 'I wonder where Grace is . . .'

Rudi gestures towards the back of the house. The back door is propped open, and the sounds of merriment can be heard from the back garden. We make our way out onto the terrace where more costumed partygoers are milling around in groups, cracking jokes and swaying to the music. I spot Grace in the corner, dressed as Alice in Wonderland in a blue dress with puff sleeves, fashioned with an old white pinafore, her tawny hair tied back with a white ribbon. She looks as if she has stepped straight out of the film screen and into real life, her round blue eyes searching the terrace until she spots us.

'There you are!' she calls, stretching up on her tiptoes and waving me over. She is standing all alone for some reason and her eyes shine with relief as they lock onto mine. 'You made it!'

'I had a little help from Rudi,' I reply, looking up at him affectionately, but he shrugs as if he shimmies up drainpipes to rescue girls all the time. Knowing Rudi, perhaps he does . . .

'Well, it is only right that you are here,' Grace says, wrapping me in a hug. 'You were invited after all. Besides, we have been looking after ourselves for years, yet now Mother is up and about again, she thinks she can boss us around and plan out our futures. Well, I'm not sure it's right and I am glad to see one of us fighting back, at least.'

No sooner are the words out of her mouth when she slaps her hand across her mouth, as if she can stuff them back in. She looks fearful for a moment, but then she starts to giggle and so do I.

'I don't think I have ever heard you say a bad word against her,' I remark, taking a sip of my gin cocktail.

'Ignore me, Clem. The champagne has loosened my tongue,' she says, looking down at the floor.

'Does this have anything to do with August?' I ask in what I hope is a casual manner, though my mouth feels incredibly dry.

'What makes you say that?' she replies sharply, snapping her head in my direction.

'I don't know, I just . . .' I pause, searching for the right words. 'I don't want you to make the wrong choices, Grace. A good match for the wrong reasons is not a good match at all.'

'So I keep hearing,' she mutters, gazing into the middle distance. 'And all anyone seems to be talking about is King Edward and Wallis Simpson. If even a king can't be free to marry whomever he chooses, then what chance do the rest of us have?'

'Oh, but don't you think it's all a bit ludicrous?' I reply. 'He's talking about throwing away everything for love.'

'I think it's the most romantic thing I've ever heard,' she says forthrightly. 'Oh, Clem, one day you will fall in love and it will hit you so hard and fast that you won't know what to do with yourself. Then, I shall ask you again what you think about the abdication.'

I wonder how she knows what it feels like to fall in love. Surely, she can't be referring to August. Everything she has said thus far has led me to believe she isn't even remotely interested in him.

'Is that how you feel?' I ask, glancing up at Rudi. He looks a little taken aback, but he tries to mask it by taking a slow sip of wine. 'About Anna,' I add. 'Would you abandon your duty to be with her?'

'What duty would I be abandoning? I am no king.'

'Your duty to ballet, I suppose.' I reply as nonchalantly as I can, but really it is a question I have been wondering for a while and I am desperate to know the answer.

'Do you mean, would I give up the Vic-Wells Ballet for her? No,' he says matter-of-factly. 'I don't consider that a duty. It is as much my dream as it is yours.'

I am relieved to hear it and I feel my shoulders relax a little. I hadn't realised how they had been inching higher and higher towards my ears.

'Where is August?' I ask, turning to Grace, but before she can answer, I hear his loud booming laugh growing nearer.

Grace looks slightly green, and she looks this way and that as if searching for an exit. 'Sorry, Clem, I just need to get a little air. I'll be right back.'

'How much fresh air do you need? You're already outside!' I snort, but she shoots me such a look of anguish that I instantly relent. 'Yes, of course, go.'

'Thank you,' she breathes, clasping my hands briefly, then slipping through the crowds and down the side of the house.

'I can't help but feel that you and your sister could solve a lot of your problems if you simply told each other the truth,' Rudi contemplates, watching Grace disappear just as August rounds the corner.

'I wonder where she is going . . .' I murmur.

'Never mind that,' Rudi replies, picking a handful of sugar-coated almonds out of a crystal bowl and popping them in his mouth. 'If you prefer to take the route of deceit rather than openness, this is your chance to woo your American.'

'Oh, Rudi, you make it all sound so clandestine,' I huff. 'I don't wish to deceive Grace, I just know that she will tell me I am too young and talk me out of it. And I would never try and woo August if I thought for even a moment that she actually liked him. I'm *trying* to do her a favour, to do us *all* a favour.'

He raises his eyebrows and sits down on the low brick wall behind us. 'I just don't understand why you are putting so much effort into someone who doesn't notice you already.'

'Yes, well, I can't imagine that is a problem you have ever had,' I reply sardonically, my face twisting into a reluctant smile. 'Look, here he comes! Quick, laugh like I have just said something terribly witty.'

'Clem . . .'

'Just do it, please!' I beg, and he barks a laugh of appreciation just as August reaches us.

He looks magnificent, dressed as a Roman emperor in a

red tunic layered with a bronze breastplate, a golden laurel crowning his head. His green eyes light up when he reaches me, and I feel my knees grow a little weak under his gaze.

'Clementine, you made it!' he says, wrapping an arm around my shoulder jovially. 'What's so funny?'

'You probably wouldn't get it,' Rudi smirks, and I shoot him a look.

'Ah, good, you brought Rudolf too.' August says this so politely that it almost sounds like he means it. 'How are rehearsals for *Giselle* coming along?'

'Oh, fine, but you don't want to talk about that. It's all very dull,' I reply nonchalantly, ignoring Rudi's incensed glare. 'Your costume is wonderful! Let me guess. Emperor Augustus?'

August gives me a knowing wink. 'How did you know?' he murmurs in my ear and I grin, feeling the blood rush to my cheeks. 'And what have you come as? Let me see if I can guess . . .'

'Oh, wait!' I exclaim. 'Let me get into character. It will help.'

I spring onto the brick wall and cling to an old oak tree, peeking out from behind it, waiting for him to guess. He folds his arms and rests his chin between his forefinger and thumb, a crease forming between his eyebrows.

'I'm not quite sure I get it . . .' he admits. 'Are you Wendy from *Peter Pan*? It looks rather like a nightdress.'

My face falls, as Rudi huffs with exasperation. 'She's a nymph from the ballet of *The Dryad*, trapped inside an oak tree and released once every ten years to find her true love.'

August claps his hands together. 'Ah, of course! I should have known there would be a ballet connection.' He steps forward and takes my hand, bowing his golden head. 'Forgive me, and may I say what a beautiful nymph you make. My oak tree is very lucky to be your captor.'

'In your defence, it is a lesser known ballet,' I admit, glowing under his praise. I glance at Rudi. His mouth is drawn in a thin line, but he isn't looking in my direction as he takes another large sip of wine.

'Forgive me,' August interrupts, and I turn my attention back to him. 'I must find your sister, but I do hope you enjoy the party and good luck in finding your true love!' He turns on his heel and I sink down onto the brick wall, disappointment unfurling in my chest like the leaves pinned to my dress.

'He was right about one thing,' Rudi says quietly, sitting down beside me. 'You do look beautiful, *solnyshko*.' His eyes gleam under the glow of the fairy lights hanging from the boughs of the great oak.

'And yet, he is off in search of Grace.' I sigh as I follow August's movements around the terrace. He glides between gatherings of friends with ease, stopping in to share a joke and departing again, always leaving everyone wanting a little more of him. 'It's over, isn't it? This was my last chance to make him notice me and I have failed.'

Rudi's lip twitches. 'What was your dream for tonight – for the American to kiss you and fall madly in love with you?'

The thought of being kissed by August makes my stomach squirm uncomfortably, but I can't deny the rush of excitement I feel at the thought of him lowering his lips to mine.

'I don't know . . .' I sigh. 'I can't help but wonder, if he did kiss me, maybe he would finally *see* me. Not just as Grace's little sister, but as a woman, perhaps even a woman he could love.'

I feel my cheeks flush as Rudi nods contemplatively.

'Have you ever been kissed before, *solnyshko*?'

My heart stops beating for a second, then starts up again more rapidly as my eyes flit to his. He is looking at me thoughtfully, a tiny crease forming in between his thick eyebrows. 'No . . .' I start slowly. 'But how hard can it be?'

'Not hard at all if it is with the right person.' He shrugs, leaning back with a look of disinterest and popping another sweetened almond in his mouth. 'But how will you know if it feels right if you have nothing to compare it with?'

147

'Are you offering to kiss me, Rudolf?' I tease, then I stop grinning because he looks rather serious.

'It was just an idea,' he replies indifferently, glancing lazily around the terrace and taking another sip of wine.

'I can't kiss you, Rudi!' I exclaim, placing my drink down and turning to look at him. 'What would people think? What would *Anna* think?'

'What people?' he scoffs, glancing around the terrace. 'You said yourself, you don't know anyone here, and even if you do, everyone is disguised in costume.' Then he shifts uncomfortably in his seat. 'And as for Anna, she is . . . not a concern anymore.'

I raise an eyebrow at him, and he looks sheepishly down at his glass of wine.

'I know what you're thinking, Clem, but this wasn't like all the other careless flings. I realised I didn't love her like I thought I did, that I never could. I didn't want to hurt her by dragging things out any longer. She deserves better than that.'

To my surprise, he actually looks repentant, and I wonder if he has started to grow a conscience at last, his long history of broken hearts finally catching up with him. I reach out and place my hand gently on top of his. He gazes down at our intertwined fingers with a stoic smile.

'So, *solnyshko*, what do you think?' he asks, looking up at me from beneath his long thick lashes, and I feel my inhibitions wane. 'Will you allow me to have your first kiss?'

'OK, Rudi, for the sake of scientific experimentation, you may kiss me.'

His eyebrows shoot up in surprise, disappearing under his mass of bronze curls, as if he is only just realising the gravity of his offer. Then he sits up very straight and inches nearer to me until our thighs are pressed up against each other. He turns to look at me, his expression uncertain, then he slowly draws his hand up to my face. His fingers trace down my cheek, and now my heart is starting to pound with anticipation. He skims his fingers along my jawline, stopping at my chin and pulling me delicately towards him. I close my eyes and try to forget that it is Rudi touching me like this, Rudi who is going to kiss me now. We are in costume, and this is just another rehearsal. I am a nymph let loose from my oak tree and he is Romeo in search of a Juliet.

'Are you sure?' he murmurs softly. He is so close that I can feel his breath on my lips, smell the sweetened almonds he had been eating, and I nod.

Then he kisses me, and for a moment it feels like we are dancing. I could swear I am floating, like he is lifting me up on his strong shoulders, high above the lights and the party, and I know I'll never fall so long as he is holding me. Sparks of electricity are spiking through me, setting off shooting stars that crackle down my spine. His finger is still crooked under my chin, his other hand resting gently against the curve of my back. I lay my palm flat against his chest and I can feel his powerful heartbeat skipping beneath my fingers. He pulls me closer, his fingertips pressing into my back, each one leaving a fiery indentation in their wake. This is Romeo, I tell myself, but I know it's not. I open my eyes. This is Rudi, I am kissing *Rudi*. I feel dizzy and disoriented like I have just spun twenty *pirouettes*.

I break away, and for a moment he looks as confused as I do. He lets out a long, low whistle as he sinks back onto the wall, but I can't think of anything to say. My head is buzzing as the electricity slowly dwindles out of me. I want to look at him and work out what he is thinking, to ask if I did it right, but I find that I can't bring myself to speak. My lips feel tingly and numb, like I've never used them properly until now. I don't know what to think, as all these feelings for Rudi flood my senses. How could I have been so foolish? I love him.

'Clem?' he asks tentatively. 'Please say something.'

What can I possibly tell him? This is terrible. Rudi is my best friend. I can't love him, yet now that I know it, there is no denying how painfully true it is. But Rudi cannot offer me the freedom I so desperately need. Even if he loved me too, there is no chance that he would ever offer me a proposal. I can feel my eyes brimming with tears, frustrated and angry at the betrayal of my own heart.

'I must go,' I tell him, and I leap to my feet like I have been stung, flying from the terrace and back into the house.

'Clem!' Rudi calls my name, but I keep running. I dash through the kitchen and down the hallway, squeezing past groups of costumed party guests. I never should have let him kiss me. I didn't need to practise. It turns out it is the most natural thing in the world, and now everything is ruined.

Rudi finally catches up with me and grabs my hand. 'Clementine, wait!' he pants, and I spin around, wrapped in fury and flame.

'Why did you want to kiss me?' I cry, and he grows bashful.

'I just . . .' he falters, shaking his curly head and looking at the floor. 'I don't see it, Clem. You don't belong with the American. You belong with—'

'Don't say it!' I interrupt, not wishing to hear the end of his sentence. A line I am sure he has used on countless girls in the past, far more foolish than me. My heart may have been tricked, but my brain is still functioning. 'You're supposed to be my best friend,' I say, fighting the lump in my throat. 'You promised me you would help me secure my future. Now all you are trying to do is scupper it.'

'*Solnyshko* . . .' he urges, taking my trembling hand in his, but I snatch it away.

'No, you don't get to call me that,' I shoot back angrily. 'I am not your little sunshine. I am not yours at all!'

His expression cracks into one of pain and I look away, unable to stomach his hurt. It is not fair for him to make me feel guilty when he is the one who has orchestrated this mess.

'I want to go home,' I say at last, looking down at my feet.

'Well, let's go then,' he says. 'Wait here one moment, I'll be right back.' He turns and takes off down the hallway, but the moment he leaves, I slip away into the night, desperate to be alone.

Chapter 16

I am woken the morning after August's party by the soft weight of Grace sitting down on the edge of my bed. I peel open one eye to look at her, and she meets my gaze with her trademark look of concern.

'Why didn't you tell me you were leaving last night?' she asks. 'I spent half an hour looking for you, and then I found Rudi holding your coat looking just as confused as I was.'

'I don't want to talk about it,' I reply, pulling the covers back over my head. The image of Rudi holding my coat and wondering where I had gone makes me feel horribly guilty about the way we left things.

Grace pulls the covers back roughly. 'What happened, Clem? I saw you and Rudi kiss, and then you left in such a hurry . . . I don't understand. Do you like Rudi?'

'I *don't* like him!' I shoot back instantly. 'It wasn't that sort of kiss, we were . . . rehearsing a scene,' I add a little listlessly, and she pulls a face of disbelief.

'I know I've always said you two have great on-stage chemistry, Clem, but that didn't seem like any sort of performance to me.'

'Well, you would know all about putting on a performance, wouldn't you?' I snap and she recoils, her blue eyes wide and hurt.

'Clem, I wish you could understand. It's not like that. I'm not misleading August or trying to trap him. Marriage isn't always about love! Sometimes it is about what is mutually beneficial to both families.'

'So, we get his money, and what does he get in return?' I ask, sitting up a little straighter and folding my arms.

'A wife,' she says dully, staring at the floor. 'That is what he wants, and I think he is going to ask me soon . . . I think he was going to ask me last night, but I panicked. That's why I took off. I couldn't face it yet – not living with you anymore, dedicating the rest of my life to a stranger . . .'

'Not to mention what Jacob would say,' I mutter, and her head shoots up.

'What do you mean?'

'Well, he made it quite clear he wasn't particularly enamoured with August the last time we were all at the library together. Why is that? Rudi doesn't like him either.'

'It's called the male ego, Clementine,' she says with a small smile.

'Why on earth would Jacob and Rudi feel threatened by August? It's not like he can dance or is vying for a position at the library.'

'Oh, Clem!' Grace chuckles, then pats my arm and stands up at last. 'You really are quite naïve sometimes.'

'Why does everyone keeping saying that?' I protest, throwing back the covers and leaping out of bed.

'I'm going to be late for work. If you swear you are fine, then I needn't bother you any longer.' She makes a swift exit before I can pester her for more information, leaving me pondering what she could possibly have meant.

I begin dressing for ballet when she leaves but I feel sick with nerves. I keep stopping and starting, urging myself to get ready and to face Rudi. This is nonsense. I have never felt nervous about seeing Rudi in my life! After Grace, he is the person I turn to in times of hardship. He is always the one who is there to offer comfort. Yet now the thought of embracing him makes me feel anxious, uncertain. Last night changed everything. We should never have kissed, not even as an experiment. We have traversed a boundary in our friendship that should never have been crossed. I am still angry at him for manipulating the situation, but I am mostly angry at myself for allowing it to happen in the first place. What was I thinking? Rudi is my best friend, my confidant, my dance partner. He cannot be anything more than that to me. Our dreams depend on it.

When I round the corner onto Montpelier Mews, Rudi is waiting outside Madame Lebedev's in his usual dance uniform of a tight white T-shirt tucked into a pair of black leggings. He is sat on the cobbled floor with his back against the wall and his head down, his beautiful curls falling around his face. I feel more and more anxious with every step I take towards him. He still hasn't noticed me, and I am considering turning back when his head finally snaps up. His steely eyes are framed with dark shadows, and his piercing gaze roots me to the spot for a second. He straightens up as I find my footing again and bows his head to light a cigarette.

'I was starting to think you weren't coming,' he croaks, his voice raw and raspier than usual, like he is getting over a bad cold.

'When have I ever missed a rehearsal?' I ask brusquely.

He raises his eyebrows but doesn't say anything so I walk ahead of him. 'Shall we get going? Your mother hates it when we start late, and I don't need to give Alice Blakely any more ammunition.'

'I was hoping we could talk about the party first.'

'There's nothing to talk about, Rudi,' I reply matter-of-factly. 'It was a silly argument. Let's just forget about it and move on. I was deluding myself to think I stood a chance with August in the first place. Why would he ever pick me over Grace?'

'Do you love him?' he asks me, and I stop in my tracks.

'No,' I admit, turning to face him. 'I just can't help but think that August and I could have had a wonderful life together,' I say, ignoring how Rudi rolls his eyes with exasperation. 'He's charming, handsome, *and* he wants to travel like I do! You and I could have performed on stages all over the world, and August could have joined us in his search for new plant specimens. It would all have been so . . . convenient.'

Rudi casts me a long look and then sighs. 'Love isn't supposed to be convenient, Clem. In fact, it is often quite the opposite. It is wholly *inconvenient*. It waits until you are finally comfortable, until you think you know exactly what you are doing with your life, and then . . .' He clicks his fingers, the sound reverberating in the long empty hall. 'It derails everything.'

I pause for thought. He is certainly right about that. Ever since last night, everything feels completely derailed and I have no idea how to get back on track.

'Do you love *me*?' He says it so quietly, I almost consider pretending I didn't hear him, but I can't do it.

'You are my best friend, Rudi,' I reply. I think it is quite a considered response – not a lie, but not the truth either. However, he looks slightly ashen, and I wonder if he had hoped I would say something else, or maybe he simply drank too much wine last night.

'Well, it's probably for the best that we keep things that way,' he says at last, not quite meeting my gaze.

'I couldn't agree more,' I lie, trying to ignore the intense ache in my chest that seems to have taken up permanent residence since we kissed.

'We'd probably end up hurting each other anyway. Nothing lasts forever.' He nods, and I swallow the lump in my throat, as if I am not already hurting.

'That's a very negative outlook, Rudi.'

'Well, I have had a lot of bad experiences to back it up.'

'Mostly your own doing,' I remind him.

'I don't just mean my own relationships,' he retorts. 'Look at my mother, look at everything she lost – she had to abandon her career, her family, her country, and start all over again in a foreign land with a small child. All because she loved the wrong man.'

A pang of guilt hits me in the chest. How could I have been so thoughtless? Here I am, feeling sorry for myself because I have fallen in love with the wrong person, when he has quite literally had his entire life torn apart by love. I think I finally understand why he has always been so afraid of commitment all these years.

'Rudi, I—'

'Come on,' he interjects. 'You said it yourself: Ma doesn't like to be kept waiting.'

In the studio, Madame Lebedev is standing by the piano, her arms crossed as she taps her foot impatiently. Alice Blakely and her usual gaggle of supporters are stretching against the barre. Madame's eyes narrow as she looks at me.

'You are both late.'

'It was my fault,' Rudi says, before I can speak up. Someone in the studio makes a kissing sound and I blush deep crimson as images of last night swim before me. There is no way they know what happened between Rudi and me, but I hate how apt their comments are.

'I don't care whose fault it is, get into position quickly. We will be practising the Dance of the Wilis. Clementine, join the other girls please. Rudolf, wait by the piano until you are needed for the *pas de deux*.' She gestures to the other side of the studio, and he does as he is told as I tie the ribbons of my pointe shoes as quickly as I can.

Mr Popov starts playing the opening music for the Dance of the Wilis and I begin. The rest of the girls are waiting on either side of me in two straight lines as I dance from foot to foot, stretching into an *arabesque*, extending the line of my body from my fingertips down to my toes. This is why I did not miss practice; I feel better instantly as I let the music consume me and my body's muscle memory begins to take over. I step lightly in quick little circles, spinning across the studio, my arms outstretched and a smile upon my face as the rest of the girls swoop in to join the dance and I filter into the group. We dance in unison, as one being with many arms and legs. At this moment, it does not matter who hates who, or who wishes they had got which part. We all have only one thought on our minds: which step comes next. It is beautiful. I watch our twenty bodies move in perfect time with one another in the mirrors until my eyes land on Rudi's and—

'Clementine!' Madame Lebedev calls. 'You are falling behind!'

I nod, blushing furiously, and skip a few steps in my attempt to catch up with the rest of the girls. I risk another glance at Rudi. He is still looking at me. There is a deep crease between his hooded eyes, and I wonder if he is thinking what is wrong with me. I never fall behind.

'*Clementine!*' Madame Lebedev calls again, and this time I stumble, catching myself just before I cause a severe injury. 'We have already done that sequence; you should be on the *balancé* now.'

The rest of the girls have stopped dancing. Some of them look irritated, some of them – namely Alice – look like Christmas has come early as they watch Madame scold me. She whispers something behind her hand and her friends snigger.

'Do we need to run through it again?' Madame asks, coming to stand in front of me. 'It's one-two-three, lift your leg, hold, and spin. Got it?' She marks the steps out in front of me, making it look easy. It *is* easy. I do this sort of thing in my sleep, so why can't I get it right?

'From the top, girls!' Madame calls and everyone falls back into formation, ready to begin again.

This time I will not look at Rudi, I will not look at anyone. I just need to get into character and forget about the things that are bothering Clementine Harrington. She does not matter right now. I am Giselle, I am Giselle, I am Giselle.

Mr Popov starts playing again and this time I do not falter. I keep my gaze in the direction I am heading, I listen to the music, and I concentrate on my body and the movement of the other girls around me. I can still feel Rudi's eyes on me, but every time the sensation threatens to overwhelm me, I focus even harder on my next steps, pushing myself to stretch further, jump higher. This time, I make it to Alice's solo with no mistakes and I kneel in position with my head bowed as she springs around the studio. She finishes with one final grand flourish as the music ends and we all spring up into our finishing poses as Madame claps.

'Excellent, girls, excellent! Alice, those turns were sublime. Now, let us move on to the *pas de deux*. Rudolf, come forwards.'

Rudi steps boldly into the centre of the studio floor as the rest of the girls melt away to the sides, leaving just the two of us on the floor. I glance at him as he approaches. The connection lasts no more than a second, but my heart begins thundering in my chest once more and the nauseous feeling returns. I swallow my nerves and lift my chin; I will simply apply the same strategy to our *pas de deux* as I did to the Dance of the Wilis. I will not look at him and that way he cannot get under my skin. This is easy at first. Rudi stands far behind me while I *bourrée* on pointe, with the rest of the Wilis waiting on each side. I unfold my leg and lift it slowly, high above my head, in time with Mr Popov's melancholy music, my eyes closed, my focus entirely on my balance. It all feels fine, wonderful in fact, as I dance on my own, and then I hear the soft pat of Rudi's footsteps. I know the musical cue; he is crossing the studio towards the Wilis and they are turning him away. There are mere moments left to steel myself for his touch, and there it is. His hands are at my waist, and it takes every piece of my resolve not to jump away from him. He seems completely unfazed as he lifts me easily into the air and places me gently back down on the ground. While he is still behind me, it makes it easier to forget that it is Rudi whose fingers are leaving small indents in my skin. Out of the corner of my eye, I see his arms perfectly mirror mine as I gracefully float them up and down. I am just starting to think this is not as difficult as I had anticipated when he lets me go and we run from one another. I turn to face him, but keep my eyes focused on the spot just above his head as I run towards him for an embrace.

'Clementine, really!' Madame Lebedev calls, and the piano music dies. She stomps across the studio as Rudi's arms fall lifelessly to his sides. Madame stands between the two of us as Rudi stares down at the floor. 'Is there something displeasing about my son?' she asks, her arms folded and a look of annoyance on her usually gentle face.

'N-no,' I stutter, feeling awfully aware of all the prying eyes upon us.

'Then please tell me why you won't look at him.'

Silence. I do not know what to tell her. I cannot say that the reason I will not look at him is because every time I do, I picture his face closing in on mine moments before he kissed me.

'You are supposed to be in love with the count,' she continues. 'So in love that his deception led to your untimely death. This *pas de deux* is supposed to be filled with romance, regret, *passion*.' She lists them off on her fingers. 'I see none of those emotions in you today.'

I can hear murmuring from the side of the studio, and I know Alice and her gossip mill are readying to tear me down.

'I was simply marking through the steps, Madame. I was going to insert the emotion later,' I lie, and I can tell by the look on her face that it falls short.

'That is not how we work, Clementine,' she replies with an air of disappointment. 'I cast you in this role because I believed you had the emotional range to carry it off. Do not make me regret my decision.'

'Perhaps she *doesn't* have the range, Madame,' Alice

suggests innocently, one hand on her hip and a challenging expression upon her face.

'If I need your suggestions, I will ask for them, Miss Blakely,' Madame Lebedev snaps, and for once, Alice shuts up. Madame Lebedev looks listlessly from left to right, from Rudi to me and then sighs. 'You are all dismissed, with the exception of Rudolf and Clementine.'

The rest of the girls filter out of the studio, their eyes fixed upon Rudi and me as they go. Alice seems to be taking an awfully long time, unlacing her pointe shoes and letting her long, blonde hair down from a tightly wrapped bun. I hope that Madame Lebedev will wait for her to leave before she begins laying into us, but we have no such luck.

'Do you need me to stay, Madame?' she asks, her voice sickly sweet. 'The Queen of the Wilis is rather instrumental to this routine.'

'That won't be necessary, thank you, Alice,' Madame Lebedev replies dismissively and turns her attention back to Rudi and me. 'I want to re-run the *pas de deux* and we shall keep doing it until you get it right.'

My shoulders droop. I know it is me letting everyone down. I just cannot get the image of Rudi kissing me out of my head every time he draws near.

'Perhaps I should start learning the Giselle role too?' Alice suggests. 'In case Clementine isn't up to it. I know how *important* this performance is.'

My skin prickles. To an outsider, it may sound like she is genuinely interested in saving the show, but I know she is simply trying to get into my head. This must be a dream come true for her, watching me struggle. I notice Madame Lebedev's expression. She does look slightly concerned, and I wonder if she is considering Alice's proposal. An understudy is quite natural in our industry, but I cannot allow it. The moment Alice scores the understudy role, she will go out of her way to sabotage me.

'I *am* up to it!' I insist. 'Let's go again. I am ready.'

Rudi glances at me out of the corner of his eye. He looks worried, but I do not acknowledge it as I take my place on the marker. I get into position then look at Madame Lebedev, my face set in determination, and she gives me a subtle nod.

'You won't be needed, Alice,' she says finally.

Alice huffs and stomps across the studio, slamming the door behind her, the sound echoing off the mirrored walls.

'She will never get what she wants with a temper like that,' Madame Lebedev mutters under her breath. 'Right, let us try again. Mr Popov, from the top please.'

Mr Popov begins playing the first sad notes of the *pas de deux*, and Rudi and I begin. He takes a tentative step towards me.

'More assertive, Rudi!' Madame calls and he immediately snaps into character.

My heart begins hammering again as he draws nearer. Images of last night are flashing through my mind, but I refuse to let them overwhelm me. I shut them out. I am not Clementine right now; I am Giselle. This time there are no slip-ups. We perform the piece perfectly and when I look into Rudi's eyes, I think of August and let my regret for what could have been be my driving force.

'That was much better,' Madame says affectionately. 'I know there is a lot riding on this performance, no one understands the pressure more than I. But if you want to do this professionally, you will need to master your brain as well as your body. You simply cannot afford to let whatever is on your mind get in the way or you will fail.'

'I understand, Madame.' I nod. 'It won't happen again.'

'See that it doesn't,' she says sternly, then her expression softens a little. 'You are a spectacular dancer, Clementine, the likes of which I have not seen in a long time. You will go far if you heed my warning.'

Rudi is lingering in the corner, stretching out his tired muscles, his curly hair damp with sweat. He takes a towel out of his bag and rubs it roughly over his face.

'I will see you tomorrow, Clementine,' Madame says, then turns to Rudi. 'I'll see you later. Good work today.'

He does not look up, but he nods as he pulls off his ballet shoes, and Madame sweeps out of the studio. The moment she is gone, a heavy silence descends. It is so peculiar. Things have never been awkward between Rudi and me, but now I do not know what to say to him. In fact, I can barely look at him. He stands, stretching his arms in the air, then grabs the cleaning supplies from the cupboard.

'You can go, Clem,' he says at last as he begins polishing the mirrors. 'I can do this on my own.'

'Don't be silly!' I remark, snatching a cloth out of the bucket. 'This is how I earn my keep.'

'I won't tell *Mamasha* if that's what you're worried about,' he says gruffly, rubbing at a particularly tough spot on the glass.

'Would you rather I go?' I ask, and I notice his head twitch up.

He turns to look at me at last. 'If anything, I thought it was the other way around,' he says sincerely. 'You are clearly – and quite rightly – still angry about last night, and I don't blame you, Clem. I overstepped the line, and I am sorry, so very sorry. The last thing I want is for my foolish mistake to impact your dancing.'

'I already said it's fine, Rudi,' I snap. 'Maybe if you stopped apologising and making everything awkward, it wouldn't *be* awkward. Last night won't impact my dancing because it didn't mean anything. I was simply playing a part, just like I was today, only last night I did it far more successfully.'

He recoils a little, his face running through a series of expressions in quick succession. First surprise, then hurt, then defiance. He turns back to polishing the mirror, giving me my cue to leave. I gather my things quickly and march towards the door, but just as I am about to leave, he speaks again.

'You dance somewhere between chasing your dreams and running from them, Clementine,' he says, and I stop in my tracks. 'Your problem is you don't know which dream to follow.'

Chapter 17

Rudi's words are still playing round and round my head as I make my way home from ballet practice. Is he right? Do I know which dreams to chase? Everything feels so confused lately. There are so many different dreams buzzing through my head, sometimes it becomes difficult to separate them all. I want to dance professionally, there is no doubt in my mind about that dream. But to do so, I need to gain my freedom from Mother. I stand outside our crumbling red-brick townhouse and gaze up at it. I dream of being free of this place, that much is certain, and I dream of travelling the world, delighting hundreds of people with my dancing in different cities every night. The sound of applause washing over me like resonant waves of love. I suppose I thought winning August's affection was a dream too, but now I am not so sure . . .

August would certainly give me the independence from my mother that I so desperately crave, but would I end up finding myself trapped in a different way? The idea of the two of us travelling the world together and following our ambitions seems wonderful, but how long would it be before he was looking for a wife to settle down, to raise his children? I could not put my ambition on hold for that. A ballerina's career is so short-lived already.

Oh, how harshly I judged Grace for doing the very same thing! I have a sudden and urgent need to hug my sister and apologise for being such an awful grump these past few weeks. I rush up the steps and pull open the front door with gusto.

'Grace!' I call, running up the stairs. 'Grace, where are you?'

I stop on the landing. My bedroom door is open and I certainly did not leave it like that. My heart skips a beat and I rush towards the door. I push it open and a feeling like being doused in ice water floods over me. Mother is sat on my bed, and she is holding Madame Lebedev's nymph costume.

'Grace isn't here,' she says crisply. 'So I think it is time that you and I have a little chat.'

'Mother, please—'

'Sit down,' she commands, and my voice dies in my throat as I do as I am told. I take a seat by the window, my eyes set firmly on the precious garment in her hands.

'So, you went to the party . . .' she begins, looking down at the dress. 'Despite my instruction for you to stay home. I thought you might try. I listened out for your footsteps on the stairs after Grace had left but I heard nothing, so I can only assume you snuck out the window?'

I nod solemnly.

'And were you helped in your endeavour?'

I think of Grace and Rudi, both of whom went out of their way to help me get to the party. They knew how much it meant to me and I have treated them both so horribly.

'Nobody helped me,' I reply quietly.

'Just imagine if you had been seen!' she hisses. 'Do you have any idea how that would look to our neighbours? Like I have raised you as some sort of unruly stop-out. You're acting like . . . like a lovesick fool.' Her eyes narrow as the realisation dawns on her, a malicious smirk spreading across her lips as I bow my head in shame. 'That's it, isn't it? You fancy Mr Draper for yourself.'

I do not say anything. I don't have to. She knows she has me. She lets out a low, cruel peal of laughter.

'Did you really think he would ever notice you?' she continues, enjoying herself now. 'You are plain, Clementine, and you are not a pleasant girl. Who would ever want you?'

Against my better wishes, fat tears start rolling down my cheeks, thick and fast. I keep my head bowed, praying she won't notice. She is right, of course she is right. My own mother didn't want me; why should anyone else? A lump forms in my throat, hard and impossible to swallow. I wish more than anything that I could collapse on the floor and let the tears roll through me like waves. I wish to shrink smaller and smaller until I simply cease to exist; anything to be rid of this torment. Mother is still hurling her tirade of abuse at me, but I only catch segments of it now.

'You will ruin everything with your selfishness!' she cries, her arms flailing for dramatic effect as she begins hobbling up and down the room. 'He was never meant for you; he is for Grace!' She stops. 'Are you even listening to me, child?'

I don't want to look up. I do not want her to see the hurt in my eyes.

'Look at me,' she commands, but I stare resolutely at the floor. All I have left is this one shred of dignity. 'There was a label in this dress, Clementine. It said, "Property of Madame Lebedev's School of Dance". That is where you have been slinking off to, isn't it? Dance classes with one of those Russian immigrants . . . and I thought this family could sink no lower. And here we are, scraping every penny we have together to keep a roof over your head, while you're wasting your money on ballet. You shall not dance again, Clementine, not while I am living. I shall make sure of it. It is time you got a real job.'

That is when I hear the ripping sound and my head finally shoots up as horror slices through me. She is holding my costume. Madame Lebedev's nymph costume. The beautiful satin folds are between her bony fingers and she is pulling them apart. My blood runs cold. I am frozen in horror. Her expression is victorious. She knows she has finally won but she keeps going. She pulls at the delicate material with all her might and it rips once more. A strangled exclamation escapes my throat, but there are no words, just pain as she tears at the dress once more . . .

Madame's beautiful dress! She trusted me and this is how I have repaid her. Mother pulls at the neck, splitting the bodice in two. She is right. I am selfish. If I had never worn the dress, this would not be happening. It isn't just a dress, it is a memory of Madame's previous life before she had to flee Russia. A memento of when she was one of the greatest dancers in the world. It is all she has left, and now it is in pieces, all because of me. With every rip and tear, it feels as if Mother is pulling my own heart apart, until eventually I buckle and fall to my knees. Satisfied, she finally tosses the dress at my feet.

'You will not leave your bedroom without my permission. You will not see Mr Draper again. And you will not defy me again.' She rises triumphantly from the bed, leaving me broken on the floor, and I hear the turning of a key in the lock as she leaves.

Chapter 18

I lose count of how many days I have been locked in my bedroom. Mother has the only key to the door; she keeps it around her neck along with the key to Father's study. The windows have been padlocked too. It would appear she has grown wiser since my flit to August's fancy dress party, and no one will be climbing the trellis to rescue me this time. She comes in twice a day with a breakfast and dinner tray, and I can still appreciate, even in this most depressive state, how the tables have turned in a few short months. I barely eat the food she brings, and every time she collects my tray, she relishes reminding me what an ungrateful brat I am. It does not matter. There is nothing she can say to me anymore. I am finally broken, and I fear nothing will lift the grey fog that has descended upon me.

For the first few days, Grace would try to sneak up the hall to speak to me through the crack in the door frame, but Mother would usher her away, and eventually threatened her with the same fate. That was perhaps a day or two ago now, and I must admit that it hurts how easily Grace gave up. We have always had each other's backs, *always*.

I lie on the bed, staring at the ceiling. I do not get up to practise ballet. What is the point? I will never be allowed to dance again, so long as I am under my mother's control. Even the thought of putting on my ballet shoes brings me no joy or satisfaction. I think of Rudi and Madame Lebedev. How many rehearsals have I missed? I try to tot them up in my head; it is impossible anyway when I have no idea what day it is. They must be wondering what has happened to me.

Madame will be going frantic with the opening of the show looming ever nearer. I know I am. I wonder if she has recast me yet. I picture Alice Blakely's smug face as she dons my costume and takes my place. It is more than I can stomach. I roll over, pulling the counterpane over my head and I weep.

When I hear the murmur of voices downstairs, I do not bother to stir from the bed, focusing my gaze on the ceiling where a spider is busily weaving a new web. Someone is climbing the staircase. I hear their footsteps drawing nearer and I close my eyes, pretending to be asleep rather than listen to more of Mother's vitriol. The key turns in the lock, and I roll over to face the wall.

'Are you planning to stay in here forever?' a familiar voice asks, though not the voice I had been expecting to hear. This voice is deep and has a Russian lilt.

I throw back the covers and sit up in bed to find Rudi standing over me with his arms folded, Grace a few paces behind him, looking fraught, the key in her hand.

'Oh, Clementine!' she cries, rushing forwards to brush the hair back from my face. 'What has she done to you?'

I try to answer, to tell her that I am fine. Instead, a strangled sob escapes my throat, quickly transforming into a bout of hysteria as I cry against her shoulder. Of course she didn't give up on me, how could I ever imagine she would? We are sisters; nothing can break our bond.

'There, there,' she coos, rubbing my back. 'Everything is going to be all right. We are going to get you out of here.'

'How can you?' I ask, looking between her and Rudi through bleary eyes. 'She will only lock me up again. Where is she now?' I add, the panic rising in me.

'Don't worry about that now, *solnyshko*,' Rudi says calmly, taking my hand in his. 'Look at you, you're skin and bones. Grace, can you find her things?'

Grace nods, springs off the bed and begins rifling through my drawers, throwing various items of clothing into a bag. 'Where are your ballet shoes, Clem?' she asks, but I just blink at her dumbfoundedly. 'Your leotards? Your tights?' she presses urgently.

'Under the bed,' I manage at last. 'But where am I going?'

'You are coming with me,' Rudi says, wiping the tears from my cheek with his thumb. 'You can stay with *Mamasha* and me until this all blows over.'

'I don't think this is ever going to blow over, Rudi,' I reply honestly. 'She has forbidden me from ever dancing again. While I live under this roof, I am powerless.'

'Precisely why we need to get you out of here,' he says simply, as if it were really that easy. 'Now come on, Clem, you need to get out of bed. We don't have long.'

He takes my hand and carefully pulls me to my feet. My legs feel unstable. I fear I will barely be able to walk, let alone dance. My head sways with dizziness and my arms shake from cold and fatigue as I take one last look around the room. Grace holds out the bag to me.

'This has everything you should need in it,' she says, her eyes wide and frightened. 'I'll come by and see you after work tomorrow.' She falters, balancing on the balls of her feet for a moment, then swings her arms around me. 'I love you, Clem.'

'I love you too, Grace,' I tell her, trying not to cry again. 'What are we going to do?'

'Don't worry about that for now,' she replies, squeezing me tightly. 'You need to get your strength back and get back into shape for your first performance.'

I turn to Rudi incredulously. 'I am still cast in the ballet?'

'Of course.' He nods. '*Mamasha* would never replace you . . . She was starting to get a little nervous, but then Grace came and spoke to me about your predicament. I knew something wasn't right. You never miss a rehearsal, not even after . . .' He blushes, and I know he is thinking about August's party. 'Well, anyway, like I said, I knew something wasn't right and Grace confirmed it. So, we hatched this plan to set you free, and *Mamasha* is more than happy for you to stay with us.'

'I don't know what to say,' I mumble, glancing between them disbelievingly. I am half-convinced this is a fever dream and I shall wake up alone in my bedroom once again.

'You don't need to say anything,' Rudi brushes me off. 'Now come on, let's go. There's a taxi idling outside, and I only just have enough fare on me.'

We hurry down the stairs and out onto the street. I notice Mrs Arbuthnot's curtains twitch as I climb into the taxi, but she doesn't come out for a better look for once. In fact, she disappears almost immediately from view. Grace leans in through the window, wrapping her arms around my neck one last time.

'I shall see you tomorrow. Please try and get some proper rest.' Then she turns to Rudi, her eyes sharp. 'Look after her, Rudolf, or you will have me to answer to.'

'Like my life depends on it,' he says solemnly, wrapping his arm around my shoulder.

'Where are we going?' the taxi driver asks, glancing at us in the rear-view mirror.

'Montpelier Mews,' Rudi replies, and I relax at last, resting my head on his shoulder. I close my eyes as the taxi rumbles to life. This is happening. We are really leaving.

Chapter 19

I do not remember falling asleep, but when I awake, I am in Rudi's bed. I have never been in Rudi's bedroom before, but I know it is his because the sheets smell like him. I have no idea how I made it up the stairs from the taxi. Yesterday feels like a blur, like some crazed fever dream, but it must have been real because here I am. I blink the sleep dust from my eyes and let my surroundings come into focus. Rudi's room is small and cramped, but he still has a barre installed on the wall. I know that, just like me, he warms up here every morning. It makes me smile to think of Rudi and I practising at the same time as one another, miles apart but somehow still connected in our shared passion. Other than that, Rudi's room is very utilitarian. He has a single shelf of books, a small chest of drawers, and a desk with one framed photograph. I climb out of bed and slowly hobble across the room to examine it. How Madame Lebedev expects me to dance the principal role in her ballet in a few days is beyond me, but I will deal with one thing at a time for now. I pick up the frame. The picture inside is bent and torn, but two women are gazing proudly back at me. They are dressed in fine silk gowns, and dripping with jewels; their hair has been swept up to reveal their long slender necks, and in the arms of the younger woman is a tiny baby, clutching a glittering brooch almost as large as his fist. I look at the young woman again. I would know those eyes anywhere. This is Madame Lebedev before she fled Russia. The older woman must be the grandmother Rudi has always spoken so fondly of, and the baby must be Rudi himself.

There is a knock at the door and I almost drop the frame in surprise. I hastily return it to its rightful place and clamber back into bed just as Rudi opens the door. He has one hand over his eyes and he is holding a steaming mug in the other.

'Are you decent?' he asks and then drops his hand at the sound of my laughter.

'Oh, Rudi, we have changed in the wings of the stage, side by side a hundred times,' I snort. 'Would it really matter?'

'Yes, well this is different,' he says uncomfortably, his eyes not quite meeting mine. 'I brought you a cup of tea, with one lump of sugar. I know it cheers you up and you could probably do with the energy.' He places the mug gently on the bedside table and I sense the heat rise in my cheeks, feeling slightly exposed by just how well he knows me.

'Thank you,' I reply, grabbing the mug to warm my hands and to give me something to focus on.

Rudi lingers awkwardly in the centre of the room, and for once I can tell it is I who must take charge.

'Won't you sit down, Rudi?' I ask him. 'You're acting like a guest in your own home.'

'I don't want to impose—' he starts, but I cut him off.

'Oh please, will you stop acting like I am a complete stranger? You speak as if we hardly know each other.'

'Well, Clementine, you have been acting quite strangely the past few months. I sometimes question how much I *do* know you these days,' he says and takes the seat at the desk, resting his elbows on his knees.

'I-I do know that,' I stutter, feeling a little pang in my chest to hear him say it. 'I'm sorry. I know I have been all over the place, and you have only been trying to help me. I just want to say how thankful I am to you, and Grace, for . . . for everything.' My eyes well up with tears. 'I don't know how I can ever repay you.'

'By getting back into rehearsal,' he says brusquely, and I realise, rightly so, that it will take more than a limp apology to win him over. 'If we are to pull off this performance, we need to get you back up to scratch as soon as possible. I will leave you to warm up, then meet me downstairs in the studio when you are ready.'

He stands abruptly, only ballet on his mind, and I watch him leave, straight-backed and serious, before rising from the bed once more and stretching my arms towards the sky. I eye the barre warily. After several weeks confined to my bedroom, the once comforting allure of the barre now fills me with dread. Madame Lebedev once told us that for every practice you miss, it takes three times as many to catch up. I have no idea how I am going to get back to where I started by the end of the month. I remember my dream, the one where Rudi and I were in Paris. I must try. Everyone is counting on me, and there is the scout from the Vic-Wells Ballet. If I can impress them, I could finally win my ticket to freedom. After all, I cannot stay in Madame's flat forever, and I certainly cannot go home.

I spend half an hour warming up at Rudi's barre. Somehow, it feels both strange yet natural to be stretching once again. Even without Mr Popov's music playing and Madame Lebedev's voice floating instructions over the top of the melody, I know by heart the steps, the timings, which muscle to control. Dancing is instinct to me; it is the only time I feel fully in control. The backs of my legs feel tight from misuse, and I know I will suffer this evening when the muscles contract and stiffen if I overstretch them now, but my heart feels light and free in a way it has not felt for weeks.

'That is what I like to see,' says a familiar voice from the doorway, and I turn to see Madame Lebedev smiling at me.

'Oh, Madame!' I exclaim, and I rush towards her open arms. 'Thank you for taking me in, thank you for saving my spot in the ballet.'

'Of course, my darling, it was always yours and this place will always be a home to you.' She strokes my hair, and my heart swells so much in my chest, I can barely take it. I squeeze her tightly as fresh tears roll down my cheeks, just when I thought I was all cried out. How do I tell her that I ruined her dress? What if she never forgives me?

'Madame?' I whisper at last, mustering the courage.

'What is it, dear?'

'There is something I need to tell you.' I sniff, and she takes a step back to look at my face.

'Whatever it is, it must be very serious if it has got you this upset.' She sits down on Rudi's bed and pats the space beside her. 'Come now, what is wrong?'

'Well, this whole mess started with the fancy dress party – the one Rudi and I borrowed costumes for. Only, I wasn't supposed to go; my mother forbade me from attending at the last minute.'

'But you still went?'

'Y-yes, I did. It seemed important that—'

'You don't need to explain your insubordination to me, Clementine.' She smiles affectionately. 'I do remember how it felt to be young.'

'Thank you, Madame.' I blush, picturing how her son's hands had brushed my cheek that night as he drew me in for a kiss.

'That is not what you are upset about, is it, Clementine?' she continues, her astute gaze resting firmly upon me.

'Oh, Madame!' I cry, dropping my head in my hands. I cannot bear to look at her. 'I borrowed your beautiful dress from *The Dryad*, and, and . . .' I see it all again, the vindictive glint in Mother's eyes as she tore the dress to shreds. 'It was ruined!' I croak at last, not able to tell her exactly what happened. I cannot bear for her to know just how weak and powerless I am.

I feel her hand on my shoulder. It is warm and she squeezes me gently. 'It is just a dress, Clementine.'

'But it was your dress, from the Bolshoi! I should never have taken it without your permission.'

'No, you should not,' she concedes with a little nod. 'But I was never going to wear it again. It is just a dress. Do you not think I remember how the satin felt against my skin? The warmth of the lights that shone down on me, the smell of sweat and perfume and make-up that clung to me and my fellow dancers? Do you think that now the dress is gone, I don't remember how it felt to be lifted by my partner? The strength of his arms, the look that would pass between us that said "I have you, and I will never let you fall"?

'I learned a long time ago, Clementine, that life does not exist in the objects that we cling to so dearly. It is not mementos we need, but memories. I lost everything when I fled Russia at the start of the Civil War, everything but my dear *mamasha* and Rudolf. They were all I needed. Does that mean I have forgotten all about my life before the men with the guns came and began kicking down doors? No, of course not. Anyway, I'm rambling, darling, all this to say do not fret about the dress. What's done is done, and I think you have been through enough. Please don't punish yourself further.'

I nod, roughly wiping away my tears. It seems silly for me to be the one crying after everything Madame has been through. I wish one day to be as resilient as her.

'Now, how about you continue your warm-up downstairs in the main studio?' she suggests. 'I suspect Rudi is already there. Don't feel like you have to hide away, Clementine. You have been doing that for far too long already.'

I grab my things and head out of the flat and downstairs to Madame Lebedev's studio. I can hear piano music tinkling on a gramaphone and the soft thud of Rudi's feet as they make contact with the ground. A smile creeps across my face, and I linger in the hallway, listening to the sound of his movements. They are so familiar to me; I can picture exactly what he is doing. He is practising his half of our opening scene. I poke my head around the corner to see if I am correct, and of course I am. Even when Rudi is practising, he dances with such passion and enthusiasm; the itch I feel to join him is unbearable. I wait for my next cue in the music and take my place beside him. If my sudden appearance surprises him, it is only given away by the merest rising of his eyebrows. He smiles graciously and I cannot help but return the sentiment. The steps do not come as naturally to me as they did a few weeks ago, and I occasionally find myself a beat behind the music, but Rudi is such a considerate partner that he slows to my tempo, allowing my brain the time it needs to send the signals to my feet. With Rudi's encouragement, the routine comes back to me, and by the time the music ends, we are in our final positions, panting heavily, our brows gleaming with sweat, and faces wreathed in smiles.

'You remember it all so well,' Rudi says at last, breaking the silence and stepping to his feet. 'I was worried you would be a little rusty. I should have known better.'

'Remembering the routines will not be the problem,' I tell him, crossing my arms across my chest and gazing at my reflection in the mirror. 'I danced them every night in my sleep. However, my body feels out of practice . . . I do not feel strong anymore. I need to take a break already.'

Rudi looks at me in the mirror, his expression stern. 'You know you will get your strength back, Clem. Remember what I told you all those years ago when we first met? Ballet made you strong once before; ballet will make you strong again now.'

'But there's so little time. Opening night is only a few weeks away—'

Rudi silences me by placing a finger to my lips and they tingle beneath his touch.

'You aren't starting from the beginning, *solnyshko*. You have only been away for a few weeks. With some extra rehearsals, you will be back to your usual stamina in no time. Trust me.'

I take Rudi's advice, and soon he and Madame Lebedev have me on a rigorous schedule. We wake at dawn, stretch at the barre for half an hour, then eat a hearty breakfast of boiled eggs and toast. We do not speak over breakfast. Rudi is not a morning person; he sips moodily at a cup of coffee, one long leg folded over the other, his long nose deep in a book. Meanwhile, I play over and over our routines in my head, occasionally getting carried away and finding myself puppeteering two pieces of toast across my plate. When the sparkle has returned to Rudi's eyes and he is once again capable of forming sentences, rather than simple grunts, we make our way down to the studio. We spend another half an hour at the barre, practising *fondus*, *tendus* and *battements* until we are entirely warmed up. Then we move to the floor and rehearse our scenes from *Giselle* together over and over. We keep going until the opening notes of the music make me want to tear my hair out. Then we break for lunch, taking a walk to the local park together, wrapped up in coats and scarves to keep the bitter chill of November at bay. We sit on a bench, sharing hot soup from a flask, watching passers-by, and spending one blissful hour talking about anything but ballet. Then it is back to the studio to iron out any flaws in the morning's rehearsal with Madame Lebedev. This usually goes on for a couple of hours, giving us one hour to rest before the official classes begin. For me, that means assisting in the teaching of the younger ballerinas. This has always been how I have paid my way for tuition to Madame, and now that I owe her for bed and board too, I feel even more indebted to help however I can. At five o'clock, our official lesson begins with the rest of the girls from our class. As Rudi and I practise our own routines earlier in the day, this is our opportunity to go through the Dance of the Wilis.

To say that Alice Blakely was frosty when I reappeared after my three-week break would be to put it lightly. Her face turned such a violent shade of purple that I thought she might faint from the pressure. I would not go as far as to say she has warmed to me, but she has finally begun to acknowledge that I am in the room again (though personally, I think I preferred it when she did not). Our class finishes at seven o'clock, but I purposefully linger in the studio until all the girls are gone. I do not want to add fuel to the fire of their suspicions by allowing them to see me going upstairs to Madame's home. Madame Lebedev, Rudi and I usually share a small dinner around the kitchen table once Rudi and I have finished cleaning the studio. Madame talks on and on about the minutiae of our performance from that day, things like, 'Clementine, I do think you could get your leg another fifteen degrees higher with a little more practice,' and we usually nod emphatically, knowing that she means well. However, when she says, 'Rudi, you were a beat behind the music in the Dance of the Wilis tonight,' Rudi throws down his fork in exasperation.

'Because I am exhausted, *Mamasha*!' he snaps despairingly, and when I look at him, I see it; two shadowy half-moons cradle his sunken grey eyes, and he looks pale.

Madame and I share a brief, wide-eyed look which he catches.

'I'm sorry,' he sighs, rubbing his face roughly with his hands. 'You're right, of course, I was behind the music. It won't happen again.'

'You know, Rudi, I was tired too, when I packed a small bag of belongings, gathered up my infant son and abandoned my home in the middle of the night while soldiers were banging down my door,' she says matter-of-factly. 'I was tired when I sold everything I had worked so hard to earn to assure our safe passage to Paris. I was tired when I arrived in Paris and the people there looked at me like I was a criminal, something less than them, an inconvenience. I was tired when I auditioned for the Ballets Russes but they said they had no place for me this late in my career. I was exhausted when I made the decision to move to London and start all over again. But did I give up? No,' she says tersely, her gaze focused on him intently. 'Lebedevs don't quit. Lebedevs don't settle for second best. They will not stand for sloppiness or tiredness in the Vic-Wells Ballet, Rudolf, and if that is truly your dream then you must work harder.'

'I think I need to go to bed,' he announces, standing abruptly. He still leans to kiss her on the cheek and bids me goodnight, but the urgency with which he exits the kitchen leaves an undeniable atmosphere.

Chapter 20

Two weeks staying in the Lebedevs' flat above the ballet studio flies by, lost in countless hours of ballet practice, evenings spent perfecting my turnout or training my leg to lift just a little higher. Ballet is my life, and always has been, but even I have found the lack of any break in routine tiresome on occasion. The only thing to break up the constant practising and striving to be better has been my visits from Grace. Every evening after her shift at the library, she has come round without fail. That was until last night. I waited up for her as long as I could, convinced that she would be over soon, but my eyes eventually grew so heavy that I had to admit to myself that she was not coming, and go to sleep. It is barely dawn, but for some reason, I find myself wide awake again. I lie in bed, listening to the sound of rain hitting the roof above my head. I rub my bleary eyes and peek through the curtains; the sky is still black, but in the darkness, I spot someone on the cobbled street below, and now I know why I have woken up.

'Grace, what are you doing here?' I hiss. 'Is everything OK?'

She does not answer, but simply says, 'Could you please let me in?'

I leap from the bed without a moment's thought, and tiptoe down the hallway, cautious of waking Madame or Rudi, as he sleeps restlessly on the sofa. I creep down the stairs and past the dark, empty studio to the front door where Grace is waiting. Her hair is frizzy and bedraggled from the rain, and her cheeks are shining with moisture, though I am starting to think these may be tears.

181

'Get inside, quick!' I exclaim, grabbing her cold, wet hands and pulling her towards me. 'What on earth are you doing wandering out by yourself so late at night?' It is highly uncharacteristic of Grace to do something so careless.

'I-I don't know.' She shivers.

'Come on.' I wrap my arm around her shoulder. 'You're freezing. Let's get you a nice hot cup of tea and you can tell me what is going on.'

We sit at the kitchen table, and I watch Grace warily, cradling a cup of tea between her slender hands. She watches the steam rise and curl from the cup, not saying anything. I feel slightly uneasy in this role reversal – usually it is me who is struggling with a problem, and Grace is always the dependable one.

'Is everything alright?' I ask timidly, knowing that, of course, it is not. Otherwise, she would not have travelled halfway across London in the middle of the night to see me.

'I just, I couldn't sleep,' she mutters, still not looking up from her cup.

I reach across the table for her hand. 'What is it, Grace? Is it Mother? Whatever it is, we can work it out together, just like we always—'

'August proposed last night,' she blurts out suddenly, and whatever I was going to say falls dead.

'And?' I squeak. 'Did you accept?'

'I did.' She says it firmly, and the stalwart sister I am used to is finally staring back at me. 'It really seemed like the best decision. I know it is what Mother wanted, and I will finally be able to move out of that house, and you won't have to stay here anymore, Clem. You can come and live with August and me. You could have the room with the lovely stained-glass window. You'd like that, wouldn't you? We could fit a barre in there. I'm sure August wouldn't mind.'

She is speaking too quickly, babbling as if to convince me that she has made the right decision, but the words just wash over me. I feel a little numb and I blink a couple of times.

'Clementine?'

I blink again and realise that Grace is gazing at me expectantly, and that I have not responded to the news yet. The numbness starts to subside and is replaced by something else, something between disappointment and desperation. I feel an anxiety mounting in me like a wild animal caught in a trap.

'If that's what you want, then I am happy for you, of course,' I say at last, but she does not look satisfied with my response.

'Is that all you have to say?' she replies with exasperation, and I have to hush her, worried that she will wake the Lebedevs.

'Well, this is what you wanted, isn't it?' I counter. 'Is this not what you have been working towards for months?'

'It is not a case of *want*, Clementine, it is a case of what is *necessary*,' she hisses, her blue eyes glinting slightly manically.

'You think it is necessary for you to marry August?' I scoff. 'Who are you doing it for – me? Mother? I would rather you marry someone who will make you happy, and nothing you do will ever be good enough for Mother, so I wouldn't bother.'

'Do you really think it's that simple? We have no money, Clem, not a penny. I can't look after us both on my salary from the library.'

'I don't need you to look after me!' I retort, my voice rising uncontrollably so that this time Grace must shush me. 'I don't ever want to be the reason you make a decision like this. If you choose to marry August because it is what you truly want, then of course I am happy for you, but if your heart desires something else, then I cannot support your choice.'

She looks torn, as if she is on the cusp of telling me something. She bites her lip and leans in slightly. I lean towards her, urging her to tell me whatever it is that is plaguing her mind, but then she shakes her head and rises suddenly from her chair.

'You can be incredibly ungrateful sometimes, Clementine. Do you know that?' she says sternly, and her blue eyes, which are usually so bright, darken as she furrows her brow.

'I am not trying to be ungrateful,' I counter. 'I am trying to be *thoughtful*.'

She pauses with her hand on the door, then looks over her shoulder at me. 'Try harder,' she says matter-of-factly, then wrenches it open and leaves.

The next evening, Grace doesn't turn up on her way home from the library. She does not come by the night after that either, and I start to feel a niggling sense of worry in the pit of my stomach. I cannot go home; if Mother gets hold of me again, that will be it, there will be no second chance for escape. I decide to go to the library myself, but when I arrive, Grace is not there.

Jacob is behind the polished mahogany counter, but he does not look his usual self. His dark brown hair hangs limply around his face like curtains, and his warm chestnut eyes have dulled to almost black. His skin looks grey, and when he looks up at me, he barely seems to recognise me, let alone produce a smile.

'Clementine,' he says monotonously, sifting through a pile of leather-bound textbooks and avoiding my gaze. 'What brings you here?'

'I was looking for my sister,' I reply steadily. 'Are you all right, Jacob? You don't look well.'

'Your sister doesn't work here anymore,' he replies abruptly and I falter in surprise. For a moment, I see a flash of the old Jacob and he glances at me in concern. 'You didn't know?'

'No, of course I did,' I lie, trying to chuckle, but even to my ears it sounds false. 'It must have slipped my mind. How silly of me!'

He looks as if he does not believe me, but he simply shrugs and returns to his stack of books.

'Jacob—' I start, but he interjects.

'Clementine, I really have a lot of work to do, especially now that your sister has left. So, if you don't mind, could you please try and look for her somewhere else?'

His words sting. Firstly, it is odd to hear him call me Clementine. It sounds so formal. He has always called me Clem, and with a warmth that is missing now. But something else is strange too, and then I realise what it is.

'Why won't you say her name?' I ask, and he freezes, his hands hovering over the book before him.

'You are being absurd now, Clem,' he says crossly, but his eyes are softer when he looks at me at last.

'Say her name.'

'What difference does it make?' he croaks.

'If it makes no difference, why won't you say it?' I counter. 'Just say it, say her name, say—'

'Grace!' he exclaims in exasperation. 'Grace is gone, and she is never coming back because she is going to marry that ridiculous botanist.'

'Are you not happy for her?' I press, folding my arms and arching one eyebrow.

He lets out a low, humourless laugh. 'Do you enjoy seeing me suffer, Clem? No, I am not happy about it, nor will I ever be.'

'And why is that?'

'Because she belongs with me,' he sighs, and as he finally admits it, I watch a weight lift from his shoulders, but he still looks so broken. 'I love her, Clem. I love her with my whole heart, but it isn't enough.'

'Does she know how you feel?' I ask, taking a step back towards him.

'Of course she does,' he replies with exasperation. 'And if I am not mistaken, she loves me too, but she will marry the American out of some sense of duty to—'

He stops himself, his eyes wide like two chestnuts, but I know what he was going to say.

'Is she marrying August for my sake?' I muster at last.

'It is not as simple as that, Clem,' he tries to assure me.

'But that is the main reason, isn't it?' I interrupt. 'She thinks she needs to provide for me?'

'She loves you very much,' he says in return, but he cannot meet my eye anymore.

Days pass and I hear nothing from Grace. Jacob's words resound in my head; he never did answer my question exactly, but the sentiment was still there. Grace is only marrying August for me. Opening night for *Giselle* is approaching quickly, and each rehearsal seems more tense than the last. Everyone can feel it, and it all comes down to the scout from the Vic-Wells Ballet. If I can just impress them, I could secure a scholarship, and Grace will be free to do whatever she wants with her life. I will finally be free to follow my dreams, and there is no way Rudi wouldn't get accepted too. The two of us, dancing on the grandest stages the world has to offer: it is all we have ever hoped for. I can feel Rudi's tension too, and it must be for the same reason. He grows more and more terse with each day, and Madame Lebedev is on his case more than ever. They fight a lot, something I have never witnessed before, but they manage to leave it all in the studio and go back to normal each evening in the cosy flat upstairs.

Day by day my strength begins to return to me, not just physically but mentally too. Now that August Draper is out of the picture, I am properly focusing on my dancing. Maybe Rudi was right all along: I never needed a husband to help secure my future, I needed to believe in my own ability and work hard. As for where that leaves me and my feelings for Rudi, I am not so sure. We have been so focused on rehearsing, that there has been time to talk of little else but the ballet. That does not stop the way my heart aches whenever he looks at me though, or the way his smile makes me feel like I am melting. There is a constant pull, drawing me towards him, no matter how hard I try to fight it. My brain tells me it is not sensible to fall in love with your dance partner, especially Rudi who goes through girls quicker than he goes through pairs of ballet shoes, but my heart tells me it does not care. Between the rigorous rehearsals and this constant internal battle over my feelings for Rudi, I am exhausted. I know I am stronger, but am I as strong as I was before? Will it be enough to impress the Vic-Wells Ballet scout on opening night?

We arrive at the Harcourt Theatre in Aldwych a few days before the show opens to begin dress rehearsals. It is such a lovely theatre, with red, plush velvet seats, just like the Royal Opera House, only on a far smaller scale and with a lot less filigree and grandeur. But to me, it is magnificent. Backstage is a warren of corridors and passageways, leading off to dressing rooms and costume cupboards, and I love the atmosphere of being behind the scenes almost as much as being on stage. There is an energy backstage, like the static in the air before a storm. Girls rush back and forth in their net skirts, there is laughter, there are tears, tantrums and arguments. We go through every emotion while preparing for a show, but when we step onto that stage, you would never know.

When opening night arrives, I have that oddly calm feeling of being in the eye of a storm. I know it will pass, I know the frantic worry is just around the corner. It doesn't matter how much I have prepared; anything could go wrong, and tonight must be perfect. Rudi's and my future depends on it.

I love being on the stage – the buzz behind the wings as we all bustle back and forth in our grand costumes, sequins and beads twinkling under lights, the rustle of a net tutu, the caustic smell of so much hairspray and greasepaint. During show week, even Alice Blakely does not get under my skin. We all have a joint goal – to pull off the show of a lifetime, bigger and better than before. None of us want to let Madame

Lebedev down. She sits by the back door, smoking cigarette after cigarette, looking as tightly wound as a violin string. She is glamorous in a black and ivory silk gown, her sharp lips painted in a deep red, and her dark hair waved and styled in a low knot at the nape of her neck.

'Clementine!' she barks, as I glide past her in my net skirt. 'Come here. You have a loose thread.' She pulls the cigarette from her mouth and runs it along the frayed edge of the netting, melting it in place. 'Do you feel ready?' she asks, her voice low, her eyes intently focused on my skirt.

'Yes, Madame.' I nod. 'I feel confident that I have caught up for my lost time. I feel as if I know this part inside out now. It is such a beautiful ballet.'

'Everything rests on tonight, Clementine. *Everything*. Chances like this can be once in a lifetime. Do not let anything distract you from your dreams.' Her voice is tough, and her eyes are sharp when she looks up at me.

I feel a tightening in my chest, and for some reason, the first thing I think of is Rudi. I wonder if he has had the same lecture already. I know she cares for me greatly, and it will do wonders for the school's reputation if I get accepted into the Vic-Wells Ballet, but she must be even more eager that her son wins a coveted place too.

As if I have wished him into being, Rudi saunters past, already in costume. He stops when he sees us, and gives me a quick nod, then leans to kiss his mother on the cheek.

'There is a gentleman in the foyer who has asked to speak with you, *Mamasha*.'

She nods and casts her cigarette out of the open door. 'Run through the opening *pas de deux* once more,' she calls after us as she swishes onto the stage and out through the theatre.

Rudi and I look at each other for a moment. It feels like an awfully long time before either of us speaks, and I can feel my heart beating rapidly beneath my leotard.

'Did she tell you how your entire future rests on tonight?' he says at last with a smirk, his eyes twinkling like silver.

'She did,' I sigh. 'Somehow that only makes me feel less prepared.'

'That is precisely what she wants, *solnyshko*,' he replies, resting a hand on my shoulder. 'She knows you well enough to know that will only have inspired you to work that much harder.'

'I am already giving it my all, Rudi,' I say, exasperated. 'What more does she want?'

'You know this is how it is, Clem.' He shrugs. 'This is the life we have chosen.'

I look down at my feet in their satin pointe ballet shoes. One of my ribbons has come loose. Rudi notices it too and kneels down to fix it back in place. I try to ignore the tingling sensation I feel whenever his fingers brush against my leg as he secures the ribbon. When he stands again, he is so close that the temptation to grab him and kiss him is almost entirely overwhelming.

'Do you ever think . . .' I start, but I don't really know what I want to say. I think I was going to ask if he thought about whether this *is* what he wants. Is it what *I* want? I have already spent my entire life being undermined by my mother. Do I want to continue to let ballet teachers and rival dancers and critics chip away at what is left of me?

'Ever think what?' he asks, his eyes growing wide.

'Nothing.' I smile. 'Come on, let's practise the *pas de deux* one more time as requested.'

An hour later, I stand before the mirror, checking over the finer details of my costume one last time. I run a hand over my hair, smoothing any flyaways, and turn my head left then right to check my make-up has blended fully. I flex my feet one at a time, and rise up onto pointe. My ankles feel strong and steady. I wish I could say I felt the same on the inside. Madame's words about the importance of this evening reverberate around my head like a flurry of flakes inside a snow globe, only they refuse to settle. The theatre feels alive, and I know that the rows of plush velvet seats will be filling up with people by now. I close my eyes and try to feel Grace's presence, but I can't sense her at all. I take a deep breath, savouring the sweet, decaying smell of the moth-eaten costumes, the salty tang of sweat, the sharp smell of leather. There is a knock on the dressing room door, and my heart stutters.

'Who could that be?' Alice asks impertinently, storming across the floor. 'We can't be anywhere close to curtains up yet.' She swings it open and lets out a little squeak. 'Rudolf! You can't come in the girls' dressing rooms.'

'I have no desire to come in,' he replies from the hall, and I can tell from his voice that he is smiling. 'Is there any chance Clementine could come out?'

'Of course,' she replies, her voice tight. 'Clementine!'

I am already at her back, and I feel a rush of unmistakable joy when I see Rudi leaning in the doorway. His face splits into a lopsided smile when he catches my eye, and he takes a step back into the hall, gesturing for me to join him. I step out into the hallway, and the temperature drops immediately. Alice still lingers by the door, as if she might hope to catch a snippet of whatever it is Rudi wants to say, but he leans forward with a broad smile and closes the door in her face.

'Is something the matter?' I ask, folding my arms across my body for warmth. I can feel the hairs on my arms and the back of my neck beginning to rise. 'Did you want to run through the *pas de deux* again? You know, I think we can over-practise too if we are not careful.'

'There is something I need to tell you,' he says, his expression suddenly more serious, a deep crease forming between his brows.

'Can it not wait until after the show? What could possibly be so urgent that you would force me to suffer the wrath of Alice Blakely?' I laugh, but the sound stops dead in my throat at the look on his face. 'What on earth is the matter?'

'Here's the thing, Clem . . .' he starts, his head bowed, then he looks up at me in earnest from his hooded grey eyes through his thick lashes. 'I love you. And I don't just mean as my best friend, or my trusted dance partner. I am in love with you. You are all I think about . . . before you came to live with me, every morning, I would wake up and wonder if you were awake yet on the other side of London. I would fall asleep imagining that you were doing one last round of *développés* before calling it a night, and when we dance together . . . *Solnyshko*, I pour all my love for you into every movement.'

I blink, but remain silent. My heart is racing and it feels as if it is trying to escape from my chest and out through my throat, but my lips seem to be glued shut. Rudi shifts uncomfortably from side to side.

'Aren't you going to say anything, Clem?' he asks, downhearted.

'I-I . . .' I stutter, searching in vain for the right words.

'It's quite simple,' he says with an air of frustration. 'You either feel the same way or you don't. If the answer doesn't come to you straight away, then I suppose you probably don't.'

'It's not that, Rudi,' I insist. 'It's just a lot to process right now. The show is starting any minute, there's a scout from the Vic-Wells Ballet out there, and—'

'Is that all you can think about?' he says, aghast. 'Clementine, I just told you that I love you and, still, all you can think of is ballet?'

'It's not all I think about!' I reply hotly. 'I just, I don't think you've thought this through. We've been pretending for so long, I think you've just got muddled up in your head.'

'I am not muddled up, Clem! I know how I feel,' he insists more ardently.

I scrunch up my eyes. I do not want to hear it. I cannot hear it, because no matter how much he might believe it, and no matter how much I love him back, it simply cannot be true. My mother's voice resounds in my head, blocking out whatever he is saying. *Who would ever want you?* I am unlovable. I cannot think about any of this now. I must secure a place with the Vic-Wells Ballet. Only then will Grace be free to be with Jacob, and I will be free from Mother forever.

'You don't love me, Rudi,' I reply quietly. 'You love Giselle, Odette, Juliet – the parts that I play – but not me, not really. It's just that most recently the parts we have been playing were not created by Tchaikovsky or Shakespeare, they were versions of ourselves, but nonetheless they were fictional. You are confusing the stage with reality.'

My heart is pounding in my chest, and I can't bring myself to look at him a moment longer. I drop my head, but my careless eyes wander back to his. He opens his mouth to respond, but his words are cut short by the arrival of Madame Lebedev as she sweeps down the corridor.

'Places, my dears,' she coos, knocking on the dressing room doors as she passes. 'Five minutes until the curtain rises.'

Chapter 21

I had worried that Madame's insistence that I give the performance of a lifetime may have finally been too much pressure for me to handle and that I would crumble on stage. I had feared that not knowing whether or not Grace was in the audience, lending me her support as she always has, would lead me to stumble and lose faith in myself. I had been completely convinced that Rudi's confession of his true feelings – mere moments before we were due on stage – would lead to a full-scale breakdown. However, somehow, I find myself on the stage of the Harcourt Theatre, curtseying to the sound of rapturous applause. My head is bowed, but I allow myself one small glimpse of the audience. They are all on their feet. I glance at Rudi; he danced spectacularly tonight, with more strength and agility than I have ever seen in him before. He smiles suavely and takes my hand as we make one final bow together.

No one in the audience would ever know what is simmering beneath the surface for the both of us. It truly was the performance of a lifetime, if not solely for that reason. The applause laps over us in wave after wave, and we hold our grinning composure for so long that I feel the muscles in my cheeks begin to twitch. I cannot help myself – I scan the audience for Grace, but it is too dark to make out anyone's face, and the lights in my eyes are blinding. Normally, this is my favourite moment, but tonight, it seems to be lasting an eternity. I am distinctly aware of how my hand feels in Rudi's as we wait for the curtain to fall. It finally begins to descend, and before it has fully hit the floor, Rudi lets go and walks off the stage.

'What on earth is his problem?' Alice sniffs beside me. 'Surely he knows he is guaranteed a place in the Vic-Wells Ballet after tonight.'

I'm not sure if she is speaking to me or not, but I do not know how to answer her either way. I want to chase after him, but before I get a chance, Madame is already on the stage, her arms around my shoulders as she sweeps me into the wings.

'Oh, *solnyshko*,' she coos, and hearing Rudi's nickname for me on a different tongue makes my heart pang. 'You were marvellous! How could the Vic-Wells Ballet not want you after tonight? Tonight was the first night in so many years that I felt transported back to my own time as a dancer. You have talent, my darling, but you have so much more than that. You have the spark they will be looking for. I know the scout will be excited to meet you.'

She guides me back to the dressing room but my eyes are swimming with tears and I can barely see. I do not know why. I should be happy, all my dreams are coming true.

'Get dressed quickly and then meet me in the foyer,' she instructs. 'I will find Rudi and meet you there.'

I change out of my costume as quickly as I can, taking care to unhook the back of my dress, and carefully unlace my shoes. I spend some time removing the greasepaint from my face, and meticulously brushing the gel from my hair, until I almost feel normal again. I stare at my reflection in the mirror, taking a moment in the silent dressing room, before the rest of the girls descend and throw the place into chaos. I touch the glass. This is the last time I shall be this girl, the girl whose dreams are all about to come true. I place a hand on my chest; there is an aching feeling in the place where my heart should be that I do not understand. If this is all I have ever wished for, why does it hurt?

Before I have time to question it further, the rest of the

girls bombard the dressing room, and I spring from my chair. Alice casts me a watchful glance. I can't tell if she is trying to read me or judge me, but either way, I find I must escape her gaze immediately. I rush into the corridor, then slow my pace as I walk towards the foyer. I can feel my heart in my throat as I approach. I can hear the humming buzz of many voices from behind the doors. I know people on the other side will want to talk to me, that they want to see me at my best, but right now I feel depleted. I take a deep breath, my hand on the door, then push it open and force my face into a wide smile.

Madame Lebedev is waiting for me just by the door; she has changed once again, this time into a black velvet gown with a glittering brooch. It is the very same brooch baby Rudi was playing with in the photograph framed in his bedroom. She has one arm around Rudi, who looks slightly disgruntled, but still perfectly composed in a pair of grey woollen trousers and braces over a white shirt. His sleeves are rolled up, revealing his muscular forearms, and beneath his open shirt collar, I can see the tensed muscles of his strong neck – a tell-tale sign that he is far more anxious than he is letting on. His eyes glide over the room, before resting on me for a split second, then he takes a sip of his drink, doing his best to look thoroughly bored.

'Here she is!' Madame cries, gesturing for me to come over. 'Clementine, this is Mr Watts, an old friend of mine from the Vic-Wells Ballet. He would like to speak with you and Rudolf.'

My heart starts thrumming in my chest and, all of a sudden, my tongue feels too big for my mouth. I swallow and take a step forward to shake Mr Wells' hand. He is a perfectly ordinary-looking man, far less intimidating than the phantom vision that has been hanging over us for so many weeks. He looks as if he is in his forties, a few lines across his brow and around his mouth. His dark hair is peppered with grey and held in gentle waves with Brylcreem.

'Miss Harrington, Mr Lebedev, it is a pleasure to make your acquaintance,' he says, his voice coarse and gravelly. 'You are both magnificent dancers in your own right, but I must say, together, you are something truly spectacular to watch.'

'Thank you, Mr Wells,' Rudi responds serenely, as if he were merely discussing the weather with a passer-by. I do not understand how he can be so calm; I can feel my hands growing clammy, and feel the rushing of my pulse in my ears. 'Clementine and I have been dancing together since we were children. We simply have a relationship built on years of amicable trust,' he pauses and glances at me before adding, 'nothing more.'

I feel it like a stab through the chest, and I know now that Rudi is still angry with me for what I said before the show. I hope that things are not going to grow awkward between the two of us. I could not bear the thought of losing our close bond, especially as we are on the cusp of this exciting new venture.

'Well, whatever it is that you have, it excited me,' Mr Wells continues. He reaches into his breast pocket and pulls out two business cards, then hands one to each of us. 'I would like to invite the two of you to audition for the Vic-Wells Ballet. Come and see me next Tuesday at three o'clock, and if you dance like you did tonight, there may well be scholarships available to you.'

I can feel my eyes widening, and my mouth drops open in surprise. It is finally happening. We are one step closer to making our dreams a reality.

'Thank you so much, Mr Wells,' I gush, shaking his hand vigorously. 'We will not let you down.'

'I hope not, Miss Harrington,' he growls. 'I do not like to be disappointed.' He gives us a curt nod, then he and Madame cut a path through the bustling foyer, leaving Rudi and me alone once more.

I glance up at him. 'Can you believe—' I start, but before

I have the chance to finish my sentence, Rudi turns and leaves, without saying a word.

Crestfallen, I stand on my own in a room full of people. I gaze around; they were all here to see me, yet somehow, I am still alone. What good is applause if it does not manifest into people who show up for you, who care about you? My heart, which had been floating so high just moments before, plummets, and I find I cannot bear to be around these crowds a minute longer. All I can think about is Rudi . . . Rudi and Grace. They are the only two people I truly care about and I have managed to push both of them away. But then something catches my eye; I spy a flash of fawn-coloured hair, and the glint of blue eyes. Grace is weaving her way through the crowds towards me. A bouquet of freesias wrapped in brown paper is in her hands, and a card is slotted carefully between the folds.

'You came!' I try to exclaim, but it is barely a whisper as I feel my throat tightening.

'Of course I did.' She smiles, and it is as if nothing ever happened between the two of us. I hug her so tightly that I crush the flowers. 'Oh, Clem, do be careful, these cost me a small fortune!' she chastises, but her eyes are shining brightly.

'Is August with you?' I ask carefully, not wanting to disturb this peace between us, but choosing to acknowledge what has passed.

She falters, her expression growing slightly wary. 'No, not tonight,' she says, and I get the sense that, once again, there is something she is holding back. 'Here,' she says, thrusting the flowers at me in a bid to change the subject. 'These are for you, of course.'

'Oh, thank you,' I reply a little absently, still pondering what it could be that she is not telling me. I reach for the card to open it, but she stops me, her fingers clasping mine.

'Don't open that yet,' she insists. 'Save it for later.' She looks down at her watch and frowns. 'Oh, Clem, I am really sorry but I must dash. Congratulations for tonight. You were so wonderful, and all this excitement around the Vic-Wells Ballet too . . . it is everything you deserve. I am so happy for you, my darling sister.'

She pulls me into another hug, and this time it is she who squeezes me so tight that my ribs begin to ache a little. I don't know why, but I get the feeling we won't be hugging each other again for a while, and I squeeze her back just as hard.

'I love you, Grace,' I murmur into her ear. It feels important that I tell her. 'I wish you nothing but happiness.'

'I love you too, Clem,' she replies, and it sounds as if she is trying to hold back tears. When she steps back, her eyes are glossy, but she smiles bravely, pats my hand and then disappears into the crowd as suddenly as she had emerged.

I leave the busy foyer and head back into the auditorium. It is empty now, except for a solitary caretaker sweeping the stage. I sit in one of the plush velvet seats and look towards the stage where I had danced like my life depended on it, a mere hour or so ago. Flashes of Rudi intrude into my thoughts: the way it felt like tiny little pinpricks of electricity whenever he touched me, the safe comfort of being in his arms . . . I scrunch my eyes tight and shake my head. He is my friend, my best friend and nothing more. I cannot afford to lose him, and I will not risk losing him for anything as silly as love. He may think he loves me, but how can he possibly feel the way I feel? One simple look from him makes my heart stutter in my chest. How could I possibly have that effect on him. He could have any girl he wants. Why would that ever be me?

A splash of warm water lands on my hand and I realise I am crying. I wipe my eyes and try my best to pull myself together. There is no use getting lost in maudlin thoughts. I must focus on the positive, on next Tuesday, when I shall dance my heart out and earn my rightful place within the Vic-Wells Ballet. I grab the bunch of freesias from Grace and the card falls to the floor. I gaze at the brown envelope for a moment, wondering why she didn't want me to open it in front of her. She is not here now, I reason, so I tear it open. It is not a card, but a letter, written in her fine, slanting script.

Dearest Clementine,

Firstly, I wanted to say how very proud I am of you. The work you put into tonight's performance, in the face of so much adversity, is truly inspirational, and I just know that you will be granted a full scholarship to the Vic-Wells Ballet. I have never doubted for one moment that you were destined for great things, and I am so glad to see them beginning to happen for you. You have worked so hard for this moment and nobody deserves it more. Look out for Rudi though, won't you? You have always had one another's backs, and you will need that close bond more than ever now. I truly believe there is nothing that boy wouldn't do for you.

Now that you are about to embark on your dream, I hope you can understand that I must too. I feel awful, writing this in a letter. I would much rather have told you in person but I couldn't risk anything going wrong with our plan. You see, Clem, I have been keeping a secret from you … and I know sisters shouldn't keep secrets from one another, but I was keeping it from myself for the longest time too. I can't marry August Draper. You were right: it is wrong to ensnare a gentleman for financial reasons. That is not me, and it is not the kind of woman I want to be. Particularly when my heart belongs to another.

This might come as a shock to you, Clem, as you always said I was so mean to him, but Jacob and I have developed feelings for one another. Quite strong feelings actually … Oh, who am I kidding? I love him with all my heart, and he loves me! Gosh, it feels good to admit that at last. We both knew our parents wouldn't approve of the match, so we fought it for as long as possible. But the heart wants what the heart wants. We are sick of being miserable apart, so we have chosen to be happy together! By the time you read this, we will be on our way to Gretna Green. Can you believe it, Clem? Who ever thought I would be the one to elope?

I don't know if I ever would have worked up the courage to follow my heart if you hadn't done so first, my darling sister. You have always been the brave one. Thank you for instilling that bravery in me.

Now, go forth and live your dream!

Forever yours,

Grace x

PS, I have been keeping another secret from you, Clem, but I hope you can forgive me. When I stole Mother's key to your bedroom, I also took the key to the study and I went through Father's documents. I found the letters Mother had told us about, and I did a little research at the library. Oh, Clem, it is not the awful scenario Mother painted it out to be. Of course he remained faithful to their marriage! I am enclosing the documents I found so that you can see for yourself and I hope, finally, be proud of your name and our father once more.

PPS, once we are settled back in London, I shall write to you with our new address. We will have you round for tea and biscuits. We can't wait to hear all about your adventures!

I read the letter through four times, letting the words sink in. I knew something seemed peculiar about her behaviour tonight. I feel another tear roll down my cheek; it lands on the paper, blurring the ink. I am half joy, half sorrow. She loves Jacob . . . of course she does! It all seems so obvious now – the cake she baked for his birthday, the listless gazes in the library, the way she used to get so easily wound up by him . . . the argument they were having at The Midnight Nest! Oh, poor Grace. She had to manage all this confusion and heartache on her own. I wish I had been a better sister, I wish we had both been open about our feelings. I should have seen the signs. Now she is gone, probably already on the train, far, far away from here, and London suddenly feels so empty without her.

I begin sifting through the extra letters she has included, letters between my father and a woman named Clementine Bodin, written after he returned from the war. It is clear he had a strong connection to this Clementine. I can tell from her responses that he must have spoken openly with her about his feelings and emotions after the war, told her how he must remain strong for his family while inside he felt as if he was crumbling. I cannot begin to imagine the horrors he went through, and I feel an outpouring of love for him. He was so strong, he always put a brave face on, he was the source of light and happiness in our home, but inside he was wrestling with such darkness.

There is one more letter, only this one is written by my father and was returned to sender. Reading it is like hearing his voice once more, and fresh tears begin rolling down my cheeks. He wrote to Clementine to say that he had another baby, a girl – me! He told Clementine that he owed her everything, not just his life, but so much more, and in honour of that he would name the baby after her. I wonder why she never received the letter . . . I begin sifting through the documents Grace found on Clementine through the library archive.

It would appear that Clementine Bodin was a retired French nurse. She took in injured soldiers at her farmhouse, and nursed them back to health. I remember Father telling me he was injured during the Somme. That was when he hurt his leg, why he sometimes used the cane. He must have ended up at Clementine's farmhouse. I read on: Grace has found her birth registration too. She was seventy-five when she met my father! Hardly likely to have been his mistress. And the date of her death is in here too. She died a couple of weeks before I was born, which explains the returned letter. I hug the documents close to my chest as if it will bring these people closer to me. I miss my father so terribly. I can't help but think how different my life would have been if he were still alive, and how I wish I could have met this woman who meant so much to him that he chose to name me after her. And Grace, my wonderful, sensitive, intelligent sister! She found all this for me, to bring me peace at last, to clear our father's good name. What on earth am I going to do without Grace?

She said I was the brave one, but I don't know how to be brave at all without her. I take a deep breath and dry my tears. I must find my courage on my own. Grace only had the nerve to leave because she thought I was finally free to live my dream. If I am truly to be brave, I must see it through, but first I need to tell Rudi how I feel, and I need to confront Mother.

Chapter 22

As I stand outside my childhood home for the first time in many weeks, I feel a sense of overwhelming dread. I look up at the three-storey red-brick house; it is no different from any of the others on this street, yet somehow feels colder, unwelcoming. This is the house where my father died, in the bedroom my mother still sleeps in. This is the house where my mother would lock herself away in the study for hours on end, ignoring us and poring over Father's documents. This is the house where our brother Edmund stood in the hall and told us he was leaving for America, immediately, and never returned. All of these memories keep me rooted to the spot on the pavement just beyond the wrought-iron gate and the red tile path, surrounded on each side by overgrown begonias.

I feel for Grace's letter in my pocket and hold on to it like a talisman. I must not forget that this is also the place where Grace and I shared many an evening, reading together under the sheets. I take a step forward. It is also where we would take it in turns to cook each other increasingly creative dinners, that would sometimes end up being downright obscure, depending on what we could cobble together in the kitchen. I take another step, and then another. This is the same place where Grace and I would make up imaginary ghost stories about the old Draper house across the street, long before our lives became complicated by its current inhabitant. My feet carry me through the gate and up the path, as if by their own volition. This is also the house where I honed my skill as a dancer, where I would practise, and bend, and stretch every morning and every night. I find myself at the front door, beside the very trellis Rudi climbed one night to whisk me away to a costume party. I glance up at the window box outside my bedroom, the room my mother locked me in for disobeying her. I know now that I will never let her have that power over me again. All I need to do is face her. I steel myself and turn the key in the door, breathing in the familiar smell of dusty furniture and damp.

It is eerily quiet inside as I close the door softly behind me. I know Grace is not here, but for a moment I wonder if Mother has gone too. I hurry upstairs to Grace's bedroom. I still cannot quite believe she is gone, but the room is bare of all signs of her. The furniture remains, but all of her belongings are gone. Her soft-bristled hairbrush, the cheap bottle of pharmacy perfume and her sewing kit are missing from her dresser. Her bed is neatly made, as always, without a wrinkle in sight, but the stack of books that was always on her bedside table has disappeared too.

'Grace?' I hear Mother's voice calling and my blood runs cold. 'Grace, is that you?'

I make a move towards the staircase. It is now or never. My heart is pounding in my chest and I feel a little sick, but I still force myself towards her bedroom, one step at a time.

'Hello, Mother,' I say as I push open the door, but she does not stir from her seat. It is like a furnace in here, the fire in the grate is blazing furiously. If she notices me enter the room, she gives no indication. She is staring at a letter that looks awfully familiar to my own. I hold mine up for her to see.

'Snap,' I say, breaking the silence.

She finally looks at me. 'Do you think this is funny?'

'No, I don't think it's funny at all,' I reply, stepping further into the room and standing by the fire. 'I think it's quite wonderful.'

'Wonderful?' she spits. 'You think it's wonderful that your sister has eloped with that Jewish boy from the library? Just when I thought this family could sink no lower . . . The nurses told me having daughters would bring me great comfort in my old age, but the two of you have been nothing but a burden.'

'That "Jewish boy" is one of the kindest, loveliest people I have ever met,' I respond pertly. 'And he makes Grace happy. Besides, I highly doubt he will come knocking for Grace's inheritance. That's all you ever cared about, wasn't it?'

She turns her head sharply towards me. 'How dare you speak to me in such a manner?' she spits. 'I am your mother.'

'You have never once shown me a single ounce of motherly love, so why should I show you any respect?' I retort. 'You have driven Grace away, just as you drove Edmund all the way to America.'

'But you are here,' she says matter-of-factly. 'You have returned.'

'Not for long,' I reply, trying to keep my voice from shaking.

'Oh?' she chuckles darkly. 'Fancy taking a shot at Mr Draper yourself, do you?'

'No, Mother, I have much higher ambitions than marrying for money or your approval. But, before I leave, there are some things I need to say.'

'Is that so?' she responds monotonously, returning her gaze to the fire crackling in the grate.

'You never loved me. You said so yourself.' I sniff, holding my head up high. 'So it should be no great loss to you when I leave. But I would be grateful if you could answer me this before I go: what did I ever do to deserve your cruelty?'

'Cruelty . . .' she echoes. 'Is that what you think it was?'

'How would you describe it?' I ask plainly. 'For as long as I can remember, you have treated me with disdain, like an inconvenience you wished you didn't have to deal with. Is it really because you believe Father named me after his mistress? Surely there must be more to it than that.'

'Is that not enough of a reason?' she ripostes. 'To be faced daily with my husband's deception? The cruel trick he played upon me by naming you Clementine . . . and how like him you have turned out to be – selfish, worthless, devious.'

Usually her words would be enough to tear me down, but I have Grace's letter to keep me strong, and I have the knowledge that I am leaving this place forever.

'Father never deceived you,' I reply simply, fishing Grace's documents out of my pocket. 'Clementine Bodin was a retired French nurse. She took in British soldiers who were injured at the Battle of the Somme, soldiers like Father who hurt his leg badly and needed a place to recuperate.'

'What are you talking about?' she froths, snatching the documents from me and scanning through them. 'Where did you get these?'

'Grace found them through the library archive,' I reply calmly. 'She is very good at her job.'

'This proves nothing,' she snaps, casting the papers into the fire.

'Clementine Bodin was seventy-five years old when Father stayed with her,' I add, retrieving the final document from my pocket. 'She died in 1918, the same year I was born.'

'I—'

'For years you have tarnished our father's reputation without any real evidence,' I interrupt. 'You have held *me* accountable for his false crimes against you, all because of a namesake.'

'You have no idea what I have been through!' she retorts, her face mingled with grief and distress. 'I was mourning the loss of my husband, I had three children to raise, and then I discovered your father's letters from this . . . this woman. How she missed him, how she wished he could return to France . . . What was I supposed to think? It seemed clear to me that he had been unfaithful while posted abroad, and he had disrespected me further by naming our child – the child he *insisted* we had – after his *mistress*.'

She spits the last word out as if it were poison. Her chest heaves up and down with distress, there is a glistening film across her brow, and as she reaches for her glass, her fingers shake a little. Despite everything, I still find I have a shred of pity left for her. She has suffered, it is true, but mostly at her own hand. Her theories were false.

'Be that as it may, Mother,' I reply shakily. 'Even if Father had betrayed and disrespected you as you believed he did, it was not me you should have condemned.' A lump grows in my throat, making it hard for me to speak, but I continue. 'I was just a child. You hated me and you punished me for something that was beyond my knowledge or control. You are my *mother*. You brought me into this world. You were supposed to care for me and love me against all the odds. Instead, you have raised me to believe I am unlovable.'

'Clementine, please—'

'No, I don't want to hear your excuses anymore,' I interrupt. 'I have spent my entire life trying to earn your affection and approval, but I don't need it anymore. I found it elsewhere: on the stage. Last night, I danced *Giselle* at the Harcourt Theatre. In another life, I would have wished more than anything that you could have been there, that you would be proud of me. I played the principal role, and I was scouted by the Vic-Wells Ballet. I have an audition with them next week, and should – no, *when* – I pass that audition, they will house me, feed me, train me and set me on course to fulfil my dreams. I am simply here as one last act of courtesy, to tell you that I am leaving and I will *never* come back.'

I don't wait for her to respond, in case she tries to break my resolve. I turn quickly on my heel and march down the landing to my bedroom. I don't stop to look at my surroundings one last time, terrified in case Mother tries to stop me. I simply empty my wardrobe of any remaining clothes as quickly as I can, grab the last of my books from the shelf, and reach under the bed for any clandestine items. I find a copy of *Lady Chatterley's Lover* and a stray pair of ballet tights. Then I dash down the stairs, closing the front door behind me, and vow never to look back.

Chapter 23

I pause for a moment on the pavement outside the house I grew up in. I daren't look back for fear that it will drag me back in. I think of how Grace must have felt, standing in this very spot earlier this evening, leaving our childhood home for the last time. Did she weep for it as I do now? The tears are running freely, but I am not sure if they are from sorrow or relief. I spy August Draper returning home across the road. He spots me as he climbs out of his car, and beckons me over with a flick of his blonde head.

'Are you going somewhere?' I ask, my eyes scanning the various packages in the back of his car.

'Yes, it is rather last minute,' he sighs, looking slightly harangued, then his expression softens as he notices the letter still clenched in my hand. 'Would you like to come inside out of the cold, Clementine?'

I nod and follow him into the house.

'Make yourself at home in the sitting room,' he calls, disappearing down the hall to lay down his bags. 'I'll put the kettle on. I know by now how much you English folk need your tea.'

The sitting room is a mess of open books, half-packed boxes, maps and scientific equipment. I gaze around at the chaos, trying to decipher where he might be going and for how long. He returns moments later with a pot of tea.

'Where are you going?' I ask pointedly.

'The opportunity has arisen for me to partake in another expedition,' he says, his usually jovial face growing rather more serious. 'I leave for India at the end of the week.'

'But you have only just arrived in London!' I exclaim. 'And you were so unwell after your trip to Peru. Is it really wise to be travelling again so soon?'

'It is the nature of my work, Clementine.' He sighs, taking the seat beside me on the sofa. 'I must admit also, after everything that has happened with your sister, I am glad of the opportunity to leave London for a while.'

I bow my head. Poor August. He had no idea what he was getting himself into when he turned up at our doorstep a few months ago. 'I am sorry, I haven't had the courage to ask how you are doing.'

'Oh, I'll be fine. Don't you worry about me.' He smiles apathetically as he pours the tea into two cups. 'Everything happens for a reason. I can only assume that this was all, perhaps, for the best.'

'You're taking this very graciously,' I reply, lifting the steaming teacup to my lips and taking a sip.

'It is unfortunate that things didn't work out with Grace,' he admits, clasping his hands together and bowing his head. 'But, ultimately, I am happy for her. She didn't love me, and if I am being perfectly honest with you, I didn't love her either.'

'You didn't?' My head shoots up and I find him gazing into the dying embers of the fire.

'No,' he murmurs. 'I suppose she just seemed like the ideal fit for a wife. She is so gentle and attentive.'

'Oh,' I reply, thinking that Grace has far better qualities than attentiveness.

'Quite,' he says with a small smile. 'But now I am starting to wonder if I should be looking for a wife at all. It would have been unfair of me to marry Grace.'

'Because you travel so much? I had thought much the same.'

'Well, yes, there is that,' he replies, rubbing the back of his neck. 'But also, I . . . I am not who you think I am, Clementine. I am a fraud.'

'What do you mean?' I ask, carefully placing down my cup and saucer.

'I told you I did not love your sister, but the truth is – and I am entrusting you with another deep secret here, Clementine,' he adds, giving me a stern, slightly concerned look. 'I am not attracted to women at all.'

I am glad I put my teacup down first, because this is not the revelation I had expected from him, and to say it comes as a shock would be a bit of an understatement.

'Did Grace know this?' I ask, finding my voice at last.

'Not at first, no, but I told her the night I offered to marry her,' he explains pragmatically. 'I said I could offer her financial stability, children even, if that was what she wanted, but I could not change who I was. I would never be able to love her, and we would be entering into a mutual understanding that, in shielding my secret, she would have her wealth and social standing back.'

'And she was willing to accept that?' I ask, astounded.

'She said she would do whatever was necessary to protect her family.'

The thought of Grace shouldering this burden on her own is awful. I remember how she looked that morning when she turned up at the Lebedevs', desperate to talk to me. She must have just found out. I can't imagine what was going through her mind, and we had a silly argument about it. I wish I had known all this before she had run so far away.

'Clementine?'

I realise it has been a long while since I have said anything. I have been staring into the fire for so long, that little blots of colour now mar my vision when I look back at August. His brow is furrowed in concern.

'I trust you will keep my secret?' he asks. 'I would very much like to return to this street when I am back from India. This a nice neighbourhood. I haven't felt this welcome in a long time.'

'Of course! Your secret is safe with me,' I assure him, clasping his hand. 'Thank you for entrusting me with it.'

'Had I known Grace was in love with this Jacob fellow, I would never have asked her to marry me,' he continues.

'I don't know what to say,' I murmur, taking my hand back and crossing my arms across my body. 'The news about Grace and Jacob was a big shock to me too.'

'You don't need to say anything, Clementine,' he says smoothly.

'Did you know I wanted to be the sister you chose?' I reminisce. 'Grace has always been the romantic one, it's all those books she reads, and she is so pretty and lovely, I thought it only fair that she should get to marry someone she truly loved. I thought if I could get you to notice me, you might have considered me instead, that I could be the one to save us from ruin.'

He raises his eyebrows in amusement. 'Of course I noticed you. How could anyone not notice you? You're a star in the making.'

'Not like that.' I blush. 'I guess I just thought, if we were both travelling so much, we could have travelled together, and maybe fallen in love along the way. Though now I see that would be impossible.'

'Unfortunately, that is very rarely how love works,' he says with a sad smile. 'Is it something you would still consider – a marriage of convenience?

I have been waiting so many weeks for August Draper to ask me this particular question, and I have always thought I knew what my answer would be, but now that the moment is here, it doesn't feel at all like I expected.

'Would you not rather wait for love yourself?' August asks me.

I think of Rudi and the way he makes me feel, like all my senses have been set on fire; the way we wind each other up, but also comfort one another. When I picture my future, it is Rudi I see, every time.

'August,' I ask tentatively. 'Will you kiss me?'

He looks slightly taken aback by the request and nearly

chokes on his tea. 'You do understand what I meant when I said I am not attracted to women?'

'Yes, yes, I know, but I assume if we were to be married, there would be instances where we would have to kiss one another,' I reply pragmatically. 'Consider this like a rehearsal.'

He laughs at that but obliges my request, setting his cup back down on the table and turning to face me.

'Are you sure?' he asks hesitantly, and for the briefest moment I think of Rudi, how tentatively he looked at me beneath the boughs of the oak tree in August's garden before he kissed me.

'Yes, I am quite sure,' I reply. 'Someone once told me that you can't possibly tell if you like someone without kissing them. I just need to figure something out, once and for all.'

He laughs again and draws nearer. He leans in the last inch and kisses me, and it is perfectly pleasant. His lips are warm and soft against mine, and there is nothing wrong with the kiss exactly, it just doesn't feel right. There are no sparks flying, no shooting stars, and I am distinctly aware that my feet are still firmly on the ground. I withdraw and look pensively at the fire; I thought that all kisses would feel the same, but this was nothing like the kiss I shared with Rudi.

'Not quite what you were expecting, I gather?' August says from beside me with a self-deprecating smile.

'Oh!' I say. 'I'm sorry. It wasn't a bad kiss at all. It was really quite lovely. It has just got me thinking that—'

'That there is someone else you are supposed to be kissing.' He finishes my sentence for me.

'Yes, I am afraid so. I'm sorry, August, I cannot marry you either. In fact, there is somewhere I need to be, right now. I must go.'

I run down the street, my feet pounding the pavement as I gasp for breath. There is only one destination on my mind. I must find Rudi. I must tell him how I feel before I lose my nerve. I don't wait for the bus, I haven't the patience for it.

I keep running, my lungs screaming for air. I have to stop every few hundred yards, doubled over as I try to catch my breath. I finally make it to Montpelier Mews and knock urgently on the door to Rudi's apartment above the studio. He opens the door on the second knock.

'Clementine!' He takes in my bedraggled appearance. 'Why do you look so . . . sweaty?'

'I ran here,' I pant. 'I need to speak to you.'

He leans in the doorway, his arms folded and his lips twitch. 'So urgently that you . . . ran here . . . from Hampstead?'

'Yes!' I exclaim with exasperation. 'Though it was really quite a long way, and I had to keep stopping to catch my breath. To be perfectly honest, I would have been better off taking the bus like usual, but I just couldn't wait for it, and the thought of sitting still was unbearable. Rudi, so much has happened since the show on Saturday. I don't even know where to start, I—'

'Why don't you come in and sit down for a while?' he interjects, stepping aside to let me into the hallway.

I follow him past the studio and up the stairs to the apartment I now know so well. The apartment is small and sparse, but immaculate. When Rudi and his mother fled Russia, they had one small suitcase of belongings between them. Only the necessities and a few trinkets Madame had been gifted over the years, in case she needed them to bribe officials to cross the border and make safe passage to Paris. Rudi said she never saw much point in material goods after that. What use are they if you have to pack up and leave in the middle of the night?

I follow him through to the kitchen and he fetches me a glass of water as I sit at the table.

'What has happened?' he asks, rolling up his shirtsleeves and resting his elbows on the table.

I fill him in on everything. I tell him all about Grace's letter, how I confronted my mother, and that Grace absconded in the night because she has secretly been in love with Jacob this whole time. He smiles at that.

'Good,' he says. 'I always liked Jacob. They both deserve some happiness.'

'I thought I knew Grace better than anybody, but now I feel like perhaps I didn't know her at all.'

'She is still the same person,' he assures me. 'She cares about you very much, Clementine. I don't think she would ever have left if she didn't think you would get into the Vic-Wells Ballet. She would probably have married the American, but once she knew that you would be safe and happy, she was finally able to put herself first.'

'I never wanted her to marry just for my sake. I feel so guilty,' I admit.

'You mustn't,' he says. 'The truth is, you didn't need Grace or anyone else to look after you. You just needed to believe in yourself. She acted with the best intentions, but she was doing you a disservice in protecting you so closely. Perhaps she was too frightened to put herself first, but she did it. She found the courage to be who she really is, to fight for what she wanted.'

'Mother was distraught,' I tell him. 'When I found her, she was just staring into the fire with Grace's letter in her hand.'

'Did you tell her about the Vic-Wells?' he asks dubiously.

'Yes, I did,' I reply solemnly. I still feel guilty for leaving her, despite everything. 'But there's more . . . Before Grace left, she had been doing some digging into my father's past. She found my namesake, Clementine Bodin.' I tell him everything I know and he nods silently, taking it all in. 'I had it out with Mother,' I say proudly. 'I displayed all the evidence and she had no retaliation.'

'I am happy for you, *solnyshko*.' He smiles warmly. 'But even if the rumours had been true, it would never have excused the way she treated you all these years. You should never have been held accountable.'

'That's what I said!' I tell him excitedly. 'I finally stood up to her, Rudi, and then I told her about the ballet and

I took my bags and I left right there and then. I'm never going back. I'm finally free . . .'

'And then you came here?' he asks expectantly, his eyebrows disappearing into his mass of curls.

'Not immediately . . .' I start. 'When I left home, I saw August on the street and he invited me in for a cup of tea. I felt I owed him an explanation. He had just been jilted by Grace after all.'

'And what did he have to say on the matter?' Rudi asks with a tone of disinterest.

'He is leaving London,' I reply. I keep my word to August and feel no need to reveal his secret. 'Travelling to India on another expedition. I felt so awful about everything that happened, but he didn't seem too cut up about it to be honest . . . In fact, he – he asked me if I would marry him. Can you believe it?'

The colour drains from Rudi's face and I notice his knuckles whiten as he tightens his grip on his glass. 'Well, there you go,' he says, his voice strained. 'It looks as if all your dreams are coming true at last.' He drains the rest of the glass and slams it down on the table a little too hard.

'No, Rudi, you don't understand—' I start, but there is a knock at the door before I can tell him why I am really here.

'Is everything alright?' I ask anxiously, when he rushes back into the kitchen several minutes later, his expression harried. 'Rudi?'

He finally looks at me, white as a sheet. 'It's *Mamasha*,' he croaks. 'She's been in an accident. Hit by an automobile . . . I-I have to go to the hospital.'

His eyes are wide, staring into blank space, his mouth slightly open. I take a step towards him, and he seems to come to his senses a little.

'I'll come with you,' I tell him, but he shakes his head.

'No, I think it should be just family,' he replies abruptly. 'I don't know how bad it is yet . . . I have to go right now, Clem.'

Chapter 24

Once Rudi has left, I sit in the dimming light for a while. Despite having stayed in his flat for several weeks, it feels strange to be here on my own. I cannot help but feel that with all that has passed, I should not be here anymore, but where can I go? Grace has eloped, August is leaving the country, I have cut all ties with Mother, and though I was confident in my statement to her that I would get into the Vic-Wells Ballet, I have not yet secured a place, so have no home there either. I wonder how Madame is, how serious the accident was. I hope she is alright. I think about Rudi. I wish I could be there to comfort him, but he made it clear he did not want me around.

My feet drag me back to Hampstead with a heavy heart. I stand by the street sign with my small bag of belongings, like a sad knapsack. I can see our house from the end of the street. Am I really going to go back, after I have just made my courageous exit? I know if I return, she will be able to make me stay forever. But what choice do I have? I have nowhere else to go. I am just about to take a step towards the house when Mrs Arbuthnot comes bustling down the street, her string shopping bag swinging in rhythm with her step.

'Clementine?' she says in surprise. 'I haven't seen you around here in a while. Your sister says you've been unwell.' She takes in my face, pale and streaked with tears. 'Oh, my dear, are you alright?'

I try to reply but my throat seems to have closed up and I cannot breathe properly. I gasp for air in short, sharp breaths. She looks around nervously, then pats my hand.

'Let's not cause a scene, dear. Come with me.' She gives me a slight tug, and I feebly follow her lead, down the road towards her house. 'You can finally meet my Archie too. Won't that be nice?'

My eyes widen at the mention of Mrs Arbuthnot's elusive son. After years of hearing her talk about him, I must admit I am more than intrigued at the prospect of meeting him.

The first thing to strike me about Mrs Arbuthnot's home is the overpowering stench of roses. It hits you like a wall the moment you walk through the front door. The layout of her house is much like ours and Mr Draper's: a long, dark hallway with a staircase and several offshoots that lead to the living room, the kitchen and dining room. However, unlike our home, Mrs Arbuthnot's is spotlessly clean. There is not a spiderweb in sight, nor a crack in the paint or the slightest inch of peeling wallpaper. It is no surprise to me that Mrs Arbuthnot is house-proud; what *is* surprising is how quiet the house seems. A grandfather clock chimes from the living room, and I start in surprise as it echoes around the house.

'Did you say your son was home, Mrs Arbuthnot?' I ask as she chivvies me down the hallway towards the kitchen.

'Yes, of course he is,' she replies as she begins unloading her string shopping bag on the counter. A pack of biscuits, some tea, a pound of bacon and some wrapped cheese. She pops the kettle on and begins to put her groceries away. 'We always have tea and biscuits at three o'clock and listen to the wireless,' she says. 'It will be lovely to have some extra company today. I think the two of you will get on very well. Archie is a splendid dancer too. Not ballet like you but, my word, how all the girls used to line up for the chance of a spin round the dance floor with him.'

I nod apprehensively, then accept a teacup from her, taking a sip instantly although I know it will be far too hot.

'Shall we set ourselves down in the living room?' she asks

kindly, grabbing the packet of biscuits and a floral china plate. 'My ankles aren't what they used to be.'

She hobbles down the hall again and I traipse after her, scanning the framed photographs that line the wall. I see a lot of pictures of the same person over and over again, from a toddler to about the age of twenty. This must be Archie. Mrs Arbuthnot is right, he is handsome. His dark eyes gaze out of the portrait, and he has a kind smile, with ears that jut out a little in quite an endearing way. An older gentleman appears in a lot of the photographs too. This must be Mrs Arbuthnot's husband, Archie's father. I don't remember ever meeting him; another thing Archie and I have in common – both our fathers passed away far too soon.

The living room is like an explosion of chintz. The over-stuffed armchairs are coated in a floral tapestry, and there is a permanent indent in the chair nearest the fire. I assume this must be where Mrs Arbuthnot sits, and just as I am thinking this, she plops herself down into the seat with a sigh.

'Sit wherever you like, dear,' she says, closing her eyes and taking a sip of tea. So I perch gingerly on the edge of the sofa, wondering when the elusive Archie will make an appearance. I feel strangely nervous, as if I am about to meet a celebrity or someone I thought was fictional and have only just found out is real.

'Will Archie be joining us soon?' I ask in trepidation, but Mrs Arbuthnot simply chuckles.

'He is already here,' she smiles warmly, then looks towards the mantelpiece where another framed photograph of Archie in his military uniform stands. Then, with a stomach-dropping realisation, I spot the framed telegram beside it, the telegram so many mothers and wives dreaded receiving.

'Oh, Mrs Arbuthnot—' I start, but she talks over me.

'He was always so charismatic. Like I said, he didn't struggle with the ladies.' She winks. 'I must admit, I do find it odd how much quieter things have been since the war. But everyone came back from that war different.'

I am too young to remember a time before the war, but the way I hear other people speak of it, it is almost as if they lived in some ignorantly blissful utopia. I consider myself lucky to have never known the difference. It is far better to have never had something at all than to have it and lose it forever.

'I am so sorry, Mrs Arbuthnot, I had no idea . . .' I feel so stupid for not realising until now, but I was only a baby during the war, and Mother would never allow any discussion of war in the house as I grew older. I don't know what to say. What words of comfort are there for a woman who has lost her whole family? I find I have a newfound respect for her. I always thought her unflinching need to be involved in everybody's business was rude and nosy, but now I can see that I have misjudged her.

She turns on the wireless, and the three of us – Mrs Arbuthnot, the spirit of Archie, and I – listen intently. A fire has broken out at the Crystal Palace, and the Penge Fire Brigade are trying to control the blaze, but the reporter does not sound hopeful. They say the blaze can be seen for miles around, and both Mrs Arbuthnot and I run to the window to check. Sure enough, there is an orange hue to the night sky.

'I almost feel like I can smell burning,' Mrs Arbuthnot remarks. 'Can't you?'

I sniff the air, and she is right. There is definitely a smell of burning. I open my mouth to respond, but before I can speak, someone screams on the street below. We both start in surprise, and Mrs Arbuthnot springs into neighbourhood-watch mode.

'Stay here, Clementine,' she says, suddenly serious. 'I will go and investigate.'

I ignore her, of course, and follow her out into the street. The smell of burning is much stronger now. The acrid smell of smoke fills my nostrils, and flecks of ash pepper the sky. Surely this cannot be coming from the Crystal Palace. We are miles away. Then I see it.

'Oh, Clementine . . .' Mrs Arbuthnot starts, but her words are drowned out by my scream.

I do not even realise that the sound has come from me at first. It is a blood-curdling, ear-splitting, guttural sound. Mrs Arbuthnot tries to hold me back but she cannot contain me, because the fire is not coming from the Crystal Palace at all. It is coming from my childhood home. The whole house is ablaze, a red glow coming from every window. I throw open the gate and stumble down the path, as if there is anything I can possibly do to stop the overwhelming inferno. The heat is unbearable already, and when I reach for the door handle, I snatch my hand back in shock from the searing hot doorknob. I try to open it again, but this time somebody has hold of me. Strong arms are wrapped around me, and they drag me kicking and screaming back down the path.

'Mother will still be in there!' I cry. 'Mother!'

'It's too late, Clementine,' a soothing voice with an American lilt murmurs in my ear. 'I am so sorry, but it is too dangerous for you to go in there now.'

August restrains me until I finally lose the energy to keep fighting, and I collapse in his arms, the sound of sirens piercing the night sky which is shrouded in thick, billowing smoke and ash.

Chapter 25

When I awake the next morning, I am in another strange bed. This is becoming a recurring phenomenon, though I suppose it is something I should get used to if I wish to spend my life travelling and performing. It does not take me long to work out where I am; the floral wallpaper pattern is an immediate giveaway. I must be back at Mrs Arbuthnot's house, in the single bed that once upon a time would have belonged to her beloved Archie.

At first, last night seems like an awful dream. It cannot possibly be real. I must have confused what happened at the Crystal Palace with all the mixed emotions about Mother and leaving home. But as I start to come to my senses, I realise that the acrid smell of burning still clings to my hair and clothes. Mother is gone. My childhood home is gone, and with it, the last physical memories of my father. Suddenly it hits me: I am an orphan. It is not as if I could ever count on Mother for anything really, but there was still some stability in knowing I had a parent and I had a home, whether it was a happy one or not. Now, I feel untethered, as if I am in the deep sea with no ships to save me, nothing to keep me afloat. I do not even know where Grace is, or if she is married to Jacob yet. It feels strange not knowing where she is, or what she is doing. I hope it won't be long before she returns to London. There is an empty space inside of me. I feel hollowed out, and I do not know how to feel whole again.

I immediately think of Rudi. I miss him terribly, and my heart aches at the thought of him. I wonder if he and Madame have returned from the hospital yet and how they are both doing. I rise from the bed and go to the window. The pane is frosted with ice, and I breathe on it, creating a perfect, clear circle. The street below is quiet. I cannot see the remains of our house from here, thank goodness. I don't know how I will feel when I have to see it again. I spot Mr Duval meandering down the road, hand in hand with his wife. They are probably on their way to the library, or to feed the ducks on Hampstead Heath. How strange it is to see people carrying on with their lives when mine has changed irrevocably.

There is a soft knock at the door and I step back from the window.

'You can come in,' I call out, and I hear how hollow my voice sounds.

Mrs Arbuthnot opens the door, her expression creased with concern. 'How are you feeling this morning, dear?'

I try to find the words, but nothing comes out, and she nods sympathetically.

'It was a silly question.' She crosses the room and rests her hand softly on my shoulder. 'I want you to know that you can stay here as long as you need, and if there is anything I can do – anything at all – you just let me know.'

'Oh, Mrs Arbuthnot, I don't want to impose,' I start but she stops me.

'Now, there will be none of that.' She tuts. 'Where else are you going to stay? Besides, I must say, it was nice having another person in the house with me again. If you won't stay for yourself, consider it a favour for a lonely, old neighbour.' She pauses and stares out the window. 'I know you and your sister must think me a terrible busybody, but I do get very lonely.'

My chest aches to hear it and I suddenly feel awful about all the snide remarks I have made about her over the years.

'I have always worried about you two girls, looking after that house and your mother, God rest her soul, all by yourselves. It is about time you let someone look after you for a change. Speaking of which, there is a young gentleman downstairs to see you.'

My heart skips a beat. Surely there is no way that Rudi could be here. How would he even know where to find me? I rush down the stairs, and burst into the living room.

'Clementine!' Mrs Arbuthnot exclaims, dashing after me, but my eyes are trained on the silver eyes of Rudolf Lebedev. He stands by the fireplace, looking at me in earnest.

'*Solnyshko*,' he whispers, as I crash into him. 'I am so sorry.' He holds me in his arms, rocking me gently from side to side as I begin to weep uncontrollably.

'I will give the two of you some privacy,' Mrs Arbuthnot says quietly, removing herself from the room.

'I'm sorry.' I sniff eventually, realising my tears have soaked his shirt and pulling away.

'Do not think on it,' he replies matter-of-factly, pulling me back to his chest and resting his chin on top of my head. I know I should not encourage this, it will only make my feelings for him grow stronger, but I cannot deny how comforting it is to be in his arms. Something about him cools the fever that often runs hot in my mind.

'How did you know where to find me?' I ask at last.

'Ah, well, Mr Draper sent his housekeeper to my flat with a note,' he replies, and I can hear how much it pains him to admit it. 'I suppose he knew you would be in need of a friend. She called by first thing this morning, so I went to see him and he told me about the fire. I came straight over.'

'That was thoughtful of him,' I point out, then add, 'and of you. Thank you for coming all this way, Rudi, especially with everything that has happened to your mother. How is she?'

'Do not worry about that now, Clem,' he says, his face creasing into an expression of conflict. 'She was badly hurt, but she is going to be OK.'

'What is it?' I ask, stepping back to look at him properly.

'It's nothing, really, it's just . . . her leg was badly broken. The doctors fear she will not dance again.'

My stomach plummets and I feel as if I am falling. 'But what does this mean for the Lebedev School of Ballet?'

'We are still working that out,' he says, the muscles in his neck clenching. 'But there is one more thing, Clem. Today is Tuesday . . .'

At first, I don't know what he means, and then it hits me. 'The audition, it's today!'

'Of course, you do not have to attend, but I thought I should tell you and let you make that decision for yourself,' he says calmly.

'But I *must* go!' I exclaim, running my hands through my hair. 'Now more so than ever. I don't have a home, I don't have anyone.'

'You have me,' he interjects.

'Rudi, I cannot take any more charity from you and your mother,' I insist, walking up and down the carpet of Mrs Arbuthnot's living room so quickly that the repeated floral patterns start to blur. 'I must put on a brave face, that is what Grace would expect me to do. It's what my father would have wanted me to do.'

'Bravery has many faces, Clementine,' he replies, tilting his head and scrutinising me with his cool eyes. 'The brave thing is finding the strength to follow what you want.'

I look at him, and for a moment everything else fades into insignificance. There is just him and me, in a bubble that no sound, no stress, no one else can penetrate. It is the most intense and all-consuming sensation, and all I can focus on is the flash of silver in his eyes, the reverberating pulse at his neck, the way his breathing has slowed right down. Then I tear my eyes away, and the moment is broken, my priorities flooding back to me.

'This is what I want,' I assure him. 'We must go to the audition, we have worked all our lives for this moment.'

He sighs and lowers his eyes, but nods and smiles. 'Very well, Clem. I have your things all ready. Let's go.'

The studio we are ushered into is very similar to Madame Lebedev's in some ways. The walls are lined with mirrors and barres, the wooden floor is springy beneath my ballet-slippered feet, and well worn in patches from the beating feet of hundreds of dancers before me. However, it is the size of the studio that is completely overwhelming. The ceilings must be twelve feet at least, and as I gaze up I feel incredibly small. I wonder if this effect has been created on purpose, in an attempt to quash any overzealous egos, and my mind immediately goes to Alice Blakely. Just like at Madame Lebedev's, there is a piano in the corner, scattered with sheet music, and I can almost picture Mr Popov sat there, tinkling the ivories.

Rudi and I are not the only ones who have been invited to audition. There is a group of about ten of us, mostly girls, but there is one other boy. We all eye each other anxiously, competitively, as we stretch and limber up for practice. The teacher is an elderly woman with tightly curled iron-grey hair. She wears a loose, black sweatshirt over a long, black skirt and a string of pearls around her neck. Though her body looks frail, she walks up and down the studio with an air that commands respect.

'Welcome, ladies and gentlemen,' she says, and the studio falls silent. 'My name is Madame Valois. You have all been invited here today because we have seen some promise in you. Not all of you will have what it takes to join the esteemed ranks of the Vic-Wells Ballet, but those of you who do will receive the highest quality training available in the country. Now, take your places at the barre and we will begin with *pliés.*'

The audition is peculiar, because it feels just like an ordinary class, but rather than receiving any instruction, Madame Valois simply watches us all like a hawk and makes notes in a small, black leather notebook. I do not know if she is looking for signs of promise or imperfections, but every time she looks at me and writes a comment in her book, I feel my stomach tighten a little more and I make extra effort to stand up straight, pull my core muscles in, and perfect my turnout. I can feel the sweat pouring down my neck by the time we finish our barre exercises. My eyes dart to Rudi and he gives me an almost imperceptible smile and inclines his head ever so slightly in a nod as if to say 'we were born for this'.

'I will now teach you a simple routine,' Madame Valois instructs, ushering us all into the centre of the studio. 'I will split you into small groups and I will be looking to see how well you perform.'

The routine is not simple at all. It involves several *pirouettes*, leaps and some very intricate footwork, as well as several changes in direction. We mark it through once and then Madame Valois splits us into groups of three so she can inspect us more closely. Rudi is in the first group, with the other boy and one other girl. He outdances the two of them spectacularly. He simply has a stage presence that you cannot teach; his limbs are that little bit more extended, his posture more commanding, his agility second to none. When he finishes, Madame Valois actually claps her hands together and her lips twitch into the barest of smiles. My heart is bursting with pride. There is no way he won't be accepted at this rate.

I have little time to dwell on it though, because before I know it, it is my turn to impress. I take my place in the middle of the studio with two of the other girls. I know I should see them as my competitors, but it is hard to look at their nervous faces and feel anything but empathy. We all want this more than anything, that is why we are here, but if I really want it the most, I have to dance to the very best of my ability. I must give even more than I did in *Giselle*. I take a deep breath and look at my own reflection in the mirror. I must not become distracted by them. I straighten my back and set my focus on the steps we have just learned. It is time to prove myself.

At first, everything is going brilliantly. I can feel the music in my veins and my body responds to the tempo in perfect unison. I fall gracefully out of each spin, and stretch my legs a little higher than they usually go. I am sure I will pay for it tomorrow, but that does not matter right now. I am completely lost in the moment, until I notice a movement in the mirror. Someone enters the studio to whisper to Madame Valois. She then looks around the room and points at Rudi. I nearly stumble. The stranger walks around the studio to speak with him. Nobody else seems to notice. I nearly fall out of my *pirouette* because I am watching Rudi rather than spotting to keep my balance. I stop looking at him. I am sure whatever is going on is not a problem and I focus all my attention on the routine. Luckily, I think Madame Valois was distracted and missed my mistakes. However, when Rudi leaves the studio, his expression resigned, it is impossible to pretend I have not noticed. The second the music ends, I dash after him, ignoring Madame Valois' cry of disgrace at my lack of respect. Nothing else matters. I need to know that Rudi is all right.

'What is going on?' I ask anxiously, rushing back into the hall where Rudi is sitting on a bench outside the studio with his head in his hands.

'*Mamasha* has taken a turn for the worse,' he says, his voice cracking with distress. 'I need to go back to the hospital.'

'Oh, Rudi, I'm so sorry,' I cry, wrapping my arms around him. 'You must go. You have finished your audition. I am sure they will understand.'

He nods sharply, then looks up and down the hall before running his hands through his curly locks again. 'I feel terrible,' he mutters. 'I was dancing, thinking only of myself, while she was lying there broken, Clem. I should have been there . . . We are all each other has. We have been through everything together. Everything. I owe her my life.' He rubs his chin and looks down. I don't know what to tell him, but before I can respond, he speaks again. 'This feels like a bad omen.'

Without another word, he rises to his feet and strides towards the door without looking back, his footsteps echoing in the hallway as he disappears from sight. I stand there for a moment, subdued by the news about Madame Lebedev, and Rudi's sudden exit. Moments before, it had felt like all of our dreams were about to come true; now it seems as if they are crashing down all around me.

I jump as the door to the studio bursts open and the rest of the dancers pour out into the hallway. Some of them cast me a pitying glance. I suppose they thought the pressure got to me and I couldn't handle it. Maybe they are right. There is a strong possibility that I have just scuppered my chances of getting into the Vic-Wells Ballet. Madame Valois leans in the doorway after the last girl has left; she tips her head and surveys me over the top of her gold-rimmed spectacles.

'I assume whatever caused you to leave my studio in such a hurry with no explanation was worth risking your place with us,' she remarks, her arms folded. 'A lot of dancers would kill to be in your position, but clearly you had other priorities.'

'Madame, I am so sorry,' I reply quickly, bobbing in an awkward half-curtsey, unsure of the protocol. 'It is just that I saw my dance partner receive some bad news during the audition, and I had to check if he was alright.'

She raises her eyebrows but her expression softens slightly. 'You are an exceptional talent,' she says, almost reluctantly, and my pulse begins to race. 'Mr Wells was right to bring you to my attention. However,' she pauses, and her gaze grows piercing once more, 'I do not have time for dancers who are not prepared to put in the effort.'

'Oh, but I am, Madame Valois!' I gush. 'This means everything to me. It is all I have ever wanted since I was a little girl—'

She holds up a hand to silence me. 'I am not a young woman, Miss Harrington. How many times do you think I have heard girls and boys, just like you, swear to me the very same thing?'

'I imagine a fair few times,' I mumble, casting my gaze down to my feet.

'Hundreds,' she says sharply. 'And most of them never amounted to anything, even those who did not run out halfway through the audition.'

'Madame, I swear I am not the type to run out on anything,' I plead with her, wringing my hands. 'It was simply—'

'Yes, yes, your friend was in need.' She nods understandingly. 'However, if you want this, if you *really* want it, you will have to put aside everything you care about and make dancing your number one priority.'

'I can do that. I will do that,' I insist, looking up at her beseechingly. 'There is nothing I want more than to join your company.'

'You will miss birthdays, weddings, funerals even,' she continues. 'You will lose friends, you will fight with family, and you will probably make more than a few ballet rivals along the way.'

I know she is trying to test my mettle, but I already know all of this, have experienced a fair bit of it already, in fact. If only she knew what I have been through, simply to make it here today, if she realised the gaping home-sized cavern within me that I am trying to ignore. I have no home left, no more family to lose... Mother and Father are both dead, and I don't know if I will ever see my beloved Grace again. I have lost so much, I cannot lose my dream too. 'I can cope with that,' I tell her. 'Dancing is all that matters to me.'

'And why is that?' she asks, quirking one eyebrow.

'Why?' I repeat, blinking. 'Because dancing is the closest thing there is to magic. It is like dreaming through your feet . . . There is nothing like it. I know it isn't an easy path that I have chosen, but I do know it will be worth it.'

She holds my gaze, and a proper smile at last warms her dark brown eyes. She unfolds her arms and extends one hand towards me.

'Welcome, Miss Harrington,' she says prestigiously as I shake her hand, 'to the Vic-Wells Ballet School.'

Chapter 26

As soon as I am able, I return to Montpelier Mews to ask after Madame Lebedev. The door opens and my breath catches in my throat at the sight of him. He is wearing a tight white T-shirt, tucked into a pair of high-waisted black trousers, his hands deep in the pockets.

'Hello, Clem.' He smiles, and as if by magic, the sun comes out from behind the clouds, casting rays of light into his silver eyes and picking up the bronze hues of his curly hair. He steps aside to let me in, and as I walk past him I catch a waft of his scent. Instantly, my mind goes blank and I struggle to remember why it is that I am here. He stops beside me in the dim-lit hall and I stare at his chest for a moment; I have an overwhelming urge to lay my hand over his beating heart.

'How is your mother?' I manage to say at last.

'She's doing alright,' Rudi says. He looks tired and a little dejected. 'Her leg is broken in three places, so she has been put on bed rest. Then she had a blood clot, that's why they had to call me away from the audition. She is on some rather strong painkillers, but at least she is alive.'

'And how are you, Rudi?' I implore. 'We haven't spoken since the audition. Have you heard anything?'

'Yes.' He pauses, and I wait anxiously. 'I went back this morning to apologise for leaving so abruptly. Madame Valois told me she offered you a place, Clem, I am so proud of you.'

'And what about you?' I ask him cautiously.

He lowers his head and my heart drops, but then he says, 'They offered me a full scholarship on the spot.'

'Oh, Rudi!' I reach out and wrap my arms around him.

'That is such wonderful news. I was sure they would. The way Madame Valois' eyes lit up when you were dancing . . . How could they not?'

'Yes, well, obviously it's a huge honour,' he replies uncertainly. 'There is a lot to consider.'

'What do you mean?'

'Well, I stand by what I said at the audition, Clem.' He shrugs. 'What happened with *Mamasha* feels like a sign. Besides, I cannot leave her as she is now. She needs someone to care for her.'

'I am sure there is something that can be done, Rudi,' I implore. 'Can I come in? Let's talk about this together, with your mother.'

'Fine,' he sighs, pinching the bridge of his long nose in frustration as he so often does when we disagree. 'But I won't be deterred, Clementine. Whatever I choose, it is my decision to make.'

I follow him upstairs to the flat that has become almost like home to me. I cannot allow Rudi to give up now. This is not how our story ends. Rudi and I will join the Vic-Wells Ballet School, work our way up to company level and take to the stage together as we always planned. We will travel the world, and wow audiences every night with our seamless chemistry.

'*Mamasha* is in her bedroom. You know the way. I shall make you both some tea,' he says, heading to the kitchen.

I linger in the hallway for a moment, unsure if I should go straight to Madame or follow him into the kitchen. I can feel the magnetic pull dragging me towards him, but I fight against it. There will be time later for Rudi and me to pick up where we left off before Madame's accident, so I shuffle down the hallway towards Madame Lebedev's bedroom. I know where it is, but I have never been inside before. I knock on the door and wait for her to say I can enter.

'Clementine!' she gushes, her eyes lighting up. 'Rudi said

you would come. How lovely to see you. We have missed having you around here.'

'I am sorry I left so suddenly.' I bow my head. 'It wasn't very courteous of me after you opened your home to me. I do hope you know how grateful I am that you did.'

'Think nothing of it, darling.' She pauses, her expression growing grave. 'I heard about what happened to your home, your mother. I am so sorry for your loss.'

I feel the same pang in my chest that comes every time someone mentions the fire, and my eyes sting with fresh tears but I blink them back.

'Thank you, Madame.' I nod my head politely. 'My childhood was not the happiest, but it is not easy to watch an entire lifetime of memories go up in smoke. And as for my mother . . . well, I suppose I always hoped one day we would find some sort of peace, but I think I had finally realised that wasn't to be. Still, I never wanted it to end like this.'

'Sometimes it is harder to lose those who we have the most complicated relationships with.' She nods understandingly. 'How can we grieve for someone we were so certain we hated? But somehow, we still do.'

She graciously turns her head to the view outside her bedroom window while I surreptitiously wipe my eyes with the sleeve of my blouse. 'Where are you staying at the moment, darling?'

'With my neighbour. She has a spare room and has kindly offered to put me up until I find my feet.' I sniff.

'I hear there is good news, too,' she says at last, turning her head back to me with a warm smile. 'You have accepted a full scholarship into the Vic-Wells Ballet School. How wonderful.'

'Oh.' I blush. 'Yes, I still can't believe it. I have to keep pinching myself to believe it is real. They have helped me find some accommodation with some fellow dancers and I am moving in next week. Then classes begin in the new year.'

'I am hoping you can talk some sense into my son,' she grumbles. 'He seems to think it best that he turns down his scholarship. He informs me that he won't be joining the Vic-Wells Ballet after all, that I will need his help with my ballet school.' She says it plainly, staring out of the window. It has started to rain again and fat droplets roll down the glass like tears. 'So, it would seem that the accident has ruined not just my career, but Rudi's too.'

I feel my heart plummet, as if whatever was holding it in place has finally given way and now I am falling. Is this really where my dancing career with Rudi must end?

'Trust me, I have tried everything to convince him to change his mind,' she says, reading the expression on my face. 'But that boy has the Lebedev stubbornness running through his veins . . . It's such a pity. I feel the loss as if it were my own, and it hurts more than this damn leg,' she says, gesturing frustratedly at her cast.

'I don't know what to say, Madame,' I croak, trying to fight back tears.

'Sometimes there are no words,' she says, taking my hand and gently squeezing it with a sad smile. 'I will miss you, darling, but you must follow your dreams, and never forget where you came from. Just be sure that you listen to your heart; it will always lead you down the right path.'

'I will, Madame,' I promise her, but my heart feels more lost than ever. I must choose my career, it is all I have ever wanted, but what would a life of dancing look like without Rudi in it?

'These blasted painkillers make me so tired,' she groans, closing her eyes. 'I must get some rest, my dear. Would you go and tell Rudi I don't need that tea after all?'

I kiss her goodbye, then make my way down the hallway to the kitchen. I can see Rudi standing in front of the stove, looking out of the window onto the courtyard below. He is humming to himself, and as I get closer I realise it is the 'Swan's Theme' from *Swan Lake,* and I wish I could tear my heart from my chest, because I think it would hurt less than listening to him hum that melancholy tune, knowing we will never dance it together at the Royal Opera House. He turns at the creak of the floorboard under my step, his curly head framed in frosted gold by the weak winter sun.

'Has *Mamasha* fallen asleep?'

'She was drifting off, and said not to bother with the tea,' I reply, coming to stand beside him.

'Well, the pot has boiled now. Would you like a cup?' he asks and I nod. I have yet to find a situation in life that can't be improved by a comforting brew, and I feel the need for comfort now more than ever. He pours the hot water methodically over a strainer into two chipped, willow-pattern teacups. He makes it just how I like it, dark and strong but with a generous splash of milk. Then, without asking, he drops in one sugar cube and stirs the cup into a frenzy. I only take sugar in my tea when I am at my most despairing, and as always, Rudi can read me like an open book. He passes me the cup, and I try to take a sip, though it is still far too hot, as I consider what to say.

'*Za zdorovie*,' he toasts listlessly, clinking his teacup against mine, and I finally meet his gaze. '*Mamasha* told you, didn't she?'

'That you're not coming?' I reply quietly.

'I'm sorry you found out that way. I wanted to tell you myself . . . The pain medication makes her forgetful.'

'Rudi, you have to come!' I insist, trying to ignore the desperation in my voice. All the words suddenly spill out at once. 'This is what we've always dreamed of . . . the Vic-Wells Ballet, Rudi! You and I, travelling the world together, performing on the biggest stages to the most influential crowds. Your mother wants you to go, and I . . . I need you to go. I can't do this without you . . .'

His cool grey eyes widen in surprise and he takes a step towards me, cupping my face in his slender hands. 'Can't do it without me? But of course you can. There is no one on this earth you couldn't dance with and hold an audience completely mesmerised.' He sweeps his fingers over my cheeks, catching the falling tears and casting them aside. 'Dry your eyes, *solnyshko*. I was only ever a pedestal for you to display your loveliness upon, and you will meet far better partners than I.'

'I don't want to leave you, but I can't stay either, Rudi,' I cry, holding his hand to my cheek and nuzzling into his palm. 'Dancing is my life, it's my escape . . . I must go.'

'I wouldn't allow you to stay, not for me.' He sighs and looks down at his feet, so all I can see is the crown of his curly head. 'I can't follow you into the Vic-Wells Ballet though, Clementine, not now when *Mamasha* needs me more than ever . . . I would be doing it for all the wrong reasons. It was never my dream, it was yours.'

'I don't understand . . .' I murmur, my head spinning with confusion. 'What do you mean it isn't your dream? We were supposed to go together, that *was* the dream!' I choke, trying to swallow the hard lump in my throat as fresh tears start to well up in my eyes.

'Clementine,' he sighs, taking my hands in his. 'How many times must I tell you that I love you before you believe me? Of course I wanted to join the Vic-Wells Ballet with you. I would have followed you to the ends of the earth, but I cannot do this anymore. I cannot live my life for you, Clem. Dancing is my life too, but I do not crave the stage like you do. I am just as happy to teach dancing to the next generation, to keep *Mamasha*'s school going, as I would be to become a star of the stage.'

His words take me by surprise. It feels like a criticism, like he thinks there is something wrong with wanting the spotlight. I stand abruptly, the legs of my chair screeching against the kitchen tiles.

'Clementine . . .' he sighs, but I interrupt.

'I am sorry if you think there is something wrong with having ambition,' I reply tersely. 'I have always been honest about what I want.'

'Have you, Clem?' he asks, standing now too so that he towers over me, but I simply stare back at him stubbornly with my chin held high. 'When are you finally going to be honest about how you feel?'

'I tried to tell you!' I insist. 'I ran all the way here from Hampstead to tell you that I loved you, Rudi, but you didn't want to hear it, and then your mother had the accident and—'

'You mean the time when you came here and told me that American you've been chasing for months asked you to marry him?' he snorts, folding his arms.

'You didn't let me finish!' I huff. 'Yes, he asked me to marry him, but I told him no, because . . . because . . .'

'Because you love me,' he says for me, but his expression is grim and resigned.

'Yes,' I say quietly, the relief finally unloading from me. 'Because I love you, Rudi.'

'But it is not enough to make you stay.'

'No,' I reply, trying to swallow the lump in my throat. It feels as if my heart is trying to escape from my chest and force its way out through my mouth.

He takes my face in his hands, wiping the tears from my cheeks with his thumb. 'I love you too, Clementine,' he says softly. 'I have never felt so sure of anything in my life.'

'But it is not enough to make you leave,' I counter, and he smiles forlornly.

'No,' he echoes. 'My place is here, and yours is at the Vic-Wells.'

I tear myself away from him, unable to bear it a moment longer. I snatch up my bag and race from the kitchen, closing the front door as quietly as possible so as not to wake Madame Lebedev. I rush down the stairs two at a time, desperate to get as far away from Rudolf Lebedev as possible. The rain has made the cobbles of Montpelier Mews shiny and slick, and I stumble across them, letting the rain soak me through. Let it wash away the last of Clementine Harrington, I think to myself. The Vic-Wells Ballet is my chance to reinvent myself. I can be anyone I want to be. I do not have to be the girl whose mother did not want her, who was picked on by the other ballerinas, the unlovable one. There is a new path stretching out before me, and it is paved with stars.

PART THREE

'It was all very well to be ambitious, but ambition
should not kill the nice qualities in you.'

– Noel Streatfeild, *Ballet Shoes*

Chapter 27

Winter 1939

There is a chill wind in the air as I step off the boat at Greenwich Pier. I had forgotten just how bitterly cold London can be in February. It is as if winter is determined to give all it's got before giving way to spring. I tuck my hands deep inside my muffler and bury my chin in the fur collar of my coat. It probably doesn't help that I am so very tired. The cold always affects me more when I am run down, and I don't sleep well on boats. Some people find the rocking motion of the sea quite soothing, but it has never felt natural to me. Returning to London makes me feel anxious too. This city holds too many memories.

'Clementine, do hurry up!' Paul calls crossly from the boardwalk. 'It's bloody freezing. I want to get to the hotel.'

Paul has a short temper, even for a dancer. He taps his foot impatiently as a porter heaves our luggage into a waiting taxi and I hurry down the ramp to join him.

'Remind me again why you accepted his proposal?' mutters my friend Sophie as she follows behind me.

'We want the same things out of life,' I reply plainly. 'And we're in the same ballet company, so we're always in the same place. It's all very convenient.'

'Ah, yes . . . convenience,' she smirks. 'Who needs love when you have convenience.'

241

I stop dead in my tracks and she nearly walks into me.

'What's the matter?' she asks, a look of concern painted across her face. 'I'm sorry, Clem, I didn't mean anything by it. You know I'm only joking around.'

'It's nothing.' I smile warmly. 'You just reminded me of an old friend for a moment there.'

'CLEMENTINE!'

Paul is now sat in the taxi, leaning out of the window with a look of vehement frustration. I glance at Sophie and she rolls her eyes. 'Run along! God forbid you keep his lordship waiting.'

I stifle my grin and kiss her on the cheek. 'I'll see you at the theatre this evening.'

The taxi crawls through the streets of London on the way to the hotel. I gaze out of the window, my eyes peeled on the passers-by, looking out for a curl of bronze hair or a pair of eyes as grey as a cygnet. I can't help myself. It has been more than two years since I have seen Rudolf Lebedev. Two years without a single sighting, a note, anything . . . Not since the night I left his flat above Madame Lebedev's studio. I don't even know if he still lives here. With the constant threat of war, perhaps he chose to move somewhere a little more rural. I can't picture it though. When I think of London, I think of Rudi.

We finally slow to a halt outside the hotel and I look up, unsurprised by our destination. Paul always insists we stay at the very best hotels when we travel. He gets in terrible fights with the producers over the cost, but he always wins. That is the sort of person Paul is. He climbs out of the taxi and marches into the lobby without looking back.

'Let me get the door for you, ma'am,' the taxi driver insists, exiting the vehicle and coming round to the rear passenger door.

I thank him and place the fare plus a tip in his hands, then make my way inside the grandiose hotel. Paul is already at the reception desk. I can hear him ordering the staff about the moment I step through the revolving doors.

'I asked for the deluxe suite, not the executive,' he demands. 'There must have been some mistake.'

'I am sorry, sir, it looks like the deluxe suite has been reserved for your partner, Miss Harrington.' The receptionist informs him, glancing nervously between the two of us.

'It's fine. He can have it,' I sigh, leaning on the desk beside him. 'I am so tired, I just need somewhere to rest my head before tonight's performance.'

'Fine,' he grumbles, snatching the key from the receptionist. 'But I shall be having words with Mr Webster. He is making a fortune from our hard work. The least he could do is put us both in a decent suite, and why did he give *you* the better one in the first place?'

'Darling, it's The Ritz,' I reassure him as we make our way towards the lift. 'They are all decent suites. You know, when I was a young girl, growing up in London, I slept on a mattress so thin that I could feel every spring. It didn't impede my ability to dance one bit.'

'Yes, so I have heard a thousand times before . . .' He rolls his eyes. 'But you are not so young anymore.'

'I am not even twenty-one yet,' I remind him. 'I'm hardly ancient.'

'For a ballerina, you should double that.'

I don't argue with him any further. I haven't got the energy for it. All I can think about is the soft, feather-filled pillow awaiting me in my bedroom. As soon as he has the door open, I glide past him, ignoring the chilled bottle of champagne in the sitting room and the bouquets of flowers sent in advance of my arrival. I flop down on the great big four-poster bed and close my eyes in bliss.

'You don't have long to rest,' Paul calls from the sitting room as he pops the champagne, causing me to jump. I wish he would just go away and drink champagne in his own suite. I long to be alone. He continues, 'A journalist is coming by to interview us both in about an hour. Then the car will be coming to pick us up and take us to the theatre . . . and don't forget you agreed to let that dance school interview you after the performance.'

I let out a groan. I had completely forgotten about that. It seemed like such a good idea at the time, an opportunity to give something back to the next generation. It still is, I know it is important, but I just want to rest.

'Then let me sleep while I can, please!' I call back from the bed, and for once he falls silent, then I hear the door to my suite quietly close behind him.

It feels as if I have barely closed my eyes when I am awoken again by the sound of laughter from Paul's suite next door. I press my ear to the wall. There are two voices: Paul's low, rich and slightly exuberant laugh, and the more restrained high-pitched lyrical chuckle of a woman. I dress quickly and rush out into the hall, rapping my knuckles on the door to Paul's suite. A young woman with dark red hair answers, and I feel my eyes widen in shock, but before I can say anything, she shakes my hand and steps aside.

'Miss Harrington, what a pleasure it is to meet you,' she gushes as I step inside and sweep my eyes over the suite. Paul is lounging over the sofa with his feet up, and another gentleman is setting up his camera equipment.

'You're here from the magazine,' I breathe with a sigh of relief, then turn towards Paul. 'Why didn't you tell me we had guests?' I ask hotly.

'Oh, Miss Harrington!' the girl squeaks, bobbing in a half-curtsey as if I am royalty. 'I am so sorry. Mr Dubrovsky said you were sleeping and that you were not to be disturbed.' I can see from her expression that she thinks this is a thoughtful act on Paul's behalf; however, I know him well enough to realise he was probably hoping to steal the interview all for himself. 'Mr Dubrovsky was just telling me all about your trip to Vienna. It sounded quite magical.'

'It was work,' I reply brusquely, then soften my tone. It is not this young girl's fault that Paul didn't wake me. 'But yes, it was quite magical. We were performing *Coppélia*. Have you ever seen it?'

'Yes,' she breathes. 'In fact, I saw you play Swanhilda right here in London, and now you're back to perform *Giselle*!'

'That's right,' I say, wiping the sleep from my eyes and taking the seat opposite her. 'Shall we get started with this interview then?'

'Do you need a moment, or are you ready to dive right in?'

'I'm as ready as I'll ever be,' I assure her.

She clasps her notebook, pen poised. 'You have been travelling a lot lately. Shows in Vienna, Paris and Rome . . . How does it feel to be back in London?'

'It feels like coming home,' I tell her, and it is not a lie. Despite how nervous I felt to return after so many months, and the memories – both good and bad, there is no denying that London is where I feel most like myself.

'Is it true that you were performing in *Giselle* when you were scouted by the Vic-Wells Ballet?'

'Yes,' I say, ignoring the pang in my chest. 'It seems as if I have come full circle. I danced the principal role of Giselle two years ago with the Lebedev School of Ballet, and that night, my life changed forever.'

'Are you still in contact with any of your old colleagues? Where are they now?'

'I write to them, but it can be hard to stay in touch when I travel so much for my work.'

That is what I tell myself. Not that Rudi simply does not wish to speak to me, but rather that his letters must arrive too late, that by the time they reach the return address I add to each envelope, I have moved on again.

'It must be hard travelling so much. Do you miss your family?'

This woman is very astute for such a young age. It is as if she already knows my life history and is simply working out how truthful I will be with my answers. I opt for a safe balance between the truth and a lie.

'I don't have much family to speak of,' I tell her. 'But I shall certainly be visiting my sister while I am in town.'

Paul sits up straight on the sofa. 'You have a sister?'

My nostrils flare as I breathe out through my nose. I must have told him a hundred times about Grace. 'Yes, an older sister. I told you, she was instrumental in keeping me dancing.' I turn my attention back to the reporter. 'We didn't have a lot of money, growing up, but my sister used to scrimp and save every penny to keep me in ballet shoes and leotards. I owe half of my success to her, the other half to Madame Lebedev.'

Her green eyes narrow. 'You're not what I expected, Miss Harrington,' she says, laying down her pen.

'What did you expect?' I ask, feeling slightly self-conscious.

Now it is she who looks uncomfortable. 'I don't know. I suppose you have a bit of a reputation for never smiling. I thought maybe you might be more . . .'

'Cold-hearted and glory-driven?' I suggest and she laughs nervously.

'Something like that,' she replies, lowering her eyes and picking up her pen once more.

'Of course, I should have known the rumours weren't true. You're clearly not cold-hearted. You and Mr Dubrovsky are engaged to be married – is that correct?'

'Y-yes,' I falter. News travels fast. I want to ask her not to print that detail, but I know it will only arouse her journalistic suspicion.

'How wonderful.' She smiles. 'It must be awfully convenient to fall in love with your dance partner. No need to worry about passing ships in the night and suchlike.'

I smile to myself. There is that word again – convenient. 'Yes,' I agree. 'We are very lucky that that will never be a problem.'

The truth of the matter is, I would never have accepted Paul's proposal, had he not asked me in such a public, grandiose way. It happened in Vienna, just a few weeks ago. It was our final performance of the trip, and as we took to the stage to take in our applause, he knelt down on one knee and produced a ring. I was dumbstruck. There must have been two thousand people watching us, and they erupted into such a loud cheer, I felt I had no choice but to accept. I had every intention of telling Paul later in private that I was flattered but I didn't think it was the right time, but every time I tried to, he would remind me how wonderful it is to fall in love with your dance partner, and – thinking of Rudi – I would lose all my confidence to go through with it. I don't believe Paul loves me, but there is no denying how well he knows me, and when I did allow myself to fall in love it ended far worse than this. Nowadays, I put all my strength into my dancing; after all, I gave up everything to be where I am today. It means there is often not much resolve left for me to deal with Paul, so I just go along with whatever he says. He knows I am weak, knows it won't take much to get me down the aisle.

The interview goes on. She asks me about rehearsals for *Giselle*, what I eat for breakfast, how many hours I practise ballet each day – all the usual things that the balletomanes long to know. Finally, she closes her notebook.

'Thank you for your time, Miss Harrington, Mr Dubrovsky. Now if my colleague could take some photographs?' She gestures to the gentleman who has finally finished setting up his equipment.

I am about to answer when Paul interjects. 'She looks awful; she's just woken up and her hair is a mess. Why don't you come by the dressing rooms later and get some good photographs before the show?'

'Oh, I don't know if we could impose like that, and the equipment is all set up—' she starts, but Paul shuts her down.

'It will be fine. Tell them you're from the magazine and that I sent for you,' he insists, with very little regard for how long the photographer has spent adjusting his equipment. 'I'll square it with the man on the door when we arrive at the theatre.'

I look at my gold wristwatch – a present from Mr Webster, the producer, on opening night. It has a midnight blue face and the quarter-hours are marked with small diamonds. It was a flashy gift, the exact sort of thing a producer would think a prima ballerina would want. I must admit, I do quite like it. It reminds me of a night sky studded with stars.

'We must get ready, Paul,' I say, showing him my watch. 'Our driver will be here to pick us up in fifteen minutes.'

Chapter 28

I hate performing at the Royal Opera House. Every time I have ever danced here has reminded me of Rudi, of the night we broke in here and danced hand in hand on the stage. How he held me in his arms and we looked at each other and some sort of mutual understanding passed between us. In that moment, I think we fell in love. We had been performing *Giselle* then too, so this time, I hate performing at the Royal Opera House even more than usual.

Once again, I am playing the titular role, but on this occasion my Count Albrecht is Paul. He is a spectacular dancer, there is no denying that. He has had the best training in the world, but I do not think that I dance my best with him. He is always trying to take the limelight for himself and he hates any choreography that involves him shadowing my moves, so performing *Giselle* puts him in a particularly foul mood. I can hear him complaining in the dressing room next to mine.

'I hate this ballet,' he groans, probably to the wardrobe mistress. 'I hate this costume.'

I try to drown him out by turning on the wireless. The station is playing the 'Swan's Theme', one of my favourites, but as an adult it has always made me feel sad. I do not know why. I hum along while I brush my hair in front of the mirror and then an image from my memory flashes before me. It is of Rudi in his kitchen above Madame Lebedev's studio in Montpelier Mews. He is making tea and humming the 'Swan's Theme', he drops a sugar cube into a cup of tea and hands it to me, so I must have been upset about something. Then it hits me. That was the last time I saw him, when he told me that he would not join me at the Vic-Wells Ballet.

'Well, look at me now, Rudi,' I mutter bitterly at my reflection. 'You should be here too.'

There is a knock at the door and I start in surprise.

'Come in!' I say as commandingly as I can muster. I have a persona to keep up after all; there is a reason that the journalist from *Pointe* magazine had heard I was cold-hearted.

The wardrobe mistress enters, looking undeterred by my tone. In the theatre, there is nothing more terrifying than a wardrobe mistress, so I have nothing on her. I bob my head politely and thank her for bringing my costumes, but she barely even acknowledges that I am there. She hangs each costume on the brass rail, then stops and turns to face me.

'How do you dance with that awful man next door?' she asks exasperatedly, and I cannot help but snort.

'It is my job,' I remind her as she brings over my peasant girl dress for the opening number. 'Just as it is yours to dress him.'

'My job is more than dressing pompous dancers, thank you very much!' she snaps, showing the fiery temperament that wardrobe mistresses are so well renowned for, and I put my hands up in surrender.

'Sorry.' She gives me a small smile.

'Theatre types love to play down the roles of those not on the stage.' She pauses contemplatively. 'Not you though. You're different, Miss Harrington.'

'You are mistaken,' I assure her as I step into the dress, and she begins to lace up the back. 'I am just as pompous as the rest of them.'

'If you say so,' she chuckles, then her face grows more serious as she catches my eye in the reflection of the mirror. 'Is it true that you are going to marry him?'

'Now you are overstepping the line,' I remark, and she blushes.

'Sorry, Miss Harrington,' she mumbles and continues to lace up my costume in silence.

Once she has gone and I am alone once more, I sit down at the dressing table and begin to apply my make-up. Am I really going to marry Paul? Once upon a time I told myself that when I left Rudi in Montpelier Mews and embarked on my future that I would completely recreate myself, but I do not seem to have managed that at all. I am the same weak-willed, lost young girl I was before. I can see traces of my mother in my features these days. In the shape of my eyes, my jawline too. Her image appears before me in the mirror. *Who would ever love you?* she whispers, even now. Rudi did not love me enough to join me, or to even stay in touch. Paul does not love me, but does it matter? I barely have time to think about it before I am being called for curtain-up. It is time to step into the loving glow of the spotlight.

Chapter 29

The performance is, by all accounts, a success. As Paul and I take to the stage to bow and curtsey in unison, the audience bursts into rapturous applause. To the untrained eye, it is impossible to see the way we fight each other for more stage presence during every *pas de deux*. When I dance with Paul, it feels like a battle; when I danced with Rudi, it felt like a dream. The applause rushes in from the auditorium, and washes over us as roses scatter the stage. Paul is still playing the audience, egging them on for more applause with unnecessary leaps and spins across the stage, but I am so tired. I take a step back in line with the rest of the ballet corps and nod to the wings for them to pull the curtain down. Paul is forced to retreat, and he comes to stand beside me with a scowl as he takes one final bow.

As soon as the curtain drops, he turns on me, his face like thunder. 'You do not get to decide when the show is over!' he bursts, spittle flying at my face.

'They had clapped enough, Paul.' I shrug. 'After a while, it just becomes meaningless noise.'

'To you, perhaps.' He sniffs, clearly still irritated, and pumped full of adrenaline from the show.

The rest of the ballet company have cleared off the stage already, though I can see Sophie lingering in the wings, waiting for me. Most of the dancers know by now that it is quite common for Paul and I to argue after a performance. Sophie does too, but that is probably why she stays.

'You nearly dropped me during that last lift,' I remark, seeing no reason to break with tradition.

'Well, you felt an awful lot heavier than last time we performed *Giselle*,' he snaps, crossing his arms. 'Your timing was out during the Dance of the Wilis.'

'My timing is never out!' I snap and his face spreads into a smug smile. He knows he has won.

He pulls me under his arm. 'Oh, Clementine, you are so easy to irritate,' he smirks. 'I just wind you up and watch you go.'

'But why do you take so much pleasure in it?' I huff exasperatedly.

'I could say the same to you.' He shrugs. 'You started this one.' He drops his arm from around my shoulders and saunters off the stage. 'Do not take too long getting changed. I want to be out of here as soon as possible.'

I stand alone on the stage for a moment, hidden behind the heavy velvet curtain. I can still hear the audience filtering out on the other side. If only they could see the real me, how disappointed they would be.

'Clem?' Sophie calls my name from the wings. 'Are you all right?'

I whip around. 'Yes, of course.' I smile and stride towards her.

'Mr Webster is looking for you, he says there are some people from the audience who would like to meet you. Some earl and countess were in the audience apparently, and he has arranged a publicity moment with some young dancers from a local school.'

I smile, the first proper smile since I arrived at the theatre. This is the part of the job I enjoy the most these days. It turns out that Rudi was right: the limelight is not all I had hoped it would be, and the effects of the applause seem to last for a shorter time with every show.

I wander backstage in search of Mr Webster and find him waiting in my dressing room, fiddling with the pocket watch attached to his three-piece, pinstripe suit.

'Darling!' he cries, easing himself to his feet. 'Another

spectacular performance, another packed out theatre! There really is no stopping you and Dubrovsky – a match made in heaven!'

I make a non-committal noise in response to this. If heaven is an eternity with Paul, then I really must start sinning more.

'The Earl of Trevellas is here with his wife. She is a famous painter, I believe,' he continues, pouring himself a glass of brandy from the drinks cabinet in the corner of the dressing room. 'I said they could come backstage and meet you. They loved the show.'

'Of course, Mr Webster,' I reply, taking a seat in front of the dressing table and beginning to remove the pins from my hair. 'Please send them in.'

He disappears and returns moments later with a handsome couple. The gentleman, who must be the earl, is very tall with dark brown hair and a matching pair of chestnut eyes. His arm is wrapped around the waist of his heavily pregnant wife. She looks perhaps a few years older than me, but not what I had expected. Neither of them are exactly what I had imagined of an earl and a countess.

'It is such a pleasure to meet you,' the young woman says warmly, extending a slender hand to shake mine. 'You dance so beautifully. We were completely captivated by your performance.'

'Thank you so much,' I reply graciously, bobbing into a small curtsey. I am not quite sure what the proper protocol is for greeting aristocracy. 'Would you like to sit down?' I add, eyeing her stomach.

'Oh, I'm fine,' she waves a hand in dismissal. 'I have just been sat down for the last two hours.'

'Birdie . . .' her husband mutters under his breath, his tone slightly reprimanding but in a way that evidently comes from adoration.

'Alexander, I am *fine*,' she sighs, looking up at him with a challenging glare. They stare one another down for a moment until they both smile and look away.

'Well, if you are sure,' I say a little awkwardly, and they return their attention to me.

'Sorry,' the countess replies. 'I wanted to come backstage to speak with you as I am an artist, you see. I am currently working on a new series, based around performing arts. I made a few sketches during the show.' She pulls a sketchbook out of the folds of her coat and flips through to show me. Her sketches are exquisite, the detail in the costumes and the way she has captured our movements are incredible.

'You did these during the show?' I ask in awe.

'I did.' She blushes. 'I hope you don't think that rude. I was simply so inspired, I had to start sketching immediately.'

'How could anyone be offended by that?' I reply, feeling the heat begin to rise in my own cheeks.

'Oh good.' She beams, her green eyes sparkling with evident delight. 'You can take one of these if you would like?'

'Really?'

'Yes, please do!' she insists, tearing it carefully from the sketchbook. 'Here, take this one. You looked so lovely in this pose.'

She hands me the page; it is the moment from the opening scene when Giselle is picking the petals off the flower. He loves me, he loves me not. I think of Rudi once again.

'I would love to arrange for you to properly model for me, if you would be interested,' she continues. 'These paintings will be part of my next exhibition, and your portrait would be the central piece.'

'That sounds wonderful,' I reply. 'I am honoured, thank you. Though I am never in the same place for very long. Is that going to be a problem?'

'I am sure we can make it work.' She shrugs. 'I am happy to travel. I have just come back from an exhibition in New York, in fact.'

'And you promised the doctor you would take it easy once you returned,' her husband reminds her with a fond smile.

'We both knew that was never going to happen, Alexander.' She winks in return, and he rolls his eyes affectionately.

I glance between the two of them. They are clearly disgustingly in love with one another, and I am torn between wanting to bask in their lovely glow and feeling horribly jealous that I have ended up lumped with someone like Paul who would never in a hundred years ask if I needed a chair, or anything for that matter.

'Have you thought about painting dancers at school, rather than performers?' I ask her, and her green eyes widen in surprise. 'I am, of course, more than happy to sit for a portrait, but it is something to think about. The relationships between dancers, their teachers, the energy in the studio . . . there really is nothing like it.' And as I say it, I realise how much I miss it. The last time dancing truly made me feel happy was when I was rehearsing *Giselle* with Rudi in Madame Lebedev's small studio in Fitzrovia.

'Thank you. That is certainly something to think about.' She nods. 'Here, she scribbles a name and a phone number on the corner of the sketch she gave me, and I look at it again.

'Birdie Graham?' I read the name aloud and suddenly I know why I recognise her. She has been profiled in almost every magazine I have read for the last couple of years. 'Gosh, you're really quite famous! Mr Webster wasn't joking.' I drop the sketch in a fluster, and bend quickly to pick it up again as she chuckles. 'Sorry.' I flush.

'Don't be.' She smiles kindly. 'I quite like being incognito.'

'But you are an international sensation!' I continue, unable to let it go, for some reason.

Her husband beams proudly while she nods and shrugs it off.

'I have had a lot of success, it's true,' she replies modestly. 'But, so have you.'

'And you still love what you do?'

'Yes, of course.' She tilts her head perceptively. I think she wants to ask if I do too, but she has better manners than me.

'What is your secret?' I ask quietly, in the hope that Mr

Webster will not hear, but when I peer over my shoulder, he has fallen fast asleep on the sofa.

She eyes Mr Webster too, then leans in and pats my arm as she says quietly, 'I only do what brings me joy. If my art didn't bring me pleasure anymore, I wouldn't be able to dedicate so much of myself to it.'

I nod and let her words sink in. Does dancing still bring me joy? It must do, but I do not feel it like I used to . . .

'Anyway, we have taken up enough of your time,' she says. 'Thank you so much for speaking with me. I do hope I hear from you soon,' she adds, tapping her telephone number on the paper. 'Thank you, Mr Webster!' she says more loudly, and he snores himself awake.

'What's that?' he grumbles. 'Oh yes, thank you so much, my lord, my lady,' he replies standing to bow deeply to each of them, before ushering them outside.

I slump down onto the sofa and gaze at the sketch for a second, before Mr Webster reappears. 'Don't get too comfortable. Your next round of guests are here, and a photographer.'

I nod and straighten up as ten young girls come flying into the room, their hair neatly swept back into tidy buns atop their heads. The photographer from *Pointe* magazine enters at the same time and begins setting up his equipment as the girls flock around me excitedly, their eager hands desperate to reach out and touch the intricate brocade of my costume. Only one girl hangs back a little. She looks at me shyly from a pair of eyes as grey and gentle as the downy feathers of a cygnet. I haven't seen grey eyes like that since . . .

'Girls, calm down and remember your grace!' someone says in a voice so familiar that it makes the hairs on the back of my neck stand up, a deep voice with an intoxicating Russian lilt that could only ever belong to Rudolf Lebedev. His eyes meet mine as he sidles into the room, leaning in the doorway with his head of magnificent curls tilted to one side, and my heart stops. 'You are ballerinas, not autograph fiends,' he reminds them, his deep-set eyes twinkling as he holds my gaze.

I struggle to regain my composure, then turn to the group of girls before me, struggling to tear my eyes away from Rudi. 'You girls are all students of the Lebedev School of Ballet, is that correct?' I ask, and they all nod enthusiastically. 'I had no idea that was who I was meeting!' I tell them. 'Well, this is very exciting for me too. I am sure you all know that I started my career under the tutelage of Madame Lebedev, but did you know that Mr Lebedev was my first dance partner?'

They all stare at me open-mouthed, then look back at Rudi to see if I am pulling their legs, and he nods in agreement. 'It's true,' he says with a warm smile. 'I used to dance with Miss Harrington.'

They gawp at him with a newfound admiration and he chuckles fondly, stepping further into the room but still maintaining his distance. He is taller than I remember, but he still has his magnificent athletic physique and commanding posture. The last remnants of his boyish face have been chiselled away, and the man who stands before me now is sharp, angular and commanding. But his eyes are just the same, and I find I can't bear the space between us for a moment longer.

'Oh, Rudi!' I exclaim, leaping to my feet and tearing across the room to wrap my arms around him. I feel him stiffen in surprise momentarily, before relaxing and wrapping his arms around me. 'Not until this point, did I realise just how much I have missed you,' I murmur into his chest, and I realise my cheeks are wet with tears that I try to dry surreptitiously before the girls notice.

'I have felt it every day, *solnyshko*.' He says it so quietly that only I can hear, and I am overcome with a desperate urge to be alone with him, but I owe it to these young girls to give them my time.

'Right!' I say, my voice wavering a little as I turn to face them and clasp my hands together. 'Who had a question for me?'

We spend a good hour talking through all their questions about what it is like to perform on the big stage, how I manage my costume changes, what I eat, how I style my hair, and all the while, the photographer snaps away, taking candid shots. The girls want to know everything, and they cling to my every word with the sort of desperate excitement I haven't felt myself in a long time. Only the girl with the dark hair and grey eyes stays quiet, but I feel her gaze on me, studying every move I make. I catch her eye and smile encouragingly, but she immediately looks down at her feet. I am sure she has questions of her own, if only she could find the courage to come forward.

'How would you all like to see the view from the stage?' I ask the group, and they start squealing excitedly as Rudi tries to calm them down again and casts me an exasperated look. 'Oh, don't pretend like you don't want to see it too!' I tease, and he relents.

I let them have a go at spinning *piqué* turns across the stage one by one, giving me the opportunity to hang back and speak to the shy girl. 'I don't think I caught your name,' I say, coming to stand beside her, and she looks up at me in mild horror, as if to double-check that I am in fact speaking to her.

'It's Charlotte,' she says quietly.

'Tell me, Charlotte, did you have any questions you wanted to ask me?' I enquire, bending down as if to correct the ribbon on my pointe shoe.

She deliberates for a moment, then leans in closer and whispers, 'How did you know that you had what it takes?'

'Oh, I didn't,' I say matter-of-factly, straightening up again. 'I worked incredibly hard, but I never really believed that I was good enough. I dreamed of it, sure, but it only ever felt like that . . . a dream. But I was very lucky, because when I didn't believe in myself, I had a dear friend who believed in me enough for the both of us. Do you know who that was?'

Charlotte shakes her head, her big, grey eyes wide with anticipation, and I look up at Rudi. His back is turned as he watches his students live out their fantasies from the wings. 'It was your teacher, Mr Lebedev,' I tell her, and she looks at him as if in a new light. 'With the support of a teacher like Mr Lebedev, there is no limit to how far you can go. Now, look, all the other girls have taken their turn. Why don't you show everyone what you've got?'

She straightens her back, lifts her chin, and steps out onto the stage. I come to stand beside Rudi and watch as she spins beautifully towards the wings with newfound courage.

'That was a very kind thing you just did, Clem,' Rudi says beside me, smiling as he watches Charlotte spin across the stage, then run the rest of the way towards the others. 'Charlotte is full of unlocked potential, if she only had a little more faith in herself.' Then he looks down at me fondly. 'She reminds me a lot of you.'

The corners of my lips twitch. 'That's funny, because when I first laid eyes on her, I thought of you. It's those grey Lebedev eyes.' He holds my gaze for a moment; I can't look away, can't breathe.

'A pure coincidence. She is no relation of mine,' he starts, but I interject.

'Why haven't you been in touch?' I ask hotly, unable to keep the pleasantries a moment longer. 'I sent you postcards every time I visited somewhere new, I scoured the papers for signs of any of your performances. I would have dropped everything to see you on the stage again.'

'I don't perform anymore,' he says matter-of-factly. 'I only teach.'

'I wrote to you both times I performed in London,' I say finally.

'And I came, Clementine,' he replies stiffly, looking out at the rows of empty velvet seats. 'I have never missed one of your performances in London.'

Somehow this hurts more than thinking he had cut me loose. All this time he had been so close, and I never knew.

'But you didn't come backstage to see me,' I reply plainly.

'I didn't think they'd let a nobody like me past the stage door.' He grins self-deprecatingly.

'You could have replied to my letters,' I point out. 'We could have met anywhere.'

'Did it ever cross your mind that I couldn't?' he says, with a desperation that breaks my heart. 'That it was simply too painful, that even sitting in the theatre and watching you, safely anonymous in a crowd of faces, was excruciating for me?'

I feel a pang in my chest, and it leaves an empty hollow sort of feeling. Of course it was painful for him. How could I have been so thoughtless? He should have been up there with me, not watching from the audience. 'Well, Rudi, all the girls have had a go on the stage,' I say, finding my words at last. 'How about a dance for old times' sake?'

He gives me a long, sideways look. 'I can't, Clem. I don't have my ballet shoes for starters, and I'm wearing woollen trousers, for goodness' sake.'

'That would never have stopped you before,' I taunt, then I disappear into the wings and return, lugging the stage manager's old gramophone with me. The 'Swan's Theme' is still resting on the turntable, and I place the needle down and watch his face transform as the music begins.

I step out onto the stage and hold out my hand to him, as the girls let out an audible gasp from the wings. His expression is conflicted, but he sighs, then unlaces his shoes and steps out to join me. We listen to the music, eyes on each other, waiting for the moment when the prince sees Odette for the first time, and as the harp flutters through the gramophone, we begin.

He walks slow, methodical circles around me as I bend down and fold in on myself, nestling on the floor with my arms outstretched, one leg pointed forward. I wait, my heartbeat drumming, as he draws down and surrounds me with his arms, and I can smell him again, that rich and spicy scent of cloves. He gently places his fingers around my wrists, his touch as light as feathers, as he unfolds me like the petals of a delicate flower, and I spin slowly into an *attitude*. He drops his strong hands to my waist, and I can feel his heart beating against my back as I curl around him and he rotates me slowly on the spot. He shadows my moves in perfect sequence, then returns to take my hand as I reach up into an *arabesque*, revolving like a tiny doll in a music box to the mournful sound of violin strings. His hands run down my arms, leaving a trail of goosebumps in their wake, and then I fall slowly backwards into his waiting arms as he lowers me to the ground. He draws me back up tantalisingly slowly and wraps his arms around my waist just as the woodwind begins, signalling the awakening of the other swans and the end of our *pas de deux*. We stay rooted to the spot for a moment longer, our chests heaving up and down, always keeping perfect time with one another, though I know mine has little to do with exertion.

He finally lets me go as the girls begin whooping from the side of the stage, assuming that the performance was only ever for their viewing pleasure. They crowd adoringly around Rudi, and I take a step back, the familiar urge to distance myself from my overwhelming feelings returning. I thought dancing with Rudi would make me happy, and in some ways it did, but now I feel overcome with a sense of mournful longing. Maybe it was the wrong music, the wrong dance. I feel all caught up in my emotions and I can't distinguish the stage from reality.

'I'm sorry, girls, but I have to go,' I call over the bubble of their voices. 'It was so wonderful to meet you all, but the wardrobe mistresses will be after my costume.'

Rudi looks up despairingly as I turn on the spot, fleeing from the stage as quickly as my pointe shoes will allow. I know I will have disappointed him once again, but it is too unbearable, too acutely painful to realise what I have passed up in favour of the stage. The feeling I have been chasing, that something which was missing, that I was convinced I would eventually find in the right role, on the right stage . . . It only ever existed in Rudi's arms.

Chapter 30

After Grace and Jacob returned from Gretna Green, married and very much in love, they settled back in London. At first, they rented a tiny flat in Hampstead as it was all they had ever known, but as their family began to grow, they soon moved to a small, terraced house in Maida Vale. It is a lovely brown-brick house, with window boxes overflowing with blousy carnations and fragrant lavender. Grace has made all the curtains herself, out of cheap cuts of material, and the two of them have spent countless weekends thrifting various bits of furniture from jumble sales, or even right off the street when neighbours have tossed something aside that Jacob sees potential in. The effect is wonderfully eclectic; it is an incredibly happy home to be in, which is why I feel so rotten to be killing the ambience with my miserable mood. I am sitting in the living room in a stripy green armchair that does not match the floral sofa in the slightest.

Grace waddles into the living room with a tray of tea and biscuits resting on top of her protruding baby bump. She sets it down carefully on the coffee table, then collapses onto the sofa with a deep sigh.

'How long do you have left now?' I ask, eyeing her stomach.

'Another two months.' She rolls her eyes and huffs, but her face is positively glowing with excitement. Grace has taken to motherhood as exceptionally as I always knew she would. She was always such a caring and thoughtful sister, and she looked after me far better than our mother did. In fact, she still does now, even though I am a grown-up and she has children of her own to worry about.

'So,' she starts, pushing the plate of biscuits towards me, even though she knows I will refuse them. 'What has happened? Is it Paul? What has he said or done this time?'

'No, it's not Paul,' I sigh. 'I saw Rudi.'

This revelation causes Grace to freeze with a biscuit mid-air, her eyes agape. 'After all this time?'

I nod. 'It was completely out of the blue. I had a publicity meeting with some young dancers and Rudi was their teacher. They were from the Lebedev School of Ballet. It all feels like some cruel trick.'

'What happened? What did he have to say for himself?' she asks protectively, sitting up a little straighter.

'Nothing. We caught up, we danced together, but that was all.' I try to shrug it off as if it were nothing, as if I can no longer feel the ghost of his touch on my skin. However, Grace knows me far too well to fall for my nonchalance.

'You *danced* together?'

'Yes!' I cry, dropping my face into my hands. 'And it was wonderful, just like it always was. I felt something, Grace . . .' I look up, my eyes welling with unwelcome tears. 'A lightness of joy that has been missing from my dancing since I joined the Vic-Wells Ballet.'

'Maybe it was not performing that you enjoyed so much, but rather it was dancing with Rudi,' she suggests, lowering her gaze and raising her eyebrows as if to say that she thought that was always obvious.

'No, it is not that simple,' I protest, shaking my head. 'I asked him why he never replied to any of my letters. He said he hadn't wanted to speak to me . . . I suppose he finally realised I wasn't worth his time. Mother was right. Eventually everyone sees the truth about me, and then they flee.'

'Clem, she's been dead for more than two years now,' she says softly, leaning forward to take my hand. 'You are not unlovable, you never were. When will you stop allowing the past to haunt you?'

'I don't know. I still feel so to blame for what happened,' I say, a lump forming in my throat, even now, even after everything she did. 'If I had been there, things would have been different. Perhaps this is my penance.'

'You didn't kill her, Clementine. It was not your fault. The fire was a terrible accident,' she insists. 'Don't you see that you are letting her win?' she says, exasperated. 'You are still living your life in her shadow. Do you remember what I said to you in my letter when I left? I said that you made me feel brave because you were chasing your dream. You made me feel like I could chase mine too, and look at me now! I have everything I always wanted – a loving husband, a family, a home. It might not seem like much to you, but I fall asleep each night and wake up every morning feeling content. Can you say the same?'

'No,' I sigh. 'I thought I knew what I wanted, that I was running *towards* it, but now I am starting to think that I ran away from it instead.'

'And what is it that you want, Clementine?' she asks, narrowing her eyes. She already knows the answer.

'Rudi,' I reply simply, and her face breaks into a smile. 'It has always been Rudi. I want to dance all of my dances with him. I don't care if they are on a grand stage in front of hundreds of strangers or alone in the kitchen in the dead of night. I simply know that I never want to dance with anyone else again.'

As soon as I say it, it all seems so obvious. I love Rudi still, of course I do, and I think he might love me too. I owe it to myself to find out, at least, and to break free from the shackles of my unhappy engagement to Paul and my contract with the Vic-Wells Ballet.

'I have to go,' I say suddenly, rising to my feet. 'I am sorry to dash out on you like this, but there are some things I need to do.'

'Good, go!' She grins. 'And good luck!' she calls as I flee from the cottage.

* * *

'Where have you been?' Paul demands, hammering at my hotel suite the moment I arrive back. 'I was waiting for you at the theatre after the matinee, and you just disappeared! We were supposed to travel back to the hotel together.'

'And yet, I see you managed to make it back alright, all by yourself,' I reply, opening the door and raising an eyebrow at him.

'That is not the point,' he intones. 'If you are to be my wife, you need to start doing as I say. You cannot simply wander around town on your own. Where were you? Who were you with?'

'We need to talk about that,' I say, removing my gloves and getting straight to the point. 'I do not think I want to be your wife, Paul. In fact, I know I don't want to be.'

He blinks a few times, as if he is unsure if he heard me correctly. 'Don't be absurd, Clementine. Now tell me, where have you been?'

He takes a step towards me, and there is a threatening glint in his eye. I grasp a brass ornament from the sideboard, just in case.

'I do not need to answer to you anymore,' I reply, trying to keep my voice from wavering. 'It doesn't matter who I was with. All that matters is that I don't want to be with you. You have never loved me, so it should come as no great loss to you. Now, if you don't mind, I will collect my things and get out of here.'

I walk quickly towards the bedroom where my suitcase is mostly packed already. It is almost as if a little part of me knew that this would happen; I had seen no need to bother unpacking. I empty the wardrobe of the few items I had seen fit to hang up and begin folding them. Paul follows me into the bedroom. He looks furious. He paces up and down, blocking my exit. My pulse quickens, but I keep my expression calm. He will not keep me from leaving.

'If you walk out now, you are ruined, Clementine,' he

snarls. 'Not just at the Vic-Wells Ballet, but everywhere. I will tarnish your reputation to anyone who will listen. No ballet company in Europe will want to touch you by the time I am through.'

'Do what you must, Paul. I really don't care,' I reply calmly, folding my belongings back into my suitcase.

I see it dawn on his face that I am not fooling around, and his anger turns to desperation. 'Clementine, you can't do this!' he begs. 'No one dances like you and I. Together we are unstoppable. You are throwing away everything you have worked for!'

'No, I'm afraid that's not true,' I say, clicking the suitcase shut and resting my hands on the smooth leather surface. I slip the engagement ring off my finger and place it on the bedside table. 'I am finally following my dream.'

Chapter 31

When I leave the hotel, there is only one place on my mind. A small mews in Fitzrovia, the only place where I ever knew true happiness. I hail down a taxi and give the driver the address. It feels as if we are crawling through the city as we circle round the statue of Eros in Piccadilly Circus, past towering buildings with advertisements for various tonics, gins and shows. I spot a poster for *Giselle* with my picture on it and I turn away, trying hard not to think about what Paul had said. I hope he doesn't make the last performances a misery, despite his battered ego. We drive on, past the Lyric Theatre, and take a left on Berners Street. There are still an awful lot of people out and about, friends crammed round bistro tables, sipping wine and smoking, laughing at one thing or another.

'Here we are, miss.'

The taxi driver stirs me from my thoughts. I open my eyes again. The car is idling on the cobbled street of Montpelier Mews, a few yards from the Lebedev School of Ballet. I lean out of the window and glance up and down the street. It looks just as I remember. The buildings are ensconced in thick vines of dormant wisteria. I remember how, in the summer, the mews is a riot of purple and blue, the flowers dripping down from on high.

'Is everything alright?' the driver asks when I do not stir.

'Yes, sorry. This is perfect.' I hand him the money and climb out of the car.

As the taxi putters away, silence descends on the mews once more disturbed only by the distant chiming of a clock tower, marking the turn of midnight. There is a light on at the studio, and I stumble down the cobbles, all the tension leaving my body as I draw closer. The door is closed but not locked and as I turn the handle, it swings open freely. I shut it behind me and breathe in the familiar smell of wood polish. My footsteps echo down the narrow hallway as I pass the noticeboard where Madame Lebedev used to pin our role sheets. There is a poster tacked to the board for *Giselle*, with my name in bold lettering and a sign-up sheet beneath it to attend the opening night. Beside it is a role sheet for their next performance, *The Nutcracker*. I scan the names until I find Charlotte's; she is down to play a snowflake. I smile, picturing her in the fluffy white costume, glittering with crystals. One day, she will make a beautiful Snow Queen if she learns to believe in herself.

I carry on down the hallway towards the studio where I spent so many blissful hours of my youth. It is dark inside; I flick on the lights and they sputter into life. In the corner is the locked door to Madame Lebedev's costume cupboard, and I remember fondly how Rudi and I spent hours in there, rustling through the various outfits and trying them on. Then I remember Madame's nymph costume, the sound of ripping fabric, and my heart wrenches. I turn my back on the cupboard, and see the old piano Mr Popov used to play still standing against the wall. I can almost hear the chiming of the ivory keys, the shuffling of sheet music. A discarded pair of ballet shoes have been left on the piano stool, forgotten in someone's haste to leave for the show, no doubt. I slip off my own shoes, remove my coat, and walk barefoot into the centre of the studio. I look at my reflection in the floor-length mirrors. I look thin and tired. I touch the shadows under my eyes, watching the mirror reflect my actions; then, as if my limbs have taken on a life of their own, I spread my feet into fourth position and spin into a *pirouette*, watching my reflection turn on the spot.

'What are you doing here?' a cracked voice asks, and I fall ungracefully out of my turn.

Rudi is standing in the doorway, his usually buoyant curls hanging limp around his eyes. His eyes are cold and hard like steel; he looks guarded. After how I left him earlier, I cannot say that I blame him.

'You shouldn't be here,' he says gruffly when I do not reply.

'I had to come,' I reply, finding my voice at last, though it sounds a little shaky. 'I needed to see you again.'

He drops my gaze as he steps into the studio, collecting up the lost ballet shoes and discarded sheet music from the piano. 'What do you want from me, Clementine?' he asks, keeping his back turned, but I can still hear the hurt in his voice.

'Would you rather I go?' I ask, and he stops fussing.

'You said that to me once before.' His lips twitch and he tries to hold back a smile as he turns to face me. 'In this very studio. Do you remember?'

'I do,' I murmur, rooted to the spot, not daring to move lest I spook him. 'It was the day after we kissed.'

His eyes are unwavering as he speaks again. 'I didn't wish it then, and I certainly don't wish it now.'

'Rudi, I'm sorry I ran away before,' I say gently, taking a few cautious steps towards him.

'Why did you?' he asks, meeting me halfway. He reaches his hand out towards me, his fingertips so close to my cheek. I wish I could take his hand and press it against my skin, nuzzling into his soft palm, but he lets it fall, stuffing his hands firmly in his pockets.

'I was afraid,' I cry softly. 'Afraid to realise what a terrible mistake I made, leaving you behind.'

'We agreed it was the best course of action,' he says calmly, but I can see from the swift rise and fall of his chest that his breathing has intensified. 'And look at the success you have had. All of your dreams have come true.'

'Then why do I feel like I'm living in a nightmare?' My voice cracks, my eyes welling with tears.

'*Solnyshko*,' he croons, closing the gap between us and taking my hands. 'No one ever said it would be easy, but surely you feel it has been worth it?'

'Is that what you think?' I ask, taking a step back from him. 'Do you believe I am that heartless?'

'You speak as if this life were forced upon you, Clementine.' He frowns, his thick eyebrows knitting together as he crosses his arms.

'Was it not?' I exclaim, my voice echoing off the walls. 'This was never my dream! My dream was to dance with *you*, Rudi. We were supposed to go *together*.'

'You cannot force people to live your dreams, Clementine!' he shoots back in frustration. He runs his hands through his hair, and I can see now why his curls have grown loose. 'If you could, do you really think I would have watched you go? It killed me to let you leave that day, but it was not my choice to stop you.'

'You had the choice to join me,' I counter.

'Yes,' he sighs, his eyes downcast. 'I had the choice and I do not regret my decision. I had a duty to my mother's legacy. I wanted to keep the Lebedev School of Ballet going.'

'How is your mother?' I ask anxiously.

'She's fine,' he says, rubbing at the tired shadows beneath his eyes. 'She has mostly retired from teaching now. Her leg never recovered well enough for her to dance on it properly, but she still does – stubborn as ever.'

'It's a family trait,' I murmur and he smiles reluctantly, then looks at me more shrewdly.

'Clem, why *are* you here?' he sighs. 'You did not answer me before.'

'I-I don't know,' I stammer. 'I followed my feet and they led me here.'

'Aren't you supposed to follow your heart?' he asks, looking up from beneath his thick lashes with a lopsided smile.

'For me, they are one and the same.'

'And neither your feet nor your heart led you to your fiancé?' he asks, raising a singular eyebrow.

'Paul Dubrovsky is not my fiancé.' I shudder. 'Not anymore.'

Rudi's shoulders drop an inch or two, but his arms remain folded. 'Isn't that going to make performing rather difficult for you now? From what I have heard of Dubrovsky, I cannot imagine he would take well to being jilted.'

'Well, it won't be a problem anymore,' I reply nervously. 'I made a decision tonight. I will not return to the Vic-Wells Ballet Company. This will be my last performance. I am done. I'm out.' I steel all my courage and let the truth flow from me like breath. 'I have danced in Paris, Berlin, Vienna, Rome . . . everywhere in search of the happiness I thought dancing professionally would bring me. I had started to believe that I would never belong anywhere, until today, when I danced with you again. I finally realised I have been chasing the wrong dream all these years. All I ever really wanted was to dance with you.'

My head drops and I stare at the floor, unsure how he will respond. I see his feet slowly pace the floor towards me until he is standing mere inches away. I breathe in his familiar scent, and it smells like home. I lift my head and my eyes find his.

'I can't tell you how long I have wished to hear you say those words,' he murmurs. 'Clementine . . . if I tell you I still love you, will you promise not to deter me this time?'

'I promise.' The hairs on the back of my neck lift in anticipation of his touch. It has been more than two years since Rudi kissed me, but not a day has passed that I haven't thought about that moment.

'I love you, Clementine Harrington,' he says earnestly, his eyes shining like two silver moons. 'I have been unconditionally, *unsettlingly*, in love with you for quite some time, far longer than I initially realised. It was not until I grasped that I might lose you to that American you seemed so focused on, that I truly understood my feelings.

I wanted to tell you I was in love with you the night we broke into the Royal Opera House and danced on the stage together. I tried to show you how truly I loved you when I kissed you in the garden at that fancy dress party . . . I loved you more still when I saw you had come back here tonight.'

'And I love you, Rudolf,' I breathe, tracing my fingertips down his cheek. 'I spent too many years believing I was unlovable, afraid to open my heart for fear of rejection. I should have listened to you; I should have listened to my heart. It was telling me all along what I needed to know. I thought I desired freedom above all else, that I could only achieve it by running, but there is nothing more liberating than to finally be able to tell you how entirely my heart belongs to you.'

I cannot wait a second longer. I clutch his head in my hands and bring his lips down to mine. The force that has held us apart for so long lifts and we collide. I cannot tell where his skin ends and mine begins. We are one and the same, our hearts, just like our feet, beat in seamless unison; and finally, I understand that there is no greater feeling than to allow yourself to be loved and to love freely in return.

Epilogue

My favourite part about teaching ballet is teaching the really little children, when they are about five years old and can barely point their toes, but are filled with an unbridled enthusiasm. At that age, there is no telling if they will be the next big thing, or if they will drop out as teenagers. We are all there simply to have fun.

Today is an even more special class, because today Grace has brought her daughter Polly along for her first lesson. She clings nervously to Grace's skirt as they enter the studio, but her face brightens when she sees me.

'See, I told you!' Grace smiles. 'Auntie Clem is here to take good care of you. It will be lots of fun.'

She looks so sweet in her pink leotard, her tawny-coloured hair swept into a bun. Luckily, Grace had plenty of practice helping with my hair when we were children. It is possibly the neatest bun in the studio. Not that I should be surprised; Grace has always been a perfectionist. Baby Arthur starts gurgling in his pram, and she looks down at him benevolently.

'Don't you start making a fuss too,' she coos, then wraps an arm around me. 'Hello, Clem, how are you doing?'

'Oh, you know.' I shrug. 'Not too bad. Business has fallen a little as some families have taken their children to the countryside, but we're confident they will return.'

'There're still plenty of families like us who won't be leaving London,' she reassures me.

'There's nowhere I'd rather be.' I smile, just as Rudi walks into the studio, lighting up the room as only he can with his wide grin.

'Grace!' he cries, opening his arms wide and giving her a big hug. 'How's the family?'

'We're doing very well, thank you.' She beams. 'Exhausted, but happy. When are you two going to have some children of your own?'

'Calm down, Grace, we only got married a few months ago!' I squeak. 'Besides, how will I teach if I can't touch my toes?'

'We will cross that bridge when we get to it.' Rudi winks, wrapping his arm around me. 'For now, we have more than enough children to look after, thank you very much.'

'Yes, well, here's one more!' Grace laughs, giving Polly a little push forward. She bends down and looks her in the eye, 'You'll have a great time with Auntie Clem and Uncle Rudi, then they are going to bring you back to Mummy and Daddy's bookshop, OK?'

Only Jacob and Grace would think it a good idea to open a bookshop during a war. I think they spend so much time with their noses in books, they are completely oblivious to what is going on in the real world. But then, I suppose Rudi and I aren't much better with our ballet. We have certainly seen a dip in income since Germany marched on Poland, but we get by, living comfortably enough in the small flat above the studio. Business is still busier than when I started, and while I was away with the Vic-Wells Ballet, before the war broke out, Madame Lebedev had expanded into the building next door. Now we can run twice as many classes, and Madame is only a stone's throw away in the flat beside ours.

Rudi finds it hilarious that I still call his mother Madame, even now we are married, but old habits die hard and I cannot seem to break it. Secretly, I think she quite likes it.

'Have you seen this?' Rudi says, unrolling a copy of *Pointe* magazine from his pocket with a smug look on his face.

'What is it?' I ask curiously, taking a step closer. 'Oh my goodness, that's the *last* person I want to see!' I exclaim as I realise it is Paul on the front cover.

'Ignore the picture. Read the headline!' Rudi insists gleefully as he taps the magazine.

DUBROVSKY DROPPED FROM VIC-WELLS BALLET FOLLOWING AFFAIR SCANDAL

'Gosh . . .' I say, a little lost for words, and counting my lucky stars I didn't go through with marrying him.

'The full story is inside, but it looks like he was having an affair with the producer's wife.'

'Oh, poor Mr Webster,' I reply, feeling genuinely quite sad for him. 'He put up with so much aggravation from Paul. How could he do this?'

'Well, he has got his comeuppance,' Rudi replies smugly. 'Serves him right for the way he tried to bad-mouth you after you left.'

'Yes, well he didn't have much luck with that, did he?' I shrug. 'As soon as Sophie stepped into my place as the new principal, she made sure everybody knew the truth.'

'Hopefully this will be the last balletomanes have to see of Dubrovsky,' he says, dropping the magazine on the piano. 'He was such a nasty piece of work. I'll never forgive the way he treated you.'

'I never give him a second thought, darling,' I reply soothingly, reaching up to kiss his cheek.

He smiles, and his grey eyes shine silver as he looks down at me and I brush a hand through his bronze curls.

'And you don't miss all the fancy hotels and the grand stages?'

'Not even for a moment,' I tell him truthfully. I have finally found everything I ever wanted: I get to dance with the man that I love every day, and I wouldn't swap it for any audience applause, ever again.

Acknowledgements

Thank you for reading *The Dancer's Promise*, I hope you enjoyed Clementine's story and I am so grateful to you for choosing to read it. A lot of people are involved in the process of turning this jumbled up story that lived in my head into the fully formed book that is now in your hands.

Huge thanks to my agent, Thérèse Coen, for your constant faith in me, your support, your excellent humour and very calm demeanour. You always have the right answers, and know exactly how to put my mind at ease and bring out the best in my writing. I am so lucky to have you as my agent.

Thank you to my wonderful editor, Cara Chimirri, for your patience primarily! This book took me a lot longer to write than I had expected, and I am so grateful for the way you supported me and allowed me the time to tell the story to the best of my ability. Thank you for your passion, and your intellect which have been invaluable in shaping the narrative and historical references in this book. And huge thanks to the rest of the team at Embla who have been so instrumental in my books – Anna Perkins, Hannah Deuce, Katie Williams and Emilie Marneur, to name a few.

A very big thank you to my family for all your support over the years. Firstly, to my sister, Sophie, who will always be my very first reader of every book I write, and this one is for you! How could a book about the bond between two sisters be for anyone else? Huge thanks to my mum, who I feel I should clarify is nothing like Clementine's mother. She did, however, introduce me to such wonderful fiction as *Great Expectations* and *Now, Voyager* which is where the inspiration for that character came from. Thank you, Mum, and thank you also to Sue Rooney, for tirelessly supporting my dance classes when I was younger: taking me to ballet, tap and jazz classes; helping backstage at shows; preparing for exams; and goodness knows what else. I may not have become a professional dancer, but at least I wrote a book about it! And a big thank you to my dad, my brother Peter, and my husband Dean, who have all been so supportive of my writing career, and pleasantly surprised to find that they enjoy a romance novel!

I would also like to say a thank you to my dance teachers, past and present, without whom this novel would not exist. Thank you to Rosemary and Samantha Groves for sparking a love of ballet in me from a young age, and a HUGE thank you to Elaine Ellis for helping me rediscover that love and passion for ballet a few years ago when I returned to adult ballet classes after a fifteen-year hiatus. I really hope I got all the ballet terminology correct!

Finally, a huge thank you to all my wonderful friends who have been so incredibly supportive from the moment I told them I was writing my first book. Thank you to Sarah, Róisín, Katrina, Becky, Steff, Kat, Helen, Lucy, Dani, Eve and Sean for your constant faith in me, your honest feedback, your live reading updates, and for just being the best friends I could ask for. Thank you!

About the Author

Olivia Horrox is the author of historical romance novels, *Beautiful Little Fools* and *The Dancer's Promise*. She studied English Literature with Creative Writing at Bath Spa University, where she wrote her dissertation on post-WWI societal changes reflected in *The Great Gatsby*. Olivia now works as a Senior Marketing Manager at Simon & Schuster, marketing children's books by day and writing books for adults by night. She lives in West London with her husband and their rather rotund cat called Maple.

You can follow Olivia on Instagram, TikTok and Twitter at @ohorrox

About Embla Books

Embla Books is a digital-first publisher of standout commercial adult fiction. Passionate about storytelling, the team at Embla publish books that will make you 'laugh, love, look over your shoulder and lose sleep'. Launched by Bonnier Books UK in 2021, the imprint is named after the first woman from the creation myth in Norse mythology, who was carved by the gods from a tree trunk found on the seashore – an image of the kind of creative work and crafting that writers do, and a symbol of how stories shape our lives.

Find out about some of our other books and stay in touch:

Twitter, Facebook, Instagram: @emblabooks
Newsletter: https://bit.ly/emblanewsletter

Printed in Great Britain
by Amazon

37654368R00164